A Knight to Remember

Realm of Honor

MICHELLE MILES

This is a work of fiction. All characters, organizations and events portrayed in this novel are either products of the author's imagination or used fictitiously.

A KNIGHT TO REMEMBER

This title was previously published.

Cover Design by Erin Dameron-Hill

Chapter 1

Henry Chase knew someone kept a watchful gaze on him even while he feigned sleep. A chill ran through him, making all the hairs on the back of his neck stand at attention and his scalp tingle. He scented the soft aroma of something decidedly feminine in the stale air of the hotel room. Nearby was the faint rustle of clothing. He shifted on the lumpy mattress and cracked open one eye to peer through the shadows at the tall, lithe, curvy body standing rigid on the other side of the room.

If he'd been in his own bed, he would have reached for his baseball bat. One could never be too careful. Since he was in Dumfries, Scotland, he had no weapon. No way to defend himself from the intruder.

Her golden hair shimmered in the half light of the room and cascaded over her shoulders in silky waves. Who she was, he didn't know? How did she get into his room? He'd locked the door. She couldn't have climbed through the window because it didn't open. A flicker of warning went through him.

"Who are you?" He sat up as he spoke, staring at the woman concealed by shadow.

She flinched, surprised by his sudden movement and outburst. She stepped into the faint moonlight slanting through the panes of glass. Her pale cheeks were flushed pink as she pressed a hand against her chest. Her features were as soft as her curves. She had a porcelain face with beautiful blue eyes and smooth-as-silk hair.

"You scared me half to death. Welcome to Scotland, by the way." Her voice was a symphony to his ears. She smiled with rose-red lips as she approached. "Took you long enough."

"Who are you? How did you get in here?"

"I'm not sure that's relevant." She glanced around the room before her gaze landed back on him. "I know who you are. I know why you're here."

Henry didn't like her cryptic nature. He didn't like being spied on either. "How do you know me?"

"You're searching for your daughter, Maggie."

"What do you know about my daughter?" Fear trickled through him as he stared at the woman standing across the room. "Are you responsible for her disappearance?"

"Gods, no! Well, not really," she added as an afterthought.

The questions poured out of him. Questions he had needed answers to for days.

"Where is she? Is she hurt? Where can I find her? "If you harmed her—"

"Calm down, Henry. I've come with a letter." She took another step toward him as she reached into the pocket of her gown. Parchment rustled against the cloth as she pulled it out. "This should explain everything to you."

He hesitated, staring at her.

The woman waved the parchment at him. "Go on. Take it. I promise it will hold the answers you seek."

He slipped it from her fingers, turning it over in his hands. It looked old. It smelled old. It had been folded neatly and sealed with red wax. He didn't recognize the seal.

"What is this? A ransom notes? Are you going to ask for thousands of dollars?"

She sighed, irritated. "No. I told you it's a letter from Maggie."

"From Maggie?"

"Aye. Read it. And then I'll be on my way, my promise fulfilled."

Henry tore past the seal and unfolded the paper. Maggie's perfect handwriting flowing down the page stunned him.

Dear Dad,

I know you must be worried sick about me by now, not having heard from me for days. I can't exactly explain where I am. It's more of a when I am.

Remember when I was a little girl and I used tell you how awesome it would be if we could go back in time? And then when I got older, I used to tell you if I could go anywhere in history, it would be to the Middle Ages? That I'd always wanted to see a live jousting tournament? Well, here I am. You probably don't believe that. You probably also wouldn't believe me if I told you

Faeries really do exist. I had a hard time believing it myself at first. But it's all true. I'm living in the Middle Ages as Lady Margaret. I'm in love with a Scottish knight. And whenever I am, I'm safe and sound.

I've entrusted Princess Elyne with the delivery of this letter. She's a Fae. Be nice to her, all right? She's been kind to me. I would have never met Finn if it hadn't been for her. I love you and miss you, Dad.

Love, Mags

He glanced back at the woman standing in front of him. She casually looked over her cuticles as if she had all the time in the world.

"What is this? A joke?"

"No joke, Henry, I assure you."

His eyes narrowed. "Are you the princess?"

"The one and only." She dipped a curtsy with a flourish. "I told you the letter would explain. Sorry it's a little crumpled. I've been a bit preoccupied."

"This can't be true." He fisted the paper and shook it at her. "You expect me to believe this? It has to be a hoax. Where is she?"

She shrugged one thin shoulder. "Believe what you will, Henry. But I saw Maggie write the letter. I promised her I'd deliver it to you. And deliver it I have. Now if you'll excuse me—"

Henry shot to his feet. "Wait, please." He couldn't allow his one link to Maggie to escape. If the letter was real then this woman was his one connection to her.

She paused, giving him a curious glance.

He had grown up with tales of the fair folk. His Irish grandmother told him the stories of the Otherworld and he knew they were a bit mischievous and caused problems. But they didn't exist. Did they? And would one go to so much trouble as to write a letter faking Maggie's handwriting and deliver it to him in Dumfries? He didn't think so. Still, he had questions. Questions he wanted answered.

"Who is Finn? What have you done with Maggie?"

"Sir Finian—Finn—McCullough. The aforementioned Scottish knight. *I* haven't done anything with Maggie. Well, that's not entirely true." She paused, tilted her head to one side as if remembering. She tapped a finger against her chin. "I *did* send her back in time to break the curse but she's the one who insisted on staying. I gave her the option to come home but she refused."

"This is madness." He raked his hand through his hair. "Am I to believe that my daughter, my Maggie, is living in the Middle Ages?"

"Hard to believe, isn't it?"

He growled his annoyance. "My daughter came to Scotland searching for information on a jousting hero. She was to finish her thesis. How did she end up in the Middle Ages?"

"Oh, *that*. Funny story. Pity I don't have time to tell it. I really must return."

"No." He reached for her, snagged her wrist before she could disappear to wherever she'd come from. She glanced down at his hand, raised an eyebrow in question. He let his hand fall away. "My apologies."

"If you must know, she came searching for Sir Derron. He happens to be my fiancé," she said. "We're to be married soon."

"You are Fae?"

"What's so hard about this? Aye, I'm a Fae of the Otherworld. The crown princess. Daughter of Queen Maeve."

"Prove it."

"You're as stubborn as Maggie. That must be where she gets it. I had to prove it to her, too."

"Go ahead," he taunted, not really believing she would do anything spectacular.

Elyne pursed her lips in a thin line. Seconds later a bright aura formed around her and then she glowed. Her golden hair shimmered. Her ears changed from rounded to pointed. Her skin took on an ethereal light. Brighter and brighter. To the point where he had to shield his eyes. The light burned into his corneas and he groaned.

"Believe me now?"

"Yes, yes. Turn it off."

She muted, the light fading. "Sir Derron is now Lord Derron. He's Protector of the Otherworld, Knight of the Realm and Guardian of the Sword of Light. Man has more titles than anyone I've ever known."

"The Sword of Light," Henry repeated, in awe the fabled relic actually existed.

He'd casually studied Celtic history as an amateur historian and teacher of medieval history. He knew of the Four Treasures and their worth to the Tuatha dé Danann. But nowhere in his readings had he discovered a guardian of the treasures.

One day, Henry, you will believe, his Irish grandmother had said when he was a young lad. Still, he didn't believe. Odd his grandmother's words echoed back to him now.

He looked Elyne over again. "It actually exists?"

"You humans think faeries are for children. That we're nothing but tales of fancy. That the sacred relics of the Otherworld don't exist. I assure you the sacred treasures do exist. And I really have to be getting back to the Otherworld. If my mother realizes I've left the realm, I'll be in trouble. Again." She sighed.

"Wait, your highness. I need to know about Maggie. Is she well?"

"She's well and happily in love with her Scotsman."

"In the Middle Ages?"

"Do I have to cover this again? Aye, in the Middle Ages. On second thought, that's not entirely true."

He narrowed his eyes. "Where is she really? I'm not leaving without her."

"I'm afraid that's not possible."

"Why not?"

"Because, Henry, your daughter is currently in the Otherworld." She gave him a sheepish grin.

He straightened. "Take me to her."

"No way. If I come back with another human, my mother will really be ticked off. I've already caused enough problems. You're staying here," she wagged a finger at him, "where you belong. In the human realm."

He reached for her again and again wrapped his hand around her wrist. His fingers tightened on her skin to press his point. "I'm not letting you go until you tell me where I can find her. Or better yet, take me there."

She stared down at his fingers encircling her wrist. "You're a stubborn man."

"That I am. Though she gets it from her mother."

Elyne chuckled. "All right, then. I can't take you there. But I *can* tell you how to get there."

"Tell me, please."

"It's a long story so I'll give you the short version. There was a war in the Otherworld. A Dark Elf tried to take over. In the process, he managed to lower the veil between the human realm and the Otherworld. We, the Fae, have managed to repair most of the veil to keep the walls from coming down completely. But there are several portals that remain open. Portals that can be found in special places. You humans think they're magical."

"Standing stones," he guessed.

"Someone was paying attention in history class." She shook her head. "But standing stones won't get you there."

"A stone circle then."

"Ding, ding, ding!"

He pursed his lips, annoyed. "Which circle? Where do I go?"

She snorted. "Am I to make it *that* easy for you? Why don't I draw you a map while I'm at it?"

"The sooner you tell me, the sooner I release you." He tightened his grip.

"A bargainer. I like it." She flashed him a grin. "There are several circles more powerful than others. The weaker ones won't push you through to the Otherworld but the ones holding stronger magic...well, they should get you there, I should think. Aberdeen would be a good place to start. You could try the Stone of Destiny on the Hill of Tara in Ireland but it's not a circle so that might not be a viable option. Let's see, where else. Oh, aye, of course there's always Stonehenge. I suppose it's up to you and how far you wish to travel to a stone circle."

She glanced down at her wrist, then back up at him. Reluctantly, he released her.

"Thank you," he said.

"Oh, and you should check out McCullough Castle before you leave Dumfries. It holds some very special things inside. You may want to put some clothes on before dashing out, though." She winked and a second later vanished.

Henry blinked with her disappearance. Then realized he stood in the middle of the empty room wearing nothing but plaid boxers.

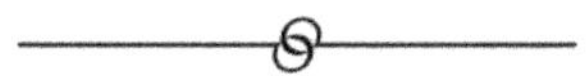

He couldn't sleep. It was impossible with the knowledge his daughter had ended up in the Middle Ages. *That can't be the truth of it.* The princess didn't seem willing to share the information either.

After Elyne's disappearance, he smoothed the crumpled parchment on the bedcovers and read it again. The handwriting looked like Maggie's. The paper felt old enough to be from the Middle Ages. But the look of age could be easily forged. Could he believe the princess?

He'd come to Scotland when Maggie failed to check in with him as she'd promised. He hadn't heard from her in days and her cell phone went straight to voice mail whenever he called. He'd been sick with worry. He had begged her to stay in the States until her friend was well enough to travel. But she was headstrong and stubborn and insisted she could make the trip alone.

I should have never let her go alone.

He flipped on the light and packed his clothes and toiletries. He would start with McCullough Castle as the Fae princess suggested. He needed to find out where he could locate the nearest stone circle. Aberdeen was a five-hour drive. He didn't want to invest that kind of time if he could find a stone circle nearby.

But what if the magic isn't strong enough?

He shook his head to whisk the thought away. Already he started to believe what the princess had said. He couldn't. Wouldn't. He would find the answers at Castle McCullough. He knew it. There was no such thing as magic stone circles or Faeries. Were there?

Dawn broke over the horizon as he checked out and left the hotel behind. He put his lone suitcase in the trunk of his compact rental. A quick consult of the roadmap and he was on his way to the site of Castle McCullough. It was a short drive, not far from Dumfries.

He'd tried to teach Maggie to read a map and even though she seemed to understand it, he'd caught her numerous times reading it upside down. What if she'd gotten lost and something horrible happened to her?

The route he took was scenic, the land lush and green. No

wonder Maggie was drawn to this place, this country. It would be hard not to love it as she did. Thinking about her letter reminded him of all the conversations they had where she talked about the Middle Ages, how she longed to be a lady in that time period.

"You realize there was no plumbing back then?" he asked.

"So what? It would be awesome to see a live jousting tournament."

"You'd hate it the second you couldn't have a shower or brush your teeth," he chided.

"Again, real jousting. Hello."

"I don't know, Mags. It's not a renaissance festival. Life was difficult for them back then. They faced all sorts of diseases and men died from injuries. Their medicine was primitive."

"Do you have to be a killjoy?"

He chuckled now at their exchange. She must have been sixteen at the time. She'd loved flipping through his medieval books, something he encouraged at a young age. Perhaps he was mistaken by persuading her to be like him. He never expected her to follow in his footsteps, though he was never prouder. When he discovered she was missing, he immediately filed for an extended leave of absence from Woodford College where he taught medieval literature.

Taking a turn, he headed down a bumpy road. He slowed the car, trying to keep the steering under control. It looked as though it had rained not too long ago. The car approached a mud puddle. Depressing the brake, he came to a halt.

On the hill a castle stood against the blue expanse of morning sky. That had to be Castle McCullough. He wondered what was so special about it and why the Fae princess—really, he still couldn't believe she was a Fae—had directed him to it. And how would he get inside? There wasn't a lot of traffic heading up to it, so it didn't seem to be a tourist attraction. In fact, he couldn't recall seeing it on any list of places that were a must-see in Scotland.

"Odd, that." It comforted him to hear his own voice.

He consulted his map again but when he looked at it, where he *thought* McCullough Castle should be, it was no longer there. Puzzled, he wrinkled his brow. He pulled off his spectacles and cleaned them with the end of his cotton shirt, then slid them back on to look at the map once again.

Still wasn't there.

"What the dickens…?"

"Hi, Henry."

He nearly jumped out of his skin at the sound of the female voice right next to him. Elyne sat in the passenger seat, her elbow propped on the car door as she gave him a broad smile.

"What the devil are you doing here?"

"Not the Devil. Fae." She thumbed at her chest. "And you still don't believe, eh?"

He growled annoyance.

"I would have thought my disappearance and reappearance would have been enough for you, but I guess not," she said. "I had to make other arrangements."

"By making the castle disappear on the map?"

"How else are you going to believe? Look again."

He glanced down. The castle had returned to the map. "What trickery is this?"

"No trickery," she said innocently. "Fae magic. We can travel through time. Sift, as we call it. This is the exact same road Maggie took when her car broke down in the pouring rain. I took pity on her and allowed the cursed castle to be visible." She nodded toward it.

"The castle is cursed?"

"Well, no. Not anymore. Not since Maggie came along."

"This is madness." He flung open the door, got out, and then spread the map on the hood of the small car to scrutinize it. "One second it's there. The next it's not. I must get my glasses checked."

"No need." Elyne had exited the other side and stood across from him, the car between them. "Your glasses are fine."

"Stop it."

"Stop what?"

"Stop whatever it is you're doing."

"I'm not doing anything but trying to convince you Faeries are real and Maggie is safe."

"Then take me to her, now!"

"No can do."

"Why not?"

She sighed. "I already told you. No more sifting humans for me.

My mother—the queen in case you didn't catch that—will have my head. Now pop on round to the castle and see what you can see. 'Kay?"

She lifted her arms, as though ready to disappear.

"What if they won't let me in?"

"Oh, I'm sure you can use your powers of persuasion. You *are* a professor, aren't you?"

And then she was gone. He blinked.

"Bloody hell," he muttered. "That Fae is going to be the death of me."

Henry got behind the wheel once again and puttered up the hill as fast as the little car would go. On the other side of the small ridge, a tow truck hooked up another compact car to the back. Maggie's car? The princess said she broke down on this road but if that were true, wouldn't the car be gone by now? It had been weeks since he'd had word from his daughter.

"Reminder! Fae magic at work!"

Her disembodied voice surrounded him but she didn't make an appearance this time. Finally, the bumpy road turned into a gravel one and headed up to the main drive through a lovely courtyard featuring a large fountain. The drive ended at the front door of the castle. No guards, no gate, just a gravel circular drive. The front door was large, oaken, with iron medieval hinges.

Henry got out of the car and stood to gaze at the structure. It had to be at least seven hundred years old, with two wings spanning out from the center. Perhaps three stories. He couldn't tell. Some of it looked as though it had been renovated where very old met new.

Taking a deep breath, he headed to the door and rang the bell. He paused in reverence of the structure that was hundreds of years old. It would be like stepping on hallowed ground.

This was no modern door chime either. This was an actual bell that *bonged* somewhere deep inside the castle. Henry marveled at the stonework as the great oaken door swung open. On the other side, a tall bearded man with a riot of red hair and twinkling silvery eyes peered out at him.

"Tours are over for the day, my good man." He had a deep and jovial voice. "But we open early in the morn."

What? He'd left shortly after dawn. He hadn't been driving that long. It *couldn't* be the end of the day yet. His brows knit as he consulted his watch. A few minutes had passed since he'd gotten out of the car.

"I don't understand. Its morning, isn't it?"

"Are ya daft, man?" He chuckled low in his throat. "It's early evening."

"That can't be right."

"Aye, it can. The sun sets there." He pointed over Henry's shoulder.

Henry followed his finger and noticed that indeed the sun was on the horizon. What the bloody…?

Fae magic!

Elyne's voice was in his head. What was she doing to him? Was she trying to make him crazy?

"My apologies. I've been driving most of the day—" He stopped short, remembering Elyne's words, and put on a winning smile. "I'm Dr. Henry Chase, professor of medieval literature from Woodford College in Pennsylvania. I was hoping to have a private tour of the castle? I understand it's spectacular."

"Chase, you say?" His brow wrinkled as he gave him a once-over. Henry wished he looked more the part of a professor. Wrinkled cotton t-shirt and jeans didn't exactly fit the mold, though tweed jacket and khakis with his glasses would probably be pushing it over the top a bit.

I'll say.

Elyne again. He wished she would get out of his head.

Not on your life. I have to make sure you don't mess this up.

"Are you by chance related at all to Lady Margaret Chase?"

Maggie's letter came rushing back to him. She'd mentioned she was living in the Middle Ages by the name of Lady Margaret. Could it be true then?

In case you missed the memo, this is where you say yes, Elyne whispered.

"Yes, I am."

"By Saint George! Patrick McCullough, my man." He grabbed Henry's hand and pumped it several times in a rowdy handshake. "'Tis wonderful to see kinfolk any time of day or night. Do come in." He pulled Henry across the threshold, then shouted, "Andrea!" Flashing a grin, he said, "My wife Andrea will want to meet you straightaway.”

Everything happened so quickly, Henry wasn't sure to what he'd agreed. Stunned, he allowed Patrick to lead him into the main hall, complete with modern furnishings and a gallery overhead.

Two young boys scampered in front of their mother, who also carried a baby girl on her hip. She was tall, lithe, with a mass of auburn waves about her face and pretty blue eyes. She smiled sweetly as she approached.

"Andrea, dear, this is Dr. Henry Chase. Lady Margaret is his ancestor." He turned to Henry. "My wife, Andrea. And these are our three monkeys." He tweaked the nose of the baby, who had pale-red hair like her father.

"Pleasure to meet you," she said with an English lilt. She was clearly not Scottish.

But Henry couldn't get past the "ancestor" thing. He wasn't an ancestor. He was her father, for crying out loud.

They welcomed him inside, offering tea and scones.

"No, thank you," Henry said. "How about a quick tour?"

"Certainly," Patrick said.

Andrea and Patrick talked about the history of the castle, how Lady Margaret was credited with the revival of McCullough Castle when she returned with the laird—a Scottish knight—from a jousting tournament in the mid-thirteen hundreds.

"Rumor was Laird McCullough had a bit of a gambling problem," Patrick said. "But the Lady Margaret set him straight. He was never seen playing cards or dice again. At least not for money. This would have been the main hall. Where most of them would eat and sleep and be entertained. It's been renovated of course for more modern accommodations. Come this way. I'll show you the portrait room."

Patrick waved him to follow and took him through the main hall to the east wing. There were numerous doors to rooms, he said, that were largely undisturbed.

"How much does it cost to keep this place running?" Henry asked.

Patrick chuckled. "It's not cheap, I'll tell you. I do most of the maintenance myself. My wife handles the staff, the planning and the finances. I'd say a million a month is a nice round number. Ah, here we are."

Henry was still processing the *million a month* when they arrived at the portrait room. Paintings stretched over every available surface of the walls from the bottom to the top. Most were in ornate frames, others in simple frames. Beneath the portraits, the walls were a garnet color. The flooring was a warm oaken color topped by a plush rug to match the walls. At the entrance, several suits of armor were on display.

"As you can see, we have a long line of McCulloughs. We're a proud brood."

"I can tell." Henry gazed around at the portraits. "Whose armor is this?"

"Ah, that's Sir Finian's jousting armor. It's seven hundred years old. He was noted for being a popular jousting hero back in his day and spent a lot of time at tournaments. That's how he met Lady Margaret. The story is she gave him her favor and he jousted for her."

"And he won her heart?" Henry asked.

"Naturally." Patrick smiled. "But I understand he never jousted again after that tourney. Seems the laird was perfectly happy to start a family with his new wife."

Henry gazed up at the walls and suddenly his heart throbbed painfully with fear, excitement, dread. "Do you…have a portrait of her?"

"Of course."

He led Henry to the center of the room to one hanging in the middle of the wall. The portrait was one of the bigger ones, with one of the more ornate frames. It had been beautifully painted, capturing the essence of Maggie. A hint of her smile drew up the corners of her mouth as she stood for the painter. She wore a gown of soft blue, belted at the waist. Beside her, a tall Scottish man with the same silvery eyes as Patrick.

But there was no mistaking the woman in the portrait was his daughter. His Maggie. He would know her sweet face anywhere. Everything Elyne had told him was true. Maggie really had ended up in the Middle Ages, really had married a Scottish knight.

Henry faltered, the room spun and the floor rose up to meet him. Andrea shouted her husband's name who grasped Henry by the arm and led him to a chair.

"I say, are you all right?" Patrick asked.

"You gave us a fright. I'll fetch you some tea," Andrea said.

Henry shook his head to clear it. "No need for all the trouble. I'm all right now. Just experienced a bit of a shock is all."

"Would you like to continue the tour?" Patrick asked.

Henry nodded, listening with half an ear as they walked through the rest of the room. He saw portraits of Maggie and her children—his grandchildren! She'd had three—two girls and a boy. The boy was the image of Maggie while the girls resembled their father. The McCullough line had survived for several generations. The more he heard about Lady Margaret, the prouder he was of his daughter.

"Patrick, is there a stone circle nearby?" Henry interrupted the description of the Laird McCullough circa 1851.

He chuckled. "There are stone circles all over Scotland. But, aye, you can find one not far from here. 'Tis about a half-hour drive southwest. Do you fancy seeing it?"

Henry gave him a sheepish grin. "I have an interest in stone circles."

"I'll give you directions after we dine, then."

"I've enjoyed your hospitality long enough," Henry said. "I would hate to impose any longer. If you could give me directions now, I'd be grateful."

"Bollocks. You can drive up in the morning."

Henry didn't want to be rude, but he couldn't wait. "I really need to get to that stone circle tonight."

Patrick and Andrea exchange a look. *They must think I've lost my mind.*

"Do you have a map? I can show you," Patrick said.

Ten minutes later, Henry bid farewell to the McCullough clan. Patrick offered him a warm invitation to come back anytime.

Night enveloped the land, the full moon shining brightly overhead. Back in the car, Henry drove away from McCullough castle down the road he came. He followed Patrick's directions and it wasn't long before he made it to the stone circle. He parked and got out.

The stones stood silent in the shimmery moonlight. The cool night air chilled, but as he approached, warmth and power emanated upward off them. There were twelve large boulders in a circle. As he peered into the circle, the veil separating the human realm from the Otherworld shimmered with an ethereal luminescence.

"Beautiful, isn't it?" Elyne materialized next to him. Her appearance and disappearance didn't startle him. Almost as though he expected it.

He gave her a quick bow. "Princess Elyne."

"You believe now, do you?" She lifted her chin and looked down her nose at him.

"Yes." He nodded to the circle. "If I go through, will I find Maggie?"

"This stone circle is not as strong as the ones I mentioned," she said.

"Aberdeen is several hours from here," he said. "I'm willing to give this one a try."

"And if it doesn't work?"

"Then I'll be driving to Aberdeen," he said. "Will I find Maggie?"

"Maggie is in the Otherworld, aye," Elyne said. "Every portal is different. I don't know where this one will take you."

"But I'll be in the Otherworld?" he asked.

"Aye."

Henry contemplated the stone circle. He had nothing to lose by stepping through, so he took a step.

"Good luck, Henry," she said.

"Thank you, princess."

He stepped past the first boulder, walking through to the center of the circle. Nothing happened. He looked up at the night sky. The stars twinkled down at him. He waited. Perhaps it didn't work. She said it wasn't as strong. Perhaps he would have to drive to Aberdeen anyway. The princess stood outside the circle. She propped her hands on her hips.

"Are you always this difficult?"

He started to reply, to take a step toward his car when she snapped her fingers and spouted something in Gaelic he didn't understand. He opened his mouth to ask her what she was doing, but the words were ripped from him as sure as his breath.

Suddenly, he fell. He gasped, his arms flailing. He tried to catch himself on something—anything—but there was nothing. He slipped through a black void that pressed all around him, stealing his breath.

Icy wind slammed into him, prickling his exposed arms. His teeth chattered. He couldn't keep his eyes open. A moment later, he blacked out.

When Henry regained consciousness, a cool wind blew across his body. He shivered. Something damp was below him. He blinked his eyes open to see he lay at the edge of a shimmering loch, half his body in the water. He crawled away from the edge and into the soft grass. He'd never been so tired.

The stone circle was nowhere in sight. Fear pounded into his veins as he realized he had taken a step he couldn't undo. What if he'd made a mistake? What if he wasn't in the Otherworld but some other realm? What if Maggie wasn't here?

He swallowed his fear and tried to calm his drumming heart. He gazed up at the stars that seemed a jumble. Not at all like the ones back home. He didn't recognize this place and the constellations looked different. He hoped he was one step closer to finding Maggie.

As Henry was about to shove to his feet, a dagger pressed against his throat. Moonlight illuminated the sharp steel. A quick glance around and he realized he was surrounded by several ugly creatures with bald heads, sharp pointy teeth, elongated hawk noses and glowing red eyes. All with swords drawn. He froze.

"Looksie what I found. A human." He licked his lips. "Humans good for roasting."

"Aye, let's roast 'im!" another said. "Let's take 'im back to camp."

"On your feet, human. You's coming to our barbecue," the first said.

That confirmed it. He knew he was in the Otherworld and the dread and panic took firm root inside him.

Chapter 2

Weeks after her brush with death, Queen Maeve finally regained enough strength to make the trek from the foothills of the Stone of Destiny to the Queen's Palace. She had wanted to leave sooner, but Seamus, the royal healer, wouldn't allow it. He had tried to persuade her to wait until she was fully recovered. But after many days of argument, he finally gave in.

At last, the camp had been packed, the horses readied, the Fae and Elves prepared for travel. With the queen in the company, Seamus insisted she be heavily guarded. No one argued with his demands.

Queen Maeve had sent the new Council ahead to the palace to begin reconstruction. They'd sifted there, leaving her behind with the remaining soldiers, a few prisoners, Seamus and the Elven royalty. When she thought she would die on the Stone of Destiny, she'd transferred all her magic to Elyne, so she had to make the journey the old-fashioned way—on horseback. She was far too proud to allow anyone to sift her to the palace. Besides, it had been years since she'd enjoyed a ride through the countryside.

Seamus mounted his horse next to her. "Are you certain about this, your majesty?"

"I have lingered here long enough, Seamus. I must return to the palace. There is much to be done."

"Aye, my queen, there is. But Elyne—"

"May be capable but I need to return. The people need to see me leading once again."

Most of the Fae had been wiped out in the war with Lord Kieran. The loss of life had been too great for Maeve to face while she recovered. Now she mourned so many of her people and the Elves. She owed a great debt of gratitude to King Urdithane for sending his Elven warriors to help fight.

The young Elven princess Allanna had returned to her father, escorted by a large group of Elven soldiers. She would impart the news of the battle to him. Prince Andahar and Lord Eldrin, two Elven princes who had helped with the fight, joined the party traveling to the palace. With the murder of the Guardians of the Spear and Club, Elyne had appointed each of them a Guardian. Andahar carried the Club on his belt while Eldrin kept the Spear close at hand. A garrison had remained behind to guard the Stone of Destiny until Maeve could find a replacement.

The black dragon Nero followed them through the sky as they traveled to the Queen's Palace. Every night when they made camp, the dragon would land nearby, curl into a ball with his tail around his big body, and sleep. And every morning when they packed up camp, the dragon would watch their caravan overhead. Maeve found it curious the great black dragon—who had been controlled by their enemy, Lord Kieran—should follow them.

"Would you like me to do something about the dragon, your majesty?" Prince Andahar asked.

He must have sensed her concern. She smiled. "No, Andahar. The dragon has posed no threat."

"Not as yet," he agreed, eyeing the beast in the sky. "But what if he attacks?"

"Lord Kieran is dead and his first-in-command a prisoner of the Fae. I doubt the dragon will attack without either of them commanding him to."

"I don't like it," Seamus put in. He rode to the left of the queen, keeping close in case she needed immediate medical attention. "He could attack any time without warning. It's dangerous to allow him to continue to follow us."

"Thank you both for your concern," she said. "But until I say otherwise, Nero is to be left alone."

"Nero?" Seamus scoffed. "You call it by its name?"

"Why shouldn't I? The other dragons have names."

"Aye, but Ambrielle, Luna and Aura did not attack us. We would have certainly perished on the Hill of Tara had they not been part of the battle," Seamus said.

Maeve knew. She was the one who brought them out of shadow. She'd put the dragons to sleep thousands of years ago when man and Fae alike hunted them to near extinction. She had promised Ambrielle she would one day release them when the need arose. With the threat of Kieran, it had been necessary to awaken them.

She hadn't seen the three dragons since the battle ended and Elyne had refused to put them back into shadow. Maeve hadn't argued with her, secretly agreeing the dragons could become an integral part of their world once again.

It seemed they had traveled forever so when the Queen's Palace came into view at long last on the horizon, it was a welcome sight. A wash of emotions passed through her—from relief to seeing her beloved home to excitement she would finally be able to return to her private chamber alone. It had been difficult to attend to her personal needs with so many men around.

She'd had some lingering pain from the injuries she'd sustained at the Stone of Destiny. The hard riding hadn't eased that much. And if that wasn't enough, she was still without her magic.

"Another few hours, your majesty, and we'll be there," Andahar said. "Welcome home."

"You may welcome me home, Andahar, when we ride through the gates and this journey is behind us at last," she said.

He laughed. They'd become traveling companions over the journey. As crown prince to the reign of the Elves and leader of the Elven warriors, mayhap Andahar felt as though he should remain by her side. He would do the same for his father, King Urdithane.

"Night falls, my queen," Seamus said. "We should make camp."

Her other traveling companion was not so amicable. Seamus constantly worried about her health and her strength. He urged her to not push herself so hard while riding, but the queen had insisted they cover as many miles as they could in a day. Now with home so close, she shook her head.

"Nay, Seamus. We continue until we reach the gates."

"My queen—"

"We continue," she repeated. Her back stiffened, her eyes straight ahead as she pinned her gaze on the palace. She was so close now she wouldn't stop.

"Ride ahead and with a message to my daughter the company approaches," she said.

"And leave your side?" Seamus shook his head. "Nay, your majesty. I cannot, as healer, leave you alone. What if something should happen to you?"

"I assure you my health is in top condition, Seamus." Even as she spoke the words, she had a pang of discomfort shoot through her. "I have Prince Andahar to protect me. Ride ahead and tell them. We will increase our speed once you're out of sight to cover more miles."

Seamus' lips thinned into a grimace as he gripped his reins. He kicked his horse into a run and galloped away, dirt clods flying in his wake.

"I think you may have insulted him, your majesty." Andahar chuckled.

"I grow tired of his hovering and constant tending. He treats me as though I'm made of glass. Therefore, I think I don't care." She flashed him a smile and gave him a surreptitious wink.

Andahar laughed out loud.

Maeve made good on her word to pick up the pace toward the palace. As soon as Seamus was out of sight, she ordered the group into a gallop. As night fell, they stopped to light torches to help lead them the rest of the way.

The gates to the outer bailey were a welcome sight but Maeve could still see a lot of damage from the attack. Tents and campfires dotted the landscape outside the walls of the palace. She scanned the dirty faces and realized these were Fae who had been displaced by the war. Men, women and children emerged from their tents. As she rode through their encampment, cheers rose up from them. Cheers of joy at seeing their queen return home at last, reinforcing her decision to return was the right one.

Lord Vaughan, her new advisor, and several of the council members waited for her arrival. Relieved to be home at last, Maeve dismounted. Her muscles ached from the long ride and she was weary.

"Welcome home, my queen," Vaughan said and bowed low.

"Thank you. This is Prince Andahar. Please make sure he is comfortable as he is one of our honored guests."

"Aye, we'll see to his needs."

"And also Lord Eldrin. Where is he?" She asked this last question of Andahar.

"He prefers to ride with his men," Andahar replied.

"Make sure that he has proper accommodations as well, Vaughan. These Elves helped keep me alive on the Hill of Tara."

Vaughan nodded understanding, then motioned for one of the servants. "Please see Prince Andahar to one of the guest bedchambers in the east wing."

Before he left, Andahar took Maeve's hand and kissed it. "Thank you, your majesty." He nodded farewell as she turned to Vaughan.

"How much damage has the castle sustained?" She started walking again, her mind on one thing—seclusion in her own private chamber.

"Quite a bit. Lord Kieran's men slaughtered our servants and burned several of the outbuildings. I've had men working day and night to rebuild," he said.

"Don't work them too hard, Vaughan. They've lost family members. There needs to be a mourning period."

As she entered, chaos reigned. Builders and soldiers crowded the palace. One of the outer walls had been breached in the battle and men worked to repair it. There weren't enough accommodations for everyone. The last thing she wanted was noise and chaos.

She heaved a sigh. "Stop the repairs for the next few nights. I'm weary, Vaughan, and need the rest. Remove all the soldiers, Fae and Elf, from the palace walls. We'll have to find someplace else for them. Find rooms for the officers. What of the prisoners we transported from the Hill of Tara?"

"They have been dealt with accordingly," Lord Vaughan said. "I saw to it personally they were put in the Reformatory."

"Make sure the wards are strong and double the guards, if possible. I don't want anyone trying to escape, especially those loyal to Lord Kieran. We don't need more trouble."

"Aye, my queen. Shortly before your arrival, the black dragon landed nearby. No one can shoo him away. He seems to have taken up permanent residence on the southeast side of the palace."

She knit her brows. "Near my private chamber?"

"Aye, your majesty. What would you like done with him?"

"Nothing." Her gut twisted, though. Why would Nero land there? "I want the dragon unharmed."

"He frightens the men," Lord Vaughan said.

"He won't hurt them." Somehow, she knew that. "Make sure no one touches the dragon."

"And if he attacks?"

"Then you have my permission to fight. Where is my daughter?"

"Hello, Mother. Welcome home."

Elyne gave her a broad smile and then embraced her. It was uncharacteristic. It took Maeve a moment to react and return the hug.

"I'll entrust you, Lord Vaughan, with your duties," Maeve said. Then to Elyne, "Come, daughter. Brief me on everything that's happened in my absence."

Maeve led Elyne to her private council chamber. Once inside, she closed the door.

"The repairs are going well," Elyne began. "Most of the interior chamber have been reconstructed. I took the liberty of using your magic." She gave her a sheepish grin.

Maeve couldn't be angry with Elyne. It was what she would have done. "Good. The sooner the palace is restored, the better. What have you learned from the commoners? How many villages did Kieran destroy?"

"Lord Derron and his men have been scouting the countryside looking for survivors. Most of the villages were wiped out. He burned them to the ground."

Hearing that, a pang of sorrow followed by anger went through her.

Elyne continued. "Kieran also managed to destroy most of the crops and stole a lot of the livestock. The survivors we've found were starving. We brought them to the palace grounds."

Maeve was pleased by her daughter's decision. As she suspected, the Fae she saw outside the walls no longer had homes. "Good. How many are housed here?"

"Several thousand, I'm afraid."

"I would like to meet with the High Council as soon as possible to begin planning our recovery," Maeve said. "What of the walls? Are they holding?"

The walls between the Otherworld and the human realm had

been fractured. Again, due to Lord Kieran. He had tried to take them down and conquer both realms to claim as his own.

"They are. The High Druid used his powers to keep them from falling completely. He also restored the Barrier between the Seelie and Unseelie realm, but there are several Unseelie here," Elyne explained.

"What is being done about that?"

"Lord Derron has sent what men he could spare to round them up and return them to the Dark," she said. "A difficult task, though, since we are short on men."

"I will ask Prince Andahar for assistance from the Elves," Maeve said.

At the mention of the Elves, her daughter shifted in her seat and looked uncomfortable. Elyne dragged her lower lip through her teeth.

"Aye, I'm sure they could help. Also, there are still portals around certain standing stones in the human realm. The High Druid said you could close them permanently," she said.

"And you still have my magic so that will have to be rectified soon. We will go see the High Druid tomorrow." Maeve laced her fingers in front of her.

"It's late, Mother. Shouldn't you rest? It's been a long journey."

"I will rest as soon as we're finished here. I sent Princess Allanna back to her father with the news of the war," Maeve said.

"Sir Drake will be disappointed she didn't return with the group." Again, at the mention of the Elves, Elyne looked uncomfortable as she glanced away from her mother.

Maeve's eyes narrowed. "Are you to tell me the humans still remain?"

"I know you detest humans, Mother, but they aren't so bad. We would have died without Sir Drake and Sir Finian here to help us."

Maeve scowled. "They don't belong here, Elyne. Send them back immediately."

"I would, but the portals around the standing stones have become unstable. And you forbid me to sift." Elyne bit her bottom lip again.

Maeve sensed her daughter had something she wasn't telling her. "That I did. What troubles you?"

"Nothing, I…nothing." Her shoulders slumped.

"Something. You've been uneasy at every mention of the Elves. What is it?"

"Wine?" Elyne jumped to her feet and poured two goblets from the brass ewer. "You look tired, Mother."

"That's the second time you've mentioned that." She took the goblet and sipped. The wine was welcome after long days and nights of nothing but water. The oaky flavor slipped down her throat and warmed her. "If there's something you need to tell me, now would be the time."

Elyne gripped her goblet so tight her nail beds turned white. "Remember when you sent me to King Urdithane to request troops to help with the fight?"

Maeve recalled it well. They hadn't enough Fae to fight the war against Kieran and his strong Unseelie army. Reaching out to the Elves for help had been her one option. Elyne had volunteered to convince their king to give them four thousand men and she had succeeded.

"What of it?"

"I was remiss in not telling you the king put a condition on giving us the men." Again, Elyne tugged her bottom lip through her teeth.

Maeve didn't like where this was going. The wine soured in her stomach. "Aye? And?"

"And, well, he made me give him my word."

"About what?" Her hand tightened on her goblet.

"He said if I gave him my word, he would honor it as the truth and give us the four thousand men to fight our cause. He said the Elves would not bleed with the Fae for nothing."

"I lose patience with this, daughter. What did you promise him?"

"That, ah, the Treaty of Separation would be abolished so the Elves and Fae may coexist as they once did."

Stunned, Maeve stared at her daughter. Her stomach twisted into a tight knot. The Treaty of Separation had been between them for over six thousand years. Elyne had promised this to King Urdithane without her consent. *To get four thousand men.* Four thousand men who fought alongside the Fae and helped defeat

Lord Kieran.

Still, Maeve would have never agreed to that term. Never. And now she was left to clean up the mess Elyne had made once again. She exhaled a deep sigh.

"Abolish the Treaty." She allowed the words to sink into her mind, the wine now forgotten. "How could you agree to that?"

"I had to, Mother." The words rushed from Elyne. "King Urdithane refused to help. But when I gave him my word the Treaty would be abolished, he offered men. If he hadn't sent them, we would have all surely died."

"You don't know that. You couldn't have known that. What happened on that field—"

"Happened because Lord Kieran killed most of our troops," Elyne interrupted. "I did what I thought was right to save us. I did the only thing I could."

"I cannot simply abolish the Treaty. The High Council will have to be involved." Anger singed her. How dare Elyne put her in this position?

"I told him the Treaty couldn't be broken without your consent and you would have to negotiate with him."

"And now you've put me in a more difficult situation with the Elves." She clenched her free hand.

"Aye, well, he intends to negotiate with you, but he wants me involved as well."

"Absolutely not." Maeve shook her head. "You have caused enough damage. The Council and I will handle this."

"But that was part of the terms of our agreement."

"I will deal with the king myself," Maeve said. "You will have no part in the renegotiations of the Treaty."

Elyne started to object, but a rap on the door interrupted her.

"Come," Maeve called.

Lord Derron eased open the door and entered, giving her a bow. "Forgive my intrusion," he said, "but I have urgent news. Welcome home, my queen."

"What is it?" Maeve asked, waving away the pleasantries.

"Most of the prisoners brought from the field at the Hill of Tara have been transferred to the Reformatory," he said.

"*Most* of the prisoners, Lord Derron?"

"It seems Cormac managed to escape." He cut a glance at Elyne. She flushed red.

Maeve gripped her goblet before taking a long swig. Her head pounded between her eyes. She wished she had bypassed this meeting and headed straight to her private chamber. Now her blood was really boiling. Cormac had been Lord Kieran's right-hand man and, she'd been told, a Fomorian. A race thought banished long ago to the Sorrow Lands and imprisoned underwater for all eternity.

"How did that happen?"

"No one knows," Derron said. "He was there one minute and gone the next."

"Of course, he was." Maeve sighed, unhappy with the situation. "Fomorians are powerful. Some are more powerful than the Fae. Find him, Lord Derron."

"Aye, my queen." He gave another bow. "I have…other news."

She sighed. "What now?"

"I've received word from the Elves that King Urdithane will be here soon."

"How nice." A bitterness lingered on her tongue. Either from the wine or this meeting, she didn't know which. "Have more guest chambers readied in the east wing, then. We can't be inhospitable despite the state of the palace."

She rose and plunked the wine on the nearby table. Weariness pressed through her bones. She needed a hot bath and her featherbed.

"I'm retiring. I trust both of you can keep things under control. Make sure I'm not disturbed. On the morrow, daughter, we will pay a visit to the High Druid to return my magic."

The queen left, her back stiff and her face flushed with anger. Guilt swarmed Elyne. Mayhap she should have told her sooner about the Elven king and his demand. But it never seemed as though it was the right time.

"She's angry at me," Elyne said. "Again."

"Once she's had time to think about it, she'll understand why you did it." Derron squeezed her hand. "Don't worry."

Her gaze fluttered to his. "And Cormac?"

"We'll find him." He pressed his lips together. "You have my word."

"I don't think we can spare any more men to search for him. I should have listened to you, Derron, and had him executed. I should have told my mother about the promise I made King Urdithane sooner."

"You can't regret your decisions, Elyne. All we can do now is move forward."

When Elyne had struggled with falling in love with Derron, Maggie had said something similar to her. Her human friend had pushed her toward him while she had resisted. Wouldn't Maggie be surprised when her father showed up in the Otherworld?

"One other thing I didn't tell her." Elyne's voice was barely above a whisper.

"More?" His brows rose. "What now?"

"When I altered time and brought Maggie to Finn, I promised her I would get a letter to her father in her time." She paused, choosing her words carefully.

"And did you?"

"I…well, I did. I visited him recently. He was in Scotland searching for her. He was worried about her because he hadn't heard from her and she'd disappeared." She swallowed.

"You didn't?"

"I found him and gave him the letter," she continued, ignoring his question. She refused to meet his gaze, though, and focused on a spot on the wall. "He didn't believe me, so I had to convince him."

"Oh, Elyne. What did you do?"

She shrugged and gave him an innocent smile. "I may have steered him toward McCullough Castle."

Derron blinked, not understanding. "Why would your mother care about that?"

"I also may have told him he could get to the Otherworld through a portal. And when he attempted to get through that portal…I might have helped him through."

He closed his eyes and shook his head. He paced, then, and scrubbed a hand down his face. "You brought Maggie's father here?"

"What was I supposed to do? He worried himself sick over her. I had to help him."

"I do believe, my dear princess, you are becoming more and more like your friend Maggie every day."

She stiffened. "What do you mean?"

"Meddling in others' affairs." His smile reached his blue eyes as he cupped her face. "And I love you for that." He kissed her softly.

"I shouldn't have brought him here," she said.

"Where is he now?"

"I don't know. I haven't found him yet."

"I suppose we'd better then. The last thing we need is for him to get captured and brought to the queen. I'll talk to Lord Eldrin to keep an eye out for him. You can give him a description of the man?"

"Aye, I can. And thank you. Another human in the realm may send her over the edge."

Nodding, Derron pulled her into his arms. "Let's worry about that on the morrow, though, aye?"

As he kissed her, Elyne was helpless to resist.

Chapter 3

It didn't take Henry long to discern he was in the company of several hungry orcs. They led him away from the loch through a copse of trees to a small encampment where others waited around a crackling campfire. Apparently, the four he was with were the hunting party.

"Dinner!"

"Get the spit ready!"

"I gets an arm and a leg."

"I's the one that found him. I gets to pick first." The orc shoved the last one who'd spoken to the ground. Then he grabbed Henry by the arm and gave him a push toward the center of the campfire. "Gets the rope."

"You's not the leader. We don't have to do what yous says."

"Gets the rope if yous want to eat." And then he growled to press his point.

It did nothing to intimidate the other orc, who growled back. They got into a shoving match then, the others cheering them on, seeming to forget about Henry. He managed to make his way from the fire toward the edge of the camp. If he could make a break through the trees, he could perhaps find his way to Maggie, though he had no idea where to begin searching.

As the two punched each other, Henry kept his eye on them. A high-pitched whistling whooshed through the air and then, seconds later, an arrow found its way into the eye of one of the orcs. It screamed in agony. Before any of them could take action, another one went down with an arrow in his head.

They scattered, skittering into the shadows like cockroaches running from light. Henry was left standing in the orange glow of the campfire with two dead orcs. He reached down to snatch the dagger from the belt of one of the dead ones, ready for anything.

He was outmatched in this strange land. The crunch of leaves signaled approaching men. A lot of men. They materialized from the brush, swords drawn and pointed directly at him. They wore uniforms and appeared to be soldiers. Friend or foe, he didn't know which.

"Drop your weapon," the one who seemed to be the leader said.

Henry released the dagger and it thumped to the ground. At least these men didn't appear to want to eat him.

"You are human," he said.

"I am." Henry nodded. Was that good or bad? Would he be punished or rescued?

"Another one." The leader sighed.

Another one? Did he refer to Maggie? Or more humans?

"Lord Derron will not be pleased," one of the soldiers said.

Clearly, they were experiencing an influx of humans in the Otherworld. Perhaps due to the open portals.

"Nay, he will not," the leader agreed. "Let's put him with the rest and take him back to the palace as ordered."

As luck would have it, Henry had fallen into good hands. They would take him exactly where he wanted to go—the palace. He assumed he would find Elyne there and perhaps even Maggie. The soldier pushed Henry into motion with his sword point.

One of the soldiers remained behind to douse the fire while the others led Henry away, through the trees. When they emerged, the small group waited on horseback, all wearing armor and carrying swords or bow and arrows. He thought he spied a crossbow with one of them. He would have expected them to be wearing suits of armor. Instead, they wore helms, padded tunics, padded pants and boots.

One thing they all had in common though—pointed ears. Elyne also had pointed ears when she revealed her true self. Her appearance had nearly blinded him but not so here. Because they were in the Otherworld? They wouldn't need to hide behind glamour here.

"Another one, my lord," the one who'd found him announced.

The leader heaved a sigh. "Bind his hands and put him with the others." He motioned toward the waiting cart where more prisoners were inside. Fear clenched his stomach.

"He doesn't look like the others." The soldier gave him a once-over. "Who are you?"

How should he respond? Not knowing if they were the good guys, he pressed his lips together and refused to answer.

"I asked who you were." The soldier pressed the tip of his sword to Henry's throat.

"It doesn't matter," the leader snarled. "He was found wandering the countryside. Our orders were to pick up anyone who doesn't belong here and bring them to the palace prison. That's where we're taking him."

"Lord Derron ordered all humans to be brought to him," he objected.

"He goes to the prison. Put him with the others."

The one who'd found him shoved him into the packed horse-drawn cart. None looked human. Pointed ears, dirty faces, tattered clothes with bloodstains. Others looked more like trolls or gnomes or nightmare creatures. Another had a mouth full of sharp, pointed teeth and no lips. His face was scarred in places and had dried blood in others. They were not like the tall, lithe men with pointed ears. Were they Fae? Or something else?

A few stared at him as he stumbled into the cart. The door slammed and locked.

Princess Elyne had mentioned a war. Were these people part of that? Had he fallen into the hands of the enemy? Could she have led him astray? Had he made a mistake about coming here? He hoped not. If this was where Maggie was, then he was determined to find her. Even so, uneasiness settled in his chest, constricting it. He should have weighed all his options before stepping through the portal. Making snap decisions was not like him. He was one to be more methodical, more thoughtful before jumping in feet first.

Well, you've jumped. Time to deal with the consequences.

Henry cowered in a corner, trying to avoid the stares. He knew he was out of place in his wrinkled t-shirt and jeans. He focused his attention on the countryside as they traveled from the portal toward the palace. His heart pounded a wild beat. Was he in the right place? He should have listened to Elyne and gone to Aberdeen. If he had stepped through the stone circle there, perhaps he would have ended up closer to the palace. Now he was at their mercy.

The countryside was much like the Scottish landscape. Rolling hills, lush green grass, pink sky. He did a double take. Pink sky? The blue intermingled with the pink, blending together. In the east, the sun peeked over the horizon, making the colors of the sky burn brighter. It was beautiful. Far more beautiful than any sunrise he'd seen at home.

The cart bounced along the bumpy road and still the strangers stared. He did his best to ignore them but he shifted in his seat nonetheless. It was disconcerting to have them eyeing him.

"You're human, aren't you?" one of the captured men asked. He had pointed ears. Dried blood splattered his clothes and hands. He scowled at Henry. "We don't like humans here."

Henry feigned a smile and shrugged one shoulder. "Sorry."

Great. Not only was he in the company of Fae soldiers, but also in the company of enemies who didn't like humans. He pressed closer to the bars of the cart, trying to put as much distance between him and them as possible. It didn't work all that well.

"Humans helped destroy us." Another glared at him with venom in his dark eyes.

Henry shifted again. That was not good news. He didn't like the way they glared at him, as though ready to tear out his throat. The one with pointed teeth licked his lips—or rather tried. All he managed was a blackened tongue wagging out of his mouth dripping with drool. Another orc.

Henry was certain orcs, trolls and gnomes existed in fantasy fiction, not here in the Otherworld. Yet he couldn't deny he faced them. He swallowed the lump of fear that formed in his throat.

"Humans look best roasting," the creature said. "Has lots of meat on him, he does."

"The human should die," a troll snarled. "Let me tear off his arms."

"And then we's eats him." The nodded agreement. More drool trickled out of the side of his mouth.

"No, you idiot." One of the pointy-eared men slapped him on the back of the head. "We kill him."

"And then we eats him," the orc insisted.

"Shut it! No one is eating the human or killing him!"

Henry breathed a sigh of relief. One of the Fae soldiers rode alongside the cart and shouted at them to get away from him. To press his point, he shoved his sword between the bars and waved it at the group of degenerates.

They slunk back into the shadows, but their gazes never left Henry. He kept a wary eye on them while also keeping an eye on the landscape, watching as it changed from rolling hills to more rocky terrain. The cart had turned and they headed toward a large palace. It looked as though it had sustained some damage—perhaps a casualty of war?

The palace sprawled across several acres and looked at least four stories tall. Flags flew from the turrets, flapping in the wind. Soldiers patrolled the highest wall. Outside the palace walls, tents dotted the landscape, clustered together. They went through the gates and halted inside the inner bailey. Morning sun beamed through the clouds, illuminating the grounds.

The Fae soldier opened the back of the cart and hauled Henry down. They led him away from the troll, orc and gnome, thankfully. He hoped he would never have to see them again or share a cell with them in the prison.

"Where are you taking this human?" One of the men intercepted the soldier. He stood taller than the Fae, with golden hair and ears more pointed than the soldier.

"All prisoners are to be taken to the Reformatory." The soldier stood his ground.

"By whose command?" He folded his arms across his chest.

"I don't have to answer you, Elf. Guardian of the Club of Dagda or not. Those are the orders I'm following." The word *elf* sounded as though it were distasteful. He lifted his chin a little higher in defiance.

Henry stared at the Elf, looking him over as though he looked at an alien. The Elf looked as he imagined one to be—tall, regal, blond. Armed to the teeth, he wore an ancient-looking club strapped to one hip, a sword to the other, and a quiver of arrows on his back. Henry spied a dagger on his belt. He wore padded vest, pants and dusty black boots.

The Elf's gaze flickered over Henry before turning back to the Fae soldier. "Humans are not to go to the prison."

"You're not in charge here, Lord Eldrin." His face flamed bright red.

"I've been appointed one of the Guardians. Lord Derron gave me orders to bring all humans to him or the princess."

Lord Eldrin pushed aside the young Fae and took Henry by the arm. Henry's hope soared. This Lord Eldrin was ordered to bring humans to Derron or the princess. He recalled Elyne mentioning Lord Derron and remembered they were to be married soon. If he could get to one of them, then he could get to Maggie.

The Elf took him through the bailey heading for the palace. The orcs and others were herded another direction.

"I doubt you wish to spend a night in the dungeons with the Unseelie and orcs," Lord Eldrin said.

"Are you taking me to Lord Derron then?" he asked.

He nodded. "He wants you with the other humans. With the portals open there are too many humans wandering into the Otherworld," the Elf said. "The High Druid is putting them into a deep sleep until they can be sifted back to the human realm. They will never even remember they were here."

Relief flooded him. He was glad he wouldn't have to spend a night in the dungeon. But then what did Lord Derron want with humans?

"However, I have a special request from someone else."

"Princess Elyne?" Henry guessed.

"Aye. She asked anyone matching your description be brought immediately to her. The request of the crown princess overrules that of Lord Derron's orders." Eldrin flashed a reassuring smile.

"And then what happens?"

"She will determine what to do with you. Though I should think it's much better than being stuck in the dungeons with Unseelie."

As they walked, he'd lost track of where Eldrin led him through the palace. He'd let his mind wander and not paid attention to where they were going. How would he ever escape? They'd gone through a maze of hallways and now entered a great hall. Henry craned his neck to see all he could. High walls made of the smoothest stone, giant candle chandeliers hanging from iron links from the ceiling, colorful tapestries along the walls, a plush garnet rug under his feet. On one side of the great hall was a six-foot fireplace complete with roaring fire.

They rounded another corner and entered a wide torch-lined

corridor. On the other end, the double oak doors swung open, the oversized iron hinges groaning. A small group entered the corridor.

"Her majesty, Queen Maeve of the Otherworld," a herald announced.

Eldrin stopped and stepped off to the side, his back against the cold wall. Henry did the same. Moments later the queen appeared behind the herald. She wore a flowing midnight-blue gown belted at the waist with a gold cord and long, flowing sleeves. Her golden-blonde hair hung in waves over her shoulders to her waist. She had perfectly chiseled features with high cheekbones, perfect blonde arched eyebrows, long, dark lashes. Her bright-blue eyes were sharp and assessing and her heart-shaped lips the color of the reddest rose. Lips shaped perfectly for kissing. Long, tender kisses.

The moment Henry saw the beauty his heart flipped in his chest. His stomach bottomed out and he knew…*knew*…he would have to have her. Queen or not. Royalty or not. Fae or not. She elicited a response in him he thought long dead.

She was flanked by a younger version of herself—he immediately recognized Princess Elyne—and a tall man with black hair and blue eyes. The resemblance between Elyne and her mother was uncanny.

"What is so urgent that you both drag me from my bed at this ungodly hour?" The queen all but growled the words.

"There is a problem in the prison," Elyne explained, her cheeks rosy. She looked as though she squirmed under her mother's scrutiny. "I would not have disturbed you, Mother, had the High Druid not specifically requested your presence."

The queen scowled. But even her scowl was beautiful. "Is someone going to explain to me what the problem is at the prison or am I going to have to guess?"

"There's been a breach." The man's tone was even and deep.

As the queen breezed by, Henry caught a whiff of her jasmine scent. He resisted the urge to close his eyes and inhale it until he couldn't inhale it anymore. Eldrin gave her a respectful bow of his head. The queen glanced at him for a brief second as they passed. She halted and turned to peer at Henry. Her sharp gaze hit him like a razorblade, cutting through him and slicing him open. Ripping his heart out of his chest and making him want her all the more.

She was the most beautiful woman he'd ever seen. But it went beyond that. He sensed a connection between them, something that told him they belonged together. Something that drew her to him.

The queen took three long strides and paused in front of him, her eyes searching his face. She looked him up and down, her beautiful heart-shaped lips now thinned into a grimace.

"What is this human doing here, Lord Eldrin?" she asked.

"I, ah…" Eldrin began.

The man next to the queen cleared his throat. "Your pardon, my queen, but Lord Eldrin is doing as I requested."

"And what is that, Lord Derron?" She never took her searing gaze off Henry.

"Humans have managed to come through the portals into the Otherworld," he explained. "Eldrin is taking him to the holding chamber with the others."

"There are more?" Her fiery gaze turned on him, her face pinched with annoyance. Waves of displeasure emanated off her. "Why haven't I been informed of this?"

"I've handled it," Derron said. "The High Druid is putting them to sleep and removing their memories of the Otherworld until we can return them to the human realm."

She heaved a heavy sigh. "Is there anything else I should know about?" She turned her heated gaze on Elyne. "Or are you planning to drop more surprises in my lap?"

"No more surprises, Mother." Elyne's words were weak and her lips were white around the edges. As though fear had taken hold of her.

The queen turned her attention back to Eldrin. "Very well. Carry on, Lord Eldrin."

She turned with a flourish, her skirts fluttering behind her as she resumed her path. Elyne and Lord Derron fell in step behind her. But Elyne glanced over her shoulder at Eldrin. The Elf gave her a nod as though agreeing with her silent request.

"Follow me." Eldrin resumed walking.

Henry followed, but his mind was on the queen. When and how would he see her again? Better yet, how could he woo her? "Where are you taking me?"

"I'm taking you to Princess Elyne's chamber as she requested.

You can wait there until she returns," Eldrin said.

"What then?"

The Elf shrugged. "I don't know."

But Henry did. He suspected he would finally see his daughter. And then what? Would he take her out of the Otherworld? Away from her Scottish knight? Knowing his headstrong daughter, Maggie would never consent to that. She would object loudly. Could he leave her here in this strange place?

He had a lot to consider.

Eldrin left Henry in the princess's chamber. Locked him in, actually. As soon as the Elf was gone, he'd tried to escape. He should have known he wouldn't be left unattended behind unlocked doors. The princess wouldn't allow him to roam the palace freely.

He spent a long time standing on the balcony, watching the repairs. Aside from that, soldiers brought in more prisoners. Others were welcomed into the palace. Henry's best guess was they were men, women and children who were victims of the war and had no place else to go. Perhaps that explained the tents outside the palace when they arrived.

When he tired of that, he turned his attention to searching Elyne's chamber. He found nothing of interest, though what he expected to find he wasn't sure. Her wardrobe was full of gowns and slippers. She had a full-length mirror in one corner. A four-poster bed dripping with gauzy curtains graced one wall. Tapestries hung along the walls, an oversized chair was in one corner and a thick rug covered the stone floor.

At one point he tried to sleep but was unable. He couldn't stop his racing thoughts. He paced the length of her room, watching the sunlight move across the floor. It was nightfall when he finally heard the rattle of a key in the lock. The door pushed open and the princess entered, closing it with a snap.

Princess Elyne turned to him, her hands on her slender hips as she looked him over. She bit her lower lip in concentration, perhaps trying to decide what to do with him.

"We have a lot to talk about," she said finally.

"Yes, we do," he agreed. "Do I have you to thank for getting here?"

"If you mean, did I push you through the portal, aye. I did."

"I thought you had a hand in that," he said.

"What was I supposed to do? You wouldn't go to Aberdeen like I suggested. That stone circle didn't have the power to get you here."

"How did Maggie get here? Where is she?" He cut to the chase.

"Whoa. One question at a time." She folded her arms and looked defiant. "First question first. It's a long story."

He checked his watch which, he noticed for the first time, had stopped. Glancing back up at her, he said, "We appear to have plenty of time."

Elyne huffed. "You may want to sit down for this." She motioned to the oversized chair. "I first saw Maggie when she came to Castle McCullough. Her car broke down on the road and she was stranded. The castle, at the time, was in ruins. And cursed."

The princess told him the story of how she haunted the then-ghostly Finian McCullough, who had been cursed for killing Lord Derron in a jousting match. She'd sent Maggie back in time to break the curse and right the wrongs, but things didn't go as planned. Sending Maggie back in time had altered the timeline. Maggie helped defeat the evil Earl of Litonshire who had been trying to blackmail Finn into giving him the McCullough lands.

Maggie had fallen hard for Sir Finian. Once the jousting tournament was over, she had decided she would stay with him. She'd written the letter—which Henry had read—and made Elyne promise to deliver it.

"But that doesn't explain how she ended up here in the Otherworld," Henry said.

"I'm getting to that, oh impatient one."

The Otherworld had been in distress—Lord Kieran of the Unseelie had attacked their realm and tried to take it over. Lord Derron's father, Guardian of the Sword of Light, had been murdered along with the other Guardians of the Four Treasures. They needed help from the Elves to defeat the Unseelie. They'd also recruited their human friends and Maggie would not be parted from Finn. She and her husband had been sifted here. Queen

Maeve had transferred all her powers to Elyne when she thought she would die in battle. Powers the princess now still possessed. The battle had been won on the Hill of Tara at the Stone of Destiny.

"I told her they could stay here as long as they wanted," Elyne concluded. "She and her husband are still here."

"When can I see her?"

"Soon," Elyne promised. "We'll have to give you some sort of disguise. I can't have you wandering around the palace looking like that." She wagged her finger up and down at him.

Henry glanced down at his attire. "Like what? This?"

"Not your clothes. You can't look like a human."

He grimaced. "And how do you propose we get around that?"

"I will cast a glamour on you. As long as I have my mother's powers, I can do that." She beamed, clearly proud of her brilliance.

"And what if you don't have your mother's powers?"

"That *will* pose a problem but I'm not worried about that yet. In the meantime, you need to look like a Fae." She looked him over once again. "And a knight."

"A knight?" His brow wrinkled. "Are you going to knight me, then?"

She grinned like a wolf. "You bet I am."

"How do you intend to do that?"

"Hello. I'm the princess." She thumbed at her chest. "I'll find you some proper clothes and then we can get the knighting ceremony underway. I'll need Derron's help with that."

"Derron is your betrothed," he said.

"You do have a memory like an elephant, don't you? Aye, he's my betrothed. Once we put a glamour on you, you can have full access to the palace. Until then, I need to keep you under lock and key."

"How long will that take? Putting a glamour on me?"

"A few seconds. But first I have to find clothes and Derron. Sit tight. I'll be back before you know it."

She yanked open the door and left, leaving Henry alone once again. He pinched the bridge of his nose between thumb and forefinger, his head suddenly throbbing. He didn't have much time to understand everything when the door came open again and closed softly.

"Daddy?"

He knew that voice. He lifted his head and there, standing with her back against the door was Maggie. He rose from the chair and she rushed to him. They hugged as relief washed over him. He held her at arm's length and took a long look at her. She was alive and well, thank goodness. She looked beautiful. Glowing, almost.

"You worried me, Mags," he said.

"I'm sorry, Dad. Did you read my letter?"

"Oh, I read it all right. That's why I'm here."

"You came looking for me?"

"I did." He nodded and stepped back. "What was I supposed to do when you disappeared?"

"I'm sorry." She frowned. "I didn't mean to make you worry."

"Princess Elyne brought me your letter but even that hadn't convinced me you were all right or that it was the truth. I started to believe when I saw your portrait in the castle."

Maggie blinked surprise, her eyes widening. "My portrait?"

"The painting. Patrick McCullough showed it to me."

"Patrick…?"

"Your descendant," he explained.

"You visited the castle in our time?" Her voice wavered with excitement.

"Yes and—oh. You wouldn't have sat for the painting of that portrait yet, would you?" He realized he might be revealing her future and quickly closed his mouth.

"We had children." She sounded as though realization finally dawned. A dreamy look came over her face and she smiled faintly.

"And what's this about you marrying a Scottish knight without my permission?"

She blushed bright red to the roots of her hair. "Wait until you meet him. You'll like him."

Henry harrumphed as he sat in the chair. "I'm old-fashioned, Maggie. I don't approve of you running off with some man I haven't met yet."

"He's not *some man*." She sounded defensive. "He's a good man. Granted, he had a gambling problem—"

"Yes, I heard about his gambling problem."

"Oh. Well, he liked to play dice and cards and gambled away a lot of money. But he doesn't do that anymore," she said in a rush. "When we married, he promised he wouldn't and he hasn't."

"Hmm," Henry said.

"What are you doing here, Dad?" Maggie changed the subject.

"I told you, I came looking for you. Elyne helped me through to the Otherworld."

"I'm not going back." She shook her head hard. She knew what he intended to say and cut him off at the pass. "I'm staying with Finn."

"You can't stay here, Mags. It's too dangerous." He didn't want to mention his run-in with the orcs. Frankly, he'd rather forget it.

"Elyne will send us back to our time soon enough," Maggie said.

"By 'our time' I assume you mean Finn's?"

"Yes."

"You intend to live the rest of your life in the Middle Ages?"

"The mid-thirteen hundreds to be exact," she said. "And yes, I do."

"How can you give up everything you worked for?" he asked. "Your friends, your life, college." *And me?* Maggie was the only family he had left. It pained him to think of her never returning home. "You were close to getting your degree, Maggie. With honors!"

"I'm not leaving, Dad," she said tartly. "My life is with Finn now and I love him. I would follow him to the ends of the earth if he asked me."

"Maggie—"

"I'm not leaving. And you can't make me." She stuck out her lower lip in an exaggerated pout.

That much was true—he couldn't make her. She was an adult. But he still didn't like the thought of his only daughter living in a drafty castle. Living without the comforts of home. How could she give up everything for this man? For love?

If he was being honest with himself, he would admit he didn't want to be alone. He couldn't face the rest of his days without his daughter. He'd already lost one to a drunk driver and his wife to cancer, how could he lose Maggie, too? She would be alive, yes, but he would never see her or his grandchildren. But he wasn't ready to admit the truth. Not yet.

He wasn't the type of person Maggie was. She was selfless, a lot like her mother. She wanted to help people and make sure they were happy. It was one of the things he admired about her.

"How can you give up your modern life?" he asked.

"I'll admit I miss some modern conveniences. Like toilet paper. And iTunes."

"Starbucks," he said. "How can you live without a latte?"

She laughed. "I got used to it. I like it here. Well, with Finn."

"Is he good to you?"

"He is. And you'll meet him soon enough."

Henry wasn't convinced. He wouldn't be until he met Finn and was satisfied that the brute of a man was taking care of his little girl. Still, he wasn't all too certain Maggie should remain here.

"Princess Elyne intends to put a glamour on me," he said. "I won't look human."

"That's because Queen Maeve doesn't like humans. Though I suppose she's gotten used to us now that Finn, Sir Drake and I have been in the palace for a few months."

The queen doesn't like humans? He did so love a challenge.

The moment Maggie said the words, Henry wanted Maeve even more. And he would do whatever he could within his power to get her. If the queen didn't like humans, he would find a way for her to love him. He was, after all, lovable. Nearly thirty years of marriage was proof of that.

Elyne returned with an armload of clothes and Lord Derron in tow. Derron closed the door and gave Henry a dubious look as Elyne dumped the clothes on her bed.

"This is Lord Derron," she said. "I wasn't sure of your size, so I guessed."

"I can't believe you did it," Derron said. "And you want me to knight him?"

"It's the only way we can keep him here in the palace without my mother knowing."

"What do you intend to *do* with him, Elyne? He's human. He shouldn't be here at all."

"Hey. What about me?" Maggie propped her hands on her hips.

"She doesn't want you or the others here either," Derron said. His gaze flickered to Elyne. "They should all be returned to the human world."

"You've said." Elyne pursed her lips in a thin line. "Henry stays and so does Maggie, Finn and Drake."

"Why? What is the purpose of keeping them here?" Derron demanded.

"I dislike being talked about as though I'm not here," Henry said.

"Me too," Maggie said.

"Maggie should return with me to our own time." Henry ignored his daughter as he addressed the others.

"Dad, we talked about this." Her voice was razor sharp.

"We did but I still think you should return with me. I know nothing about this Finn."

"Dad!"

"Aside from that, it's not safe for a modern woman here, Maggie," he continued. And what about Finn? He'd seen the portrait of the man. He looked overbearing and gruff. How did he know his daughter was in safe hands with the man? How did he know he wasn't some controlling monster? Men were cruel to women in this time. Women died in childbirth. Not to mention all the diseases that could kill. He couldn't help but worry about her.

She balled her fists. "I already told you I'm not leaving here. I met the love of my life at that jousting tournament and I'll not leave him behind."

"Can you settle your family differences later? We have business. Derron—"

"I'll not knight him, Elyne." Derron shook his head.

"Stop being so stubborn. He has to be knighted or he'll never be able to fit in here."

"Fit in here how? I don't understand what you mean by that," Derron said.

"I intend to put him in the Queen's Guard. He'll be safe there and I can keep an eye on him." Elyne smiled, looking well pleased.

"You plan to do *what*? Have you lost your mind?" Derron, however, did not look pleased.

"If you won't do it, then I'll find someone else who will." She glared at Derron, fire flashing in her blue eyes.

Henry heaved a sigh and rubbed his forehead. He was tired. Bone-weary exhausted and tired of all the bickering. "I don't care what any of you do. All I want is—"

Loud bugles interrupted him, announcing someone of importance. The sound came through the open balcony doors as if the horns were right next door. Elyne and Derron rushed outside. Maggie grabbed Henry by the sleeve and dragged him behind her. The procession of a long line of horses headed for the palace.

"Who is that?" Maggie squinted against the darkness as if that would help her see better.

"That is his royal majesty, the king of the Elves," Elyne said. "He's come as he promised." She rubbed her temples with the tips of her fingers. "He's come to negotiate the Treaty of Separation."

Chapter 4

Cormac couldn't believe how easy it had been to escape the Fae. But then they never expected him to use his magic, either. Had the princess realized how powerful he was as a Fomorian she would have found another way to keep him contained.

He had also managed to breach the walls of the Fae prison, breaking down the wards. It had been a good day. He'd released several of his people before the Fae caught on and were able to reinstate the wards and the walls. Pity, that.

But he had what he needed—his fellow Fomorians and freedom. They'd already gone their separate ways and he had begun the arduous task of finding his family Lord Kieran had hidden away.

Princess Elyne had promised she would find them, but he couldn't wait for her. For all he knew they were already dead or dying. He would start looking in the Unseelie realm.

But it had taken him a lot longer to cross the realm of the Seelie. The Fae were crawling all over the countryside looking for enemies of the crown. He couldn't afford to be captured again, so he traveled at night when he could be concealed by the shadows.

On the second night, as he traveled through a densely packed forest, he kept his eyes open for any moving shadow and his ears attuned to all the night sounds. He was unable to procure a sword or dagger or anything. And he'd lost his link to the black dragon Nero, though he could still sense him. He thought it strange the beast kept vigil at the Queen's Palace. He'd tried to reconnect the mental link with the dragon but was unsuccessful. He suspected it was because the dragon resisted him.

He also had to be wary of the other three dragons roaming the Otherworld. The silver, emerald and azure dragons had been released from shadow by Queen Maeve to fight the war. He hadn't seen them since the defeat on the Hill of Tara. The last thing he needed was to become a crispy dragon treat.

Cormac had found the river that would lead him through the Seelie realm to the Barrier in the Heartlands. There he would cross into the Unseelie realm. Moonlight sparkled on the glassy surface and bounced off the jagged rocks lining the bank. Somewhere in the distance, the sound of rushing water. Hope was the one thing keeping him sane on his trip through the realm.

As he crested a small hill, he saw the woman standing atop one of the jagged rocks.

She was beautiful. Ethereal. Her skin was as pale as the moonlight, her eyes black as the night fringed in dark lashes. Straight blue-black hair cascaded over her shoulders to her waist. Her gown was the color of midnight, with a plunging neckline to her navel and a scarlet belt at her narrow waist. Cormac halted to drink her in. He had never seen anyone more beautiful.

"You are Cormac of the Fomorians?"

Her voice was smooth as velvet, beckoning him to her darkness. He couldn't help but nod and take another step toward her.

"You aided Lord Kieran in his quest?"

Another question lined in velvet. So sensual. It ignited the heat inside him and the thought of her talking to him again made him hard. He continued advancing, closing the space between them.

"I did."

Her smile shattered his soul. She stepped down from the rocks and paused in front of him. Her once-over made him shiver and her tongue dampened her perfect lips. "I've been searching for you, Cormac."

"I-I was a prisoner of the Fae."

"This I know. I also know how you broke free." She flattened a palm against his chest over his heart. "You will aid me, aye?"

"Aid you?"

"That fool Kieran failed. I watched him from my prison in the underworld, hoping he would defeat the ice queen and her stupid daughter. Now I look to you, Cormac of the Fomorians, to aid me. As you aided him. Will you?"

"Who are you?"

"I am Morrigan." She gave him a devastating smile as her hand slid down his body and cupped his crotch. She squeezed gently.

His brain melted. He lost all sense of right and wrong. All that mattered was doing what she wished. Helping her. Being with her. He would be her slave for eternity if she asked him. "What is it you wish me to do?"

"Destroy Queen Maeve," she said. "I want her dead."

"If you kill her, Princess Elyne will be crowned."

"I don't care about her. Her fate does not matter to me. I want the ice queen dead." She leaned into him, both hands pressing his chest. Her lips brushed his. "Will you help me?"

Alluring. Tempting. *Must. Resist. Can't. Resist.*

He wanted to say no. He *had* to say no. If he agreed to help her, his soul would be hers. *Family. Bargain. Aye.*

"I know where he hid them," she whispered. She feathered kisses along his jaw. "Help me and I will release your family."

Cormac gripped her wrists, his fingers digging into skin. He jerked her away. "Are they alive?"

"For now." She cocked a grin. "And will remain that way." She paused, the threat lingering between them.

"As long as I agree to assist you," he said.

"I like you, Cormac. You catch on quickly." She pushed his hands away and leaned into him again. Her lashes fluttered as she looked up at him with those dark eyes. "You desire me."

"No."

The lie barely left her lips as she kissed him. Oh, aye. He wanted her. Every part of his body wanted her and betrayed his words.

"You can have me." Her hot breath cascaded over his neck. She sucked his earlobe. "Take me, agree to help me, and I will grant you anything you wish."

What was it he wanted? He had some burning desire, something he needed to find. He had to find. He couldn't remember. Her hand was on his crotch again. Her fingers tugging at his waistband. Her breasts pressing into his chest.

He couldn't remember why he was here or what he searched for. He'd forgotten. All he knew now was he wanted her. Oh, aye, he would take her. He would give her whatever she wanted.

Morrigan shoved him to the ground. She pushed her gown

from her shoulders, the material pooling at her feet. Standing over him, he had a moment to drink her in. His mouth watered at the sight of her.

"Will you help me, Cormac? Say you will."

"I will help you." He couldn't tear his eyes from her naked form.

"You will do anything I ask?"

"Anything."

A smile played at the corners of her mouth as she dropped to her knees. She tugged his breeches off his hips. He was powerless to stop her. She straddled him, hovering over his body and snapped her fingers. The landscape changed abruptly and they were no longer by the river. Now they were in a four-poster bed.

Her hands raked up his chest, pushing aside his tunic as she lowered her body onto him. She rode him hard until she finally collapsed on him, her breathing heavy. He blinked, clearing the fog from his addled brain and then gave her a violent shove. She tumbled away with a giggle.

She'd put some sort of spell on him. His quest for his missing family interrupted yet again. The thought sickened him as he realized what he'd done. Cormac sat up too fast, pinpricks of light bursting behind his eyes. She laughed and ran a finger down his arm. He flinched.

"Where am I? Take me back."

"Ah, dear Cormac. You are in my castle."

He stood, looking for his breeches. But she'd tugged them off before snapping her fingers and bringing them here.

"You can't leave." She didn't hide the threat in her voice. "You gave me your word you would help me."

Heat prickled the back of his throat. His stomach twisted in a tight knot. "You tricked me."

"You wanted to be tricked." Her wicked smile froze his insides solid. "And now you are mine."

"No. I belong to no one." He spun to face her. His hands fisted. He would not be forced to follow evil again. He'd made that mistake with Kieran. He would not make the same mistake with Morrigan.

Her eyes narrowed and the darkness consumed her. As she sat

up, her hair tousled fell over her shoulders. "You cannot defy me. I am the Goddess of War. You belong to me until I decide to release you."

"All I want is my family back. I have no interest in killing Queen Maeve or Princess Elyne."

"Oh, but I do. Kieran was nothing more than a fool. I hoped he would dispose of the queen for me but he failed. You will not fail me, will you, Cormac?"

"I don't…"

"You wouldn't want me to hurt your family, would you? Or you? After all, if you're dead, you can't ride to the rescue."

He clenched his jaw until it ached. "No."

"As I thought." The smile she gave him did not reach her eyes. "Now, Cormac, do what you will with the princess but I want the queen's head on a platter."

Cormac bowed his head in servitude. "As you wish, Goddess."

The arrival of King Urdithane sent the palace into a flurry of activity. Maeve didn't like being disturbed from her solitude with his arrival, but her royal duties were to greet him and his entourage. When the call went up, she left her chamber and waited in the courtyard. Princess Elyne and Lord Derron joined her.

"These negotiations could be disastrous, Elyne," she said.

"Have faith, Mother. King Urdithane isn't all that unreasonable," Elyne replied.

"Mayhap but I have my doubts. At first light, you and I will be calling on the High Druid to get my magic back. If I'm to negotiate the terms, I will need to be fully recovered."

"Aye, Mother. As you wish." Elyne exchanged a look with Derron.

Maeve was not so oblivious she missed it. A flicker of a glance passed between them. There was some other secret her daughter held. Soon, she would discover what that was.

Now she had to greet the king of the Elves. She put on her best regal face, lifting her head high and straightening her back. The king rode a great white stallion, his daughter Princess Allanna at his side. Behind them, several Elven guards. One carried the heraldry of the Elves—a white flag with Celtic knotwork in the shape of a leaf from the Woodland trees in which they lived.

The king and princess stopped inside the courtyard and dismounted. He approached with his daughter at his side and paused in front of Maeve with a respectful bow of his head.

"Queen Maeve, thank you for greeting us," the king said. "I apologize for our late arrival but the roads have proven to be unsafe."

"Aye, I've heard the orcs and other Unseelie are roaming freely. We are doing our best to contain them all but it's an arduous task."

"Understandable, of course. If the Elves can be of any assistance, I hope you'll let me know."

"I appreciate your willingness, King Urdithane. Welcome to the Queen's Palace," she said. "I'm afraid we've sustained some damage from Lord Kieran's attack. Accept my apologies for the current state of the palace." She swept her hand toward the repairs.

"You have my deepest condolences on the loss of your four Guardians. Lord Malcolm was a good man, as were all the Guardians." The king's gaze flickered to Derron as he referred to the death of his father and the Guardian of the Sword of Light.

"Thank you," Maeve said.

"Both our races have suffered great loss in the war against the Unseelie."

"I owe you a debt of thanks for sending your Elven warriors to fight with us," she said.

"Princess Elyne assured me we could negotiate the abolition of the Treaty of Separation. I hope we can set aside our differences and remove the barrier that has existed between us far too long," Urdithane said.

Maeve raised one thin brow. "Negotiating already, Urdithane?"

Annoyance flickered over the king's face before he quickly got it under control. "I'm merely stating I look forward to our united front once again, your majesty. As I hope you are. I do hope Princess Elyne will be present," the king said. "She was quite convincing when she asked for my help."

"Was she?"

Her daughter stiffened next to her. "Mother." Elyne's tone held warning.

But Maeve ignored her and abruptly changed the subject. "You must be weary from your travels. Allow me to offer you and your daughter comfortable chambers. I'm afraid the only space we have available is for your royal majesties. The others will have to bunk outside."

"We gratefully accept your offer." Urdithane gave a bow of his head. "I hope you don't mind my men erecting their own tents outside your walls."

"Not at all. Before we begin the Treaty negotiations, let us celebrate our victory at the Hill of Tara. I have special festivities planned on the morrow followed by celebratory games."

Maeve didn't miss the look of surprise on Elyne's or Lord Derron's faces. Aye, neither knew of her plans, but their formal bonding ceremony was long overdue and something she planned to rectify as soon as possible.

"Your generosity is great, your majesty." Urdithane had a hint of a smile on his lips.

"Lord Derron, please show the king and the princess of the Elves to their chambers in the east wing. Make sure their needs are tended."

"This way, your majesties."

Urdithane fell in step behind Derron but Allanna lingered behind a moment. "Princess Elyne, might I inquire about Sir Drake?"

Maeve shifted from one foot to the other as Elyne cleared her throat.

"What of the knight?" Elyne asked.

"Is he…still visiting the Otherworld?" The girl blushed to the roots of her hair.

"Aye, he is." Elyne cut Maeve a surreptitious glance.

Allanna dipped a quick curtsy as her face flooded with a bright smile. "Thank you, princess." She hurried to catch up to her father and Lord Derron.

Maeve folded her arms across her chest. "The Elf fancies the human knight?"

"Aye, she does."

Maeve looked after the girl, watching as her white-blonde hair swept down her back and her skirts kicked up as she struggled to catch up. "Does she realize they will never be allowed to be together?"

"I'm not sure, Mother." Elyne sounded a little sad. "She's in love with him, though, there's no denying that."

Poor girl. How would she take the news when she realized her father would never allow her to marry a human? It would likely break her heart. Though, Maeve mused, she couldn't understand how the girl could fancy a human anyway.

"Mayhap I have been too rash in not allowing you to be part of the negotiations," Maeve said.

Elyne's eyes widened in surprise. "Aye?"

"If the king expects you to be there, he may become obstinate if you're not. Therefore, I expect you to be there."

"As you wish, Mother." But there was no hiding the smile in her daughter's voice.

"Now get some rest. We visit the High Druid at dawn."

Henry paced the length of the princess's chamber, hands clasped behind his back. She and Lord Derron had left him there while they greeted the king of the Elves. Henry had stood on the balcony for a long while, watching the procession, their way lit by numerous torches.

Maggie yawned widely and made her escape but not before he made her promise to introduce him to the Scottish man and soon. Henry was old-fashioned. He disliked his daughter marrying the man without being properly courted.

While he waited, he changed from his street clothes into the clothes Elyne had brought him. Now he wore a forest-green tunic with billowing sleeves, leather vest, breeches, belt and tall black boots. All he lacked was a sword strapped to his waist.

The door opened and the princess entered. She paused to give him a once-over and then nodded approval.

"You'll do."

"Gee, thanks." He scowled.

"All that's lacking is a glamour."

"What about knighting me?"

"Oh, that. Derron wouldn't agree to it. So now I'm going to do it my way."

"With the glamour?" he asked. She nodded. "Will it hurt?"

"You won't feel a thing, I promise. And you won't need the glasses." She held out her hand.

"But I can't see without them."

"It won't matter once I cast glamour." She wiggled her fingers.

Reluctantly, Henry handed over his spectacles. The princess waved a hand over him and then stood back to examine her handiwork. She nodded, grinning and looking proud of herself.

"That will do nicely. Take a look."

She waved him toward the full-length mirror. Henry stared at his reflection with wide eyes. He looked like himself…but didn't. Like a younger version of himself. His green eyes were brighter, sharper. And she was right—he didn't need his glasses. He still had the same auburn hair but instead of being cropped short with a touch of gray at the temples, the ends brushed the collar and there was no gray. His face sported a three-day growth of beard, nearly hiding his clefted chin. And his ears! They were no longer rounded on top. They were pointed. Like Elyne's and Derron's.

He flexed his arms, saw the muscle bulging in his biceps. He ran his hands over his chest, felt the sinew drawn together there and grinned. Elyne had made him into a Fae. A young, virile handsome Fae.

"I look—" He halted, trying to decide what he looked like.

"Perfect." Elyne clapped. "My mother will never recognize you."

"And that's good, right?"

"If you want to stay in the Otherworld, it is," Elyne said.

"I do. I need time to convince Maggie to return with me."

Elyne blinked, looking at him as though he'd grown a second head. "*That* will never happen."

"It will if I have anything to say about it."

"Nope. It won't." She shook her head. "She's totally in love with Finn. She will never leave his side. And besides she's pregnant." Realizing what she'd said, she clapped her hand over her mouth, her eyes wide.

"She's *what?*"

"Oops."

He advanced on Elyne until he had her cornered. "Maggie never mentioned it to me. Why didn't she tell me?"

"Probably because she, herself, doesn't know," Elyne said. "Promise me you won't tell her!"

"I will do no such thing. She needs to be home where there are doctors who can take care of her. Not here in this barbaric world."

"Excuse me, but this *barbaric world* happens to be my home. And if she stays in the Otherworld, the royal healer will tend to her when her time comes."

"What about prenatal care? The vitamins she needs to take? All the testing that has to be done? She's fragile. She needs—"

"She's stronger than you think. She can take care of herself."

Maybe she could. But Henry wasn't all too confident. She couldn't even read a map, for crying out loud. He clenched his jaw, the muscles ticking.

"Maggie will never go with you," Elyne said, more gently.

"Then why am I here?" It was more of a rhetorical question. He hadn't expected the princess to answer.

"Because you wanted to see her. You didn't believe me when I gave you her letter. You had to see for yourself she was all right."

She was right. And he had made the spur-of-the-moment decision to come here. He was not accustomed to making quick decisions. He was a thinker. He usually considered all options before leaping into a dangerous situation. But the thought of losing Maggie made him lose his head.

Determination settled through him. Would he leave and give up so easily? No. He had nothing to go back to anyway except for his lonely life as a professor. Not hearing from Maggie after she disappeared had nearly driven him mad. He couldn't—wouldn't—leave here without her.

He focused on Elyne then. "You're going to send me back with Maggie."

"Against her wishes? I will not." She folded her arms over her chest.

"Maggie doesn't belong here and neither do I. You're going to wave your magic wand and get us home."

"First of all, I don't have a magic wand." She rolled her eyes. "Second of all…I can't."

"What do you mean you can't? You brought me here, didn't you?"

"Aye, I did, but—"

"If you won't help me, then I'll find another portal."

Henry started for the door, as if he had a clue where he was going and what he was doing. When, in reality, he hadn't a clue. He had no idea how to get back to the place where the orcs found him. He was pretty much screwed.

"You can't go through a portal. They're unstable. Humans can come through, but they can't get home."

"Then sift me and Maggie home. I know you can do that."

"I can't."

"Why not?" he roared.

"I want you to stay." Slowly, he turned to face her. She flushed, her cheeks turning pink.

He clenched his fists.

"Maggie won't admit this, but she misses you. She misses her connection with home. That is why I brought you here."

Hearing that took all the wind out of his sails. It was a comfort his daughter missed him, even though she had her Scottish husband. His shoulders slumped in defeat.

"She has Finn but it's not the same," Elyne continued. "She turns to him for comfort but he's a medieval man. He doesn't understand her grief or the things in the modern world she talks about. I know of your loss."

Hearing her mention the loss of his wife and eldest daughter sent a pang of sorrow through him. He had never properly dealt with their deaths, mostly because he'd buried his grief long ago. Stinging pain sliced through him.

He realized their deaths weren't his fault—his wife had died of cancer and his daughter had died in a tragic car accident. There wasn't anything he could have done to prevent either death. With them gone, Maggie was his only family. The only one left he could call his own. If she stayed, if he lost her it would kill him.

"Maggie lost them, too, and she feels as though she's lost you. She needs you to stay for a little while. She needs you to understand she loves Finn and she *wants* to live in the Middle Ages."

Henry's hands relaxed, his fingers opening. He nodded slowly. "I'll stay."

"Good, I'm glad." The princess smiled broadly. "The palace is a little cramped these days so you can use my chamber as your own. I've had the linens changed for you so please make use of the bed."

"Where will you be staying?"

"With Derron." She flashed him a sheepish grin. "But don't tell my mother. We're bonded but not officially in her eyes."

"What did you do? Elope?"

"You could say that."

He almost chuckled at her admission.

"Get some rest. We have a busy day on the morrow."

As she headed for the door, Henry couldn't stifle his yawn. He sank on the edge of the bed as she reached for the handle.

"Princess Elyne?"

She paused, turned to look at him with question in her blue eyes.

"Thank you," he said.

She nodded. "Sleep well, Sir Henry."

As the door closed behind her, Henry stretched out on the bed. Moments later, he was fast asleep.

Chapter 5

"Have the final preparations been made, Lord Vaughan?" Maeve paced the length of the hallway, trying to think of anything to keep her mind off the interminable waiting.

"Aye, my queen. They have. The wedding will commence as you requested this afternoon."

"Good. And the feast? Have the kitchens been able to prepare enough food for everyone?"

"Of course. All the arrangements are in hand."

Maeve halted in the foyer and glanced up and down, looking for Elyne. She hadn't made an appearance as yet and it was far past the first light of day. The time they were supposed to meet to visit the High Druid. She tapped her foot impatiently.

"Where is that girl?"

Lord Vaughan waited patiently with her. He glanced around the hall. "I'm afraid I don't know, my queen."

"Well, find her. I told her we would leave for the High Druid at first light." The blood in her head pounded, causing a headache of massive proportions.

As Lord Vaughan nodded to do her bidding, Elyne came skittering around a corner. She looked frenzied with her hair a scraggly mess and her gown disheveled.

"There you are. What kept you?"

"I'm sorry, Mother, I…was detained."

Maeve could guess by whom. She grimaced. "Come."

They left the palace behind, the queen's personal guards followed closely. The High Druid lived in a small cottage not far from the palace. Though he'd been part of her court for years, he preferred to live away from the bustle of court life. Maeve indulged his request, allowing him to be somewhat of a hermit.

At the cottage, Maeve knocked. A moment later, the door opened and the old man ushered them inside.

"Welcome, welcome. A pleasure to see you both again." He waved them to the wooden chairs in front of the fireplace where a great fire roared. "To what do I owe the pleasure of your visit?"

"Akram, you know why we're here," Maeve huffed. "I need my magic back."

"Ah, right, right. Because you transferred it all to Elyne when you thought you'd die." He nodded, stroked his beard. "Aye, aye."

When he made no other move to help them, Maeve heaved a heavy sigh. "Well?"

"Well, I'm afraid that can't be done."

"Why not?" Anger surged through her veins. "You are the High Druid, are you not?"

"Ah, I am, indeed. But magic is tricky. A very tricky thing. Magic cannot simply be passed from user to user."

"I was able to pass it to her," Maeve pointed out.

"Well…since the magicks have been combined, it makes it more difficult to separate yours from hers."

"Akram, I need my magic back. Elyne is far too powerful with mine and hers combined. She's not experienced enough yet to handle it."

"Gee, thanks." Elyne sounded all too much like her human friend Maggie.

Maeve shot her a warning glance.

"'Fraid there's not much I can do."

"Unacceptable. I cannot rule this realm without magic. And Elyne is not ready to rule."

"Your confidence in me is reassuring, Mother."

She narrowed her eyes at Elyne then said to the High Druid, "There must be something you can do. You knew we were coming here today. Why aren't you prepared?"

"Oh, I did prepare, my queen. I've searched through my spell books, my potion books, my herb books. But I've found nothing that will yield the results you seek." He clasped his hands together and his face paled. No doubt fearful of her retribution. "Even if there was some way to reverse the magic transference, your majesty, I don't know how to separate hers from yours."

"There has to be a way. I refuse to believe all is lost. Can't she simply transfer the magic to me as I did to her on the Hill of

Tara?"

He cleared his throat. "Were it that simple, your majesty, it could have already been done by now. And at the time you transferred your magic, you were standing on the Stone of Destiny."

"And the Stone thought I was turning over the realm to her," Maeve said.

Akram gave a nervous glance at Elyne, then back at Maeve. "Aye, your majesty. It could also be that, ah, the princess doesn't want to give up the powers."

Maeve's head whipped in Elyne's direction. "Is that true?"

Elyne paled, her face washed of all color. "No, Mother. I don't know how to transfer the magic back to you or I would have done it by now. Why else would we be here with the High Druid?"

Maeve returned her venomous gaze to Akram. "Keep looking. There has to be something somewhere in some spell book that will allow Elyne to give my magic back."

"Aye, your majesty. I'll keep searching." He bowed his head in respect.

Maeve picked up her skirts and spun around, leaving the cottage behind. Elyne walked silently next to her. She could sense Elyne wanted to say something, mayhap apologize again. But Maeve didn't want to hear any more apologies. She wanted results.

"Is it true what the High Druid said? That you don't wish to return the magic?"

"No, it's not true. I don't know how to return your magic." Her daughter's razor-sharp voice had a hard edge.

"I hope for your sake, Elyne, you are telling the truth."

"I am," she snipped. "Why do you always do that?"

"Always do what?"

She stopped and squared off with her. "Why do you always think the worst of me?"

"Do not raise your voice to me, young lady. You are still my daughter and still under my command."

"Aye, I know all too well. A fact you never allow me to forget. You always have to be in control of everything. Even my magic."

"Part of that magic is *mine* and, aye, I do need to be in control of it. You have no idea how powerful you are right now."

"Oh, I have an idea." Elyne started walking again.

Maeve let her go, guilt swarming over her. Mayhap she'd been too hard on her. She'd treated her as inferior, as though she were incapable of controlling her magic. Her daughter had defeated Lord Kieran, after all. And she hadn't destroyed the kingdom yet.

"Elyne, forgive me." Maeve hurried after her. "It seems as though things are spinning out of my control since that day at the Stone of Destiny. And now I have to discuss the Treaty of Separation with King Urdithane."

Elyne relaxed some, her grip loosening on her skirts. "Nay, Mother. I should apologize for that. I shouldn't have agreed. I thought it was the only way we could get help from the Elves."

She put her hand on her daughter's arm, stopped her. Elyne faced her, her cheeks flushed. "You did what you had to do to ensure we would survive. You made the right decision. Having my magic back would…make me feel as though the realm is still under my rule."

"It is, Mother. I don't wish to take that away from you." She grinned then. "Not yet anyway. I realize I have much to learn. And you're the only one who can teach me."

Pride flooded Maeve. Pride and guilt. She *had* been too hard on her. She would never allow that to happen again. Smiling now, she hooked her arm in Elyne's and they started walking again toward the palace.

She'd been thinking about the official bonding ceremony of Elyne and Derron for a while now. In fact, before leaving the Hill of Tara, she'd sent word to begin secret preparations. She couldn't have them running around the place together any longer. What would her people think? It simply wasn't proper.

"I should tell you I have arranged for your official bonding ceremony for this afternoon," Maeve said, breaking the uncomfortable silence.

"You have?" Elyne blinked surprise.

"I expect you and Lord Derron will be there and on time?" She gave her a cursory glance.

"Aye, Mother. We will."

"And your human friends? What of them?"

"I would like them to be there." At least she had the wherewithal to glance down.

Maeve harrumphed. She disliked humans, though she couldn't deny they had helped during the war. If it hadn't been for Sir Finn, Lord Derron would be dead. And her, too, if she was being honest with herself.

"Is that acceptable?" Elyne's voice was quiet.

"I suppose, though you know it's against my better judgment. Once the bonding ceremony is over and the ensuing celebration has ended, I want them sifted back to the human realm. All of them. Even the ones who managed to wander into the Otherworld through the portals. Is that understood?"

"Aye."

Maeve halted then and turned to her. She gripped her by the arms and held her in place, making her meet her eyes. "I know you're fond of the human girl, Elyne," she said. "But there is no place for them here in the Otherworld."

"I know, Mother. I…needed them here."

"I find it difficult to understand your fondness for the humans. But I understand your wish to have your friends close."

She dropped her arms, desolation pressing into her. Many long years had passed since she had someone to turn to, someone she could confide in. Thousands of years had passed since her husband King Adhamh had been murdered. She had never loved another. Part of her envied Elyne's friendship with Maggie and her romance with Derron.

"We will need your focus once the negotiations of the Treaty begin. There will not be time to entertain them," Maeve said.

"I understand." Elyne nodded.

"Now…you have a wedding to prepare for." She smiled, turning Elyne back toward the palace and walking once more. "The palace seamstress has been hard at work on your gown. I'm sure you'll want to see her and have the final adjustments made as soon as possible."

Elyne dipped a quick curtsey. "Thank you, Mother."

She hurried away, leaving Maeve alone in the courtyard. Alone. Again. She had been alone for so many years. Ruling and keeping the peace in the Otherworld.

Heaving a sigh, she sought out Lord Vaughan to find out how the final preparations were going for the bonding ceremony and the following celebration. Duty, it seemed, always called.

At the princess's urging, Henry joined the company as one of the spectators, wearing his Fae glamour and his knightly clothes. Princess Elyne had not managed to convince Lord Derron to knight him, but he still wore the clothes befitting one. He lacked a sword strapped to his side, though.

He arrived in the grand hall alone, and scanned the crowd. Fae nobles dressed in their finery, knights in polished steel and ladies wearing beautiful gowns packed the hall. A small group of musicians played softly toward the front of the room. There were numerous candelabras burning brightly, giving the room a pale-yellow—romantic—glow.

What was he doing here? Really? He was as out of place as a peacock in the desert. He smoothed his hands over his tunic, ready to bolt when he saw her—his Maggie.

She bobbed through the crowd. Her auburn hair bounced behind her in soft waves. She wore a pale-blue gown trimmed in gold with bell sleeves. Henry couldn't help but notice how she glowed. She dragged a tall Scotsman behind her. That must be Finn. Already Henry formed his opinion of the man. He didn't like him.

Maggie gave him a jaunty wave as she approached, coming to a halt in front of him. Immediately, he and Finn sized each other up. The man had several inches and a whole lot of muscle on him. It didn't stop Henry from doing the fatherly thing of stiffening his back and widening his stance. Had they been in their time, he'd be cleaning his shotgun. Just to scare the boy.

Not that Finn was a boy. Henry was fairly certain the man could snap him in two.

"Dad, I want you to meet Sir Finian McCullough. My husband." She beamed at him, her hand resting in the center of his chest.

Henry scowled. Finn glared.

"He doesna look human," Finn said.

"Shh!" Maggie admonished. "Elyne put a glamour on him so he could blend in. I told you that."

"*Och*, aye?" Finn gave him another once-over. Then nodded as though approving. "'Tis a good disguise."

"Thanks."

"*Dad*," Maggie whispered roughly. She jerked her head toward Finn.

"Oh, right. Henry Chase. It's a pleasure." Reluctantly, he extended his hand to the man. Finn took it, pumped it once and then released it. But Henry wasn't immune to the man's death grip. His hand throbbed from the crushing.

Even after the official introduction, he didn't like the man. He knew it was for the simple fact he was with his little girl and no one was good enough for her. No one ever would be. He knew he would have to get over that—eventually—but for now he contented himself with disliking the man.

"I've heard much about ye," Finn said. "Maggie speaks of ye often."

"Does she?" He glanced at her with a raised eyebrow as if to ask if that were true.

"I do. Finn knows how much I miss you."

"Yet you will not return with me."

Her jaw clenched. "No, Dad."

"Ye intend to take her from me, then?" Finn asked.

Henry was certain he saw the man's chest expand. If he were a rooster, Finn's crest would go up.

"We've discussed it."

"Aye?" Now Finn raised an eyebrow and looked at his wife. "'Tis true, lass?"

"No. Dad, stop it. I already told you I'm not leaving him."

For now. But Henry would continue to try to change her mind. A trumpet sounded, signaling the beginning of the ceremony. He followed Maggie and Finn and took a seat. He expected a processional. The queen entered the room from the side. The officiant looked like a wizened old man. His silver hair hung long and straight to his waist. His eyes were the color of moonlight and there were a few crinkles around his eyes and mouth. He wore a long white robe trimmed in gold, indicating he was someone of importance.

"That's the High Druid." Maggie's voice was low as she nodded in his direction.

But Henry couldn't stop staring at the queen. Tall, beautiful, with long flowing blonde hair. Her skin was smooth, supple and looked about as soft as silk. She wore a gown of deep blue, bringing out the color of her eyes.

Lord Derron entered next, taking his place by the queen. He smiled as he caught sight of his princess then. All eyes turned to watch her enter. She wore a gown of gold trimmed in ivory fur at the hem and sleeves.

As she took her place beside Derron, the High Druid reached for Derron's left hand, then Elyne's right hand and placed it with the lord's. They laced their fingers together, clasping palm to palm. Turning, the High Druid retrieved a long silken piece of material and wound it around their wrists and hands, creating an infinity over their joined hands.

Once the binding was complete, he placed one hand over theirs and addressed the crowd.

"Your royal majesty and honored guests, we welcome you to witness the eternal binding of her royal highness Princess Elyne and Lord Derron, Protector of the Otherworld, Knight of the Realm, Guardian of the Sword of Light." He looked at first to Elyne and then Derron. "Is it your wish today, my lady and my lord, that you be joined and that your hands be fasted in the ways of auld?"

"It is," they answered together.

The High Druid removed his hand and dropped it to his side. "Lord Derron, if it is truly your desire to become one with this woman present her with the symbol of your pledge and token of your love."

With his free hand, Derron removed his sword and placed the flat side of the blade across their hands, the steel glinting in the candlelight.

"Princess Elyne, Lord Derron has pledged his sword to you. The pledge of his sword is the pledge of his soul. A symbol of his power, his passion, his fire, his strength, his courage. His ability to protect, defend and care for you. The strength of his blade and endurance of the Sword of Light represents what is in his heart. Do you, as his beloved, accept his pledge of heart and steel?"

"Aye, I accept his pledge of heart and steel. Now and always." She smiled as Derron sheathed his sword.

Something about her smile sent Henry's stomach to his toes. She looked completely joyful and radiant. Completely happy and content. He glanced at Maeve perched upon her throne, who kept her emotions in check and her face passive. How could she, he wondered, be so in control? Not even a glimmer of a smile for her daughter?

"Princess Elyne, if it is truly your desire to become one with this man present him with the symbol of your pledge and token of your love."

She turned to one of the servant girls, taking a chalice and holding it over their clasped hands.

"Lord Derron, Princess Elyne has pledged the chalice, a symbol of all that is within her, her rapture, her devotion. Yours is the voice of reason and steadfast support. You are the spark of her passions and yours are the arms in which she will come to rest. The red wine within foretells the richness of your future together. Will you, as her beloved, take the chalice in which she offers and drink from the bounty within?"

"Aye, I will accept the chalice. Now and always." Derron took the chalice and sipped, handing it off to the High Druid.

Henry felt as though he were an intruder on a private ceremony. That he shouldn't be seeing something so personal, so intimate. Yet he couldn't look away. Next to him, Maggie sniffed and quickly wiped away a tear.

As the High Druid slowly unwound the material from their hands, he spoke the final words. "May you forever be united as one. May your hearts forever beat as one. I bind you to each other until the sun no longer burns. Until the moon no longer glows. Until the Otherworld is no more. You may kiss your bride."

Even the staunchest Fae noble's eyes misted with tears. Henry choked up a few times. Especially when Maggie cried buckets when the two sealed it with a kiss.

With the formal bonding complete, Queen Maeve rose from her throne. "This is indeed a great and wonderful day. In addition to celebrating the bonding of Princess Elyne and Lord Derron, we also celebrate the arrival of Urdithane, King and Ruler of the Elves. Without his Elven warriors, the Otherworld would surely be lost to the Unseelie."

A chorus of cheers went around the room. King Urdithane,

who sat to the queen's right, gave a humble nod as if in thanks for her kind words.

"The royal palace kitchens have been preparing for days for these events. Now come and let us feast!"

"Wasn't the ceremony beautiful?" Maggie still wiped tears from her eyes.

Henry knew she asked of no one in particular and wasn't inclined to reply. Oh, sure, it was nice to see two people come together forever. But was anything really forever? He'd lost his beloved wife. He would never be the same without her. He shifted from one foot to the other.

The crowd dispersed, heading for the dining hall where there were rows and rows of tables set up to accommodate the guests. Henry, Maggie and Finn paused at a table. A human knight stood with a young blonde woman—Fae or Elf he couldn't tell. And he wondered why there was another human knight when the queen was so dead set against them.

"That's Sir Drake," Maggie explained, following his gaze. "He helped us defeat the Unseelie. I first met him at the jousting tournament."

"He is a fine knight," Finn said. "And a good friend."

"Who's the girl?" Henry asked.

"That's Princess Allanna, she's the Elven princess. She has a fancy for Sir Drake," Maggie said and sighed wistfully.

"Ye canna be matchmaking everyone, lassie," Finn said.

"I can try."

"You, a matchmaker, Mags?" Henry asked.

"People deserve happiness," she said. "They deserve to be with the one they love." She gave him a pointed look. He didn't miss the way she squeezed Finn's hand either.

Before he could reply, Elyne and Derron made their way through the crowd as servants filtered their way into the room with steaming trays. Girls filled tankards. Elyne and Derron approached them. Elyne clutched his hand in hers and kept giving him adoring eyes.

"I'm so glad you were here, Maggie," she said.

"I don't mind claiming some responsibility for getting you two together finally." She hugged Elyne and it was clear to Henry his daughter and the princess really were close friends.

"Lord Derron, you have my congratulations," Finn said.

"Thank you, Sir Finian."

"We best go," Elyne said. "My mother will want us at the head of the table."

Derron kissed her hand. "As you wish, my princess."

As the two guests of honor left, the rest of them made their way to a table and sat. Servants filled their pewter plates with roasted meat and vegetables. As they dined, Henry was aware of the queen the entire time. Being smitten with her was completely ridiculous. She didn't care for humans. What made him think she would come to care for him? Even with his Fae glamour firmly in place.

The musicians played a lively tune and some of the guests got up to dance. The queen, Henry noticed, remained firmly in her seat. Next to her the king of the Elves seemed to be doing most of the talking. She responded infrequently—probably when she had to. She looked positively miserable. Henry considered asking her to dance. Would she shun him? To her, he was nothing more than a lowly Fae knight. Even then he didn't look the part. He looked more like a commoner.

He must be crazy to even consider asking her to dance. She looked so bored though. As though she might die of it any moment.

Henry stood, his palms damp with sweat. No, he couldn't do it. He sat again, picked up his tankard and took a healthy swig. Perhaps if he drank more, he would have more gumption to ask her. He took another quaff of the—what was this stuff? Mead? He liked the way it warmed his veins. He stood again. But his damn palms still sweated.

"Dad, what are you doing?" Maggie's rough whisper came from his left. She tugged on his tunic. "Are you all right?"

"I'm fine."

Yes, he *was* going to do this. He was going to ask the queen to dance. And if she rejected him, he would hang his head in shame and leave. She would never see him again.

"I'm going to ask the queen for a dance."

"Are you mad?" Maggie jumped to her feet next to him, her hand on his arm, keeping him in place. "You can't do that."

"Why not?" It sounded more like a challenge than a question.

"B-because she's the *queen*." Maggie stole a glance at her before looking back at him. "And I forbid it."

He nearly laughed. "You forbid it?"

"You…you can't, Dad."

"Why not?" This time he wanted a real answer.

"She's the mother of my best friend. It would be weird."

"Mags, you're a grown woman. Married. I seriously doubt it would be *weird* to ask her for a dance." He paused, thought about his words when his daughter raised an eyebrow. "Okay, aside from the fact she's a queen and I'm a…you know."

"Human," she whispered roughly.

"But *she* doesn't know that."

"Not yet!" She fisted her hands and perched them on her hips. "What if she says no? Then what?"

"Then I'll look silly, won't I?" He straightened his tunic. "Don't worry, my little magpie. If she says no, I swear not to bother her again. But I don't think she will. I may be old, but I still have *some* charms."

Maggie scowled, looking every bit like the teenager he remembered. "Dad. Ew."

"Hey, don't look so disgusted. Your mother and I—"

"All right, all right. I get it. No need to explain." She held up her hands in surrender. "But be careful. She doesn't like humans."

"Hey, who you calling human? I'm a Fae now." He thumbed at his chest as he winked and Maggie laughed. "See you later, magpie."

He headed for the front of the room, steeling his nerves. The delay with Maggie made him nearly lose his nerve. But no. He was seriously going to do it. He wouldn't let the fact she was royalty and he was…nothing, deter him. He stepped up to her, held his hand out across the table.

"Your majesty, would you do me the honor of this dance?"

The Elven king dropped his chicken leg in shock. Elyne stared at him wide-eyed. Derron clenched his jaw. Maeve's expression hadn't changed from bored and annoyed and he wondered if that was now directed to him.

"Sir Henry…?" Elyne's words waned and she didn't continue.

"It would be my honor," he said.

"And who are you, exactly?" Her silky voice caressed his senses.

He dropped his hand and gave a quick bow. "Sir Henry. At your service, my queen." That sounded convincing, didn't it? He almost believed it himself.

"Are you new to the Queen's Guard?" She still didn't seem convinced as she looked him over, sizing him up.

"I am," he said, feeling rather confident. She was going to say yes. He knew it.

"And how did you end up here?"

Crap. A question he didn't have an answer to. Thankfully, Elyne piped up.

"He helped round up some of the orcs and humans wandering the realm, Mother. He came to the palace yesterday."

Not an untruth. Points to Elyne for thinking fast and offering an explanation. He liked the princess more and more.

Maeve's gaze never left his face as she peered at him with something he couldn't read. Not mistrust. She seemed to trust him. It was something else. Curiosity. Interest. She bit her lip as though on the verge of agreeing to dance with him. He held out his hand again.

"Do me the honor of a dance?"

"I don't think that's—"

"I will." Maeve cut Derron off as she rose.

Henry's heart leapt as she rounded the table. Her grace and poise were impeccable. She was every bit the dignified queen she appeared to be. She took his hand, his fingers closing around hers. Her warmth penetrated him to his soul. His heart hammered a happy cadence as he led her to the dance floor. The tune had been lively, upbeat. Now it was something slower. Softer. He cheered at the thought of holding her close and feeling her press against him.

As he took her in his arms, he realized he had no clue what the dances were of this realm. How did the Fae dance here? He gave the room a quick cursory glance. The others had practically deserted the floor to give way for their queen. A few brave couples remained dancing side by side, their fingertips barely touching.

Henry would not do that. He wanted her in his arms, next to him. He wanted to smell her beautiful, heady scent of jasmine. She was exotic and ethereal. He was acutely aware of the gawks and stares from those around the room.

Had it been a bold move to ask her to dance? Because he was a lowly Fae knight did that mean he was not allowed to speak with his queen? Knowing she really wasn't his queen made it okay in his mind. He slipped his arm around her waist, pulled her close, while holding her other hand shoulder height.

"What are you doing?" She flinched and for a moment he thought she might pull away.

He tightened his grip, keeping her firmly in place. "Where I come from this is how we dance. I'll show you. All you have to do is follow my lead."

"Where exactly do you come from?" An eyebrow quirked in question.

Ah, yet another question he couldn't answer. "Across the realm." Did that sound plausible?

"Hm," was her response.

He led her through the steps, keeping her as close to him as possible. Then turned with her still in his arms.

"You learned to dance like this there?" she asked.

"I did."

Actually, he learned before his wedding. Maggie's mother had made him take lessons so they could dance together and not look like fools. Her words, not his. He had reluctantly agreed. He wasn't for the ballroom dancing but now he was glad he had learned. Now he was with this lovely woman whose curves seemed made for him.

"I have never seen such a dance," she said.

"Mayhap, your majesty, you should relax and enjoy it instead of questioning it every few seconds."

She blinked surprise. Had no one talked to her like that before?

"I would remove the head of most who spoke to me like that."

"Like what?"

"In that insolent tone."

"Apologies, your majesty. I hope I can keep my head. For my lips are attached and they've yet to have a taste of you."

"You are bold, aren't you?" She tilted her head back, gave him a look down her nose that he suspected she'd perfected eons ago.

"Too bold for her majesty?"

"That remains to be seen," she said. And her mouth quirked into almost a grin.

Henry's heart thumped and for the first time he could acknowledge the attraction he had for her. His nerve endings tingled and even his buddy in his pants was in agreement.

"Too bold to kiss you here?" He knew he pushed it but he didn't care. He wanted to see what she'd say.

Her face hardened. "Definitely too bold."

He slanted his head, as though ready to kiss her. She licked her lips, as though ready to let him. His mouth was close to hers. Oh, so close. Her warm breath tickled his face.

"Tempting me, your majesty?"

"Telling you not to kiss me here in front of my court is tempting you?"

"It is. Because you're a beautiful woman. I find I cannot resist your charms."

"Ha. Do you tell me this so you can have your way with me?" she asked.

He grinned and pulled her closer. He delighted in the way she molded to him in his arms. "Would you allow me to have my way with you?"

Her response was stony silence. Her face turned impassive as though she suppressed her emotional response. But Henry was aware of the jump of her pulse in her long, slender throat. Her heart beat quicker as she pressed against him.

"Would you like me to tell you what I'd do should I have my way with you?" He dropped his voice to a near whisper.

"You wouldn't dare." Her attempt to sound offended fell far from the mark. A pale flush creeped along her milky-white skin. He also heard the imperceptible hitch of breath in her throat.

"Wouldn't I?"

"I should have you drawn and quartered."

"I should have your lips upon mine while I thoroughly kiss you." Henry was not to be dissuaded.

"I should have you tied up and roasted alive." Her eyes narrowed.

"I should have your soft curves under me in my bed."

His last statement shocked her to silence. She merely gaped at him. When she didn't reply, he decided to push it further.

"I should like to have you cradled against me while I whisper love words in your ear—"

"Insolent man!" Despite her outburst, she didn't try to pull free. If anything, she wiggled closer.

"Tell me, your majesty, do you not enjoy my advances? If you tell me no, I won't believe you. Your emotional reaction to me is all the evidence I need."

"And what emotional reaction, pray tell, is that?"

"The flutter of your pulse in that gorgeous throat of yours for starters. The widening of your beautiful, perfect eyes in a shade of blue that rivals the ocean. The coloring of your high cheekbones in the softest shade of pink I've ever seen. Shall I continue?"

"No, Sir Henry, you—"

"It was worth a shot." He winked. "You can't blame me for trying."

"I should have you arrested. Thrown in the stocks."

"But you won't, will you?"

"I *should*," she repeated.

"But you won't." He pressed his hand into the small of her back to make sure she couldn't get away. By doing so, it pulled her closer to him making him aware of the rapid beat of her heart. He *had* affected her whether she chose to admit it or not. "I don't fear you, Queen Maeve. I'm enchanted with you."

His head dipped closer to hers. Her breathing was ragged. He was so close to claiming her lips. Before he could, someone bumped into them, breaking the contact. Elyne and Derron had twirled into them. When had they stepped onto the dance floor? Clearly, he had been too enamored with Maeve to pay attention to anything around them. To his dismay, the queen slipped out of his arms and stepped away.

"Thank you, Sir Henry, for the dance. It was…interesting."

He bowed as she walked away, leaving him cold and empty.

"Whew. That was a close one." Maggie joined them without Finn, the relief evident on her face.

Apparently, his daughter decided he and the queen needed an intervention. Elyne was all too happy to comply.

"Were you going to kiss her?" Disbelief was in Elyne's voice.

"What if I was?"

"You can't do that, Dad. She's *the queen*," Maggie said.

"I'm well aware who she is. You keep reminding me." Henry gave his daughter a searing look. "Did you think maybe she *wanted* me to kiss her?" This he directed to Elyne.

"Whether she did or didn't is beside the point," Derron said. "Your actions are inappropriate. In fact, this whole situation is inappropriate."

"I must agree. It can't happen again. In fact, my mother made me promise to send the humans back after the ceremony," Elyne said. "All of them."

"What? No!" Maggie exclaimed. "I won't go. Not yet. Please, Elyne. Not yet. I haven't been able to spend much time with my father." Maggie looped her arm in his.

"I'm sorry, Maggie, but it's out of my hands."

"But you have all the queen's magic. You don't have to send us back yet."

"Maggie, she said it's out of her hands." Secretly, Henry thought that was a small victory. If they had to go back, they'd go back together whether his daughter liked it or not.

Elyne glanced at her mother, who had returned to her seat at the table. "Well…"

"Elyne, no. We have to do what she says. She's still our ruler, magic or no."

Henry smiled at Derron who was clearly the voice of reason. But Derron didn't return the smile. Oh, no. He was still glaring at him, probably due to the kiss attempt.

"I understand." Elyne gave him an innocent look and fanned her eyelashes. Any man within a two-foot radius would know she was up to something.

"Shall we retire?" Her husband held out his elbow for her to take.

She kissed his cheek, still trying the demure look. "You go ahead. I'll be right there."

His response was to narrow his eyes in suspicion.

"No funny business. I promise," she said. "I'll be right behind you. I want to say goodnight to my mother and Maggie."

He looked doubtful as he walked away, out of earshot. As soon as he was far enough away, she turned to Maggie and Henry and lowered her voice. "I'll see if I can buy some time before sending you both back."

"How?" Maggie asked.

Elyne shrugged. "I'll tell her I forgot." She flashed a smile.

Chapter 6

Morrigan had waited thousands of years for the right time to attack Queen Maeve. She'd long dreamed of the day she could finally destroy the woman who had taken away the man she loved. At last, she would pay for that with her life.

All this went through her head as Cormac moved off her and settled on the bed next to her. She probably should keep her thoughts on him but she found the very idea of Maeve dead distracted her. Putting him under her spell had been the first step. Finding his Fomorian army had been the second. Now she was ready to give the bitch queen a warning.

"Do I not please you?" Cormac asked, his chest rising and falling after his exertion.

Morrigan rolled to her side, her fingers slipping over his chest. "Oh, aye, you do. My mind is elsewhere today."

"The queen?"

"She vexes me deeply, Cormac."

He turned to her. There were moments of clarity when his mind broke through her dark spell. As he looked at her now, he blinked. His gaze seemed to sharpen. He shook his head as if to clear it and glanced around, realizing he was in her dark palace. Cormac slid off the bed and grabbed his breeches, pulling them on.

"What do you think you're doing?" she asked, snapping her fingers.

He paused, gave her a look over his shoulder. Normally, a snap of her fingers would bring her back to her spell but not his time. Now he merely looked at her with all the hatred he had for her.

"Leaving."

"No," she said. "You cannot leave me. I will not permit it."

"You don't control me," he said.

Morrigan jumped off the bed and rounded on him. His gaze raked over her naked form. He still wanted her, even though he hated her. Good.

"Have you forgotten our deal, Cormac?"

"You coerced me into agreeing to help you by using your dark magic."

"Then you wish for me to kill your wife and children?"

His angry glare was scorching. "What is your bidding?"

Since he'd managed to break one holding spell, she would attempt another. She waved her hand in front of his face. His eyes turned to black orbs and she smiled. He was under her control once again.

"I want to warn her first. Let her know who is in control of her life…and her death."

Morrigan placed her hands on either side of his cheeks, the roughened three-day growth abrasive on her palms. She leaned in and kissed him.

"For that, I need your help. Your magic." She whispered the words against his mouth.

His hands tangled in her long dark hair. "As you wish. I will do whatever you ask of me."

"Oh, aye, you will," she breathed. "Or I will kill your wife and have her head brought to you in a basket."

His hands fisted in her hair and jerked her head backward—mayhap another moment of clarity? She gasped with the sweet agony.

"Careful, my pet. You wouldn't want to anger me, would you?"

His eyes clouded over once again. His mouth brushed hers seconds before he nipped her lower lip.

"I need a Shade, Cormac. One that will mark her. Can you do that?"

"Oh, aye. I can. You will have your Shade. For it to be effective, I will need something belonging to the queen. A strand of hair. An article of clothing. Anything that has touched her body will do."

Morrigan released him and turned away from him. "That, my sweet, can be arranged."

"Where are you going?"

"To get what you need." With a wave of her arms, she was fully dressed. "Don't move. I'll be back."

Before Elyne could walk away, a loud explosion rocked the entire palace, shaking the walls and rumbling the floor. Maggie grabbed Finn to steady herself. Derron had paused to wait for Elyne. Now he hurried toward her and grasped her to keep her steady on her feet. Dishes rattled, drinks spilled and there were shouts throughout the room.

"What was that?" Maggie asked.

The doors flung open as if in answer. A woman entered wearing a long black gown and hair the color of midnight flowed over her shoulders. Eyes black as night pierced through everyone in the room. She had pale skin, offsetting the darkness of her gown, hair and eyes. Princess Elyne gasped at the sight of her.

"Who is that?" Maggie whispered.

"That…" Elyne's eyes were wide and the color had drained from her face. She inched closer to Derron. "Is the Goddess of War. Morrigan."

"How did she get here?" Derron asked. "I thought she was imprisoned in the underworld."

"She was," Elyne agreed with a nod. "Mayhap with the rip in the walls, it freed her."

Morrigan advanced toward the queen, who remained seated and glared at the goddess. She looked strangely calm. Not at all flustered by her presence. Silence descended on the room and all eyes were on her as she walked closer and stopped in front of the queen's table.

"Morrigan," Maeve said in greeting and stood. Her tone, though, was far from cordial. It was downright frigid. "State your business. And then be gone." Maeve lifted her chin a little higher.

Morrigan laughed, her voice dark and melancholy. "After all this time, I'm surprised you don't know why I'm here."

Guards crowded toward Maeve to protect her. Morrigan's gaze flickered over each one before looking back at the queen. But they didn't deter her. She stepped closer, the four feet of wood all that separated the two of them.

With his heart hammering in his chest, Henry inched closer, trying not to call attention to himself.

"I could guess," Maeve said.

"If you guessed I've come for your head, oh great one, you'd be correct."

"You think to come here and threaten me? I've defeated Lord Kieran. I can defeat you."

"*You* defeated him? Tsk, tsk, Maeve, darling. I know the truth. You couldn't do it. You had to involve the *Elves*." She looked at the Elven king who remained seated to Maeve's right. Then back to Maeve. "I came to finish the task."

"You sent Kieran here, didn't you?"

"Why, Maeve, you wound me. Why would I send someone to do my own dirty work? Especially when it's something I will take great pleasure in. Kieran was nothing more than a fumbling fool who had delusions of grandeur. I, on the other hand, want *you* dead."

"You'll not destroy me. You can't," Maeve said.

"How wonderful you've challenged me." A small smile played at the goddess's mouth. "I do so love a challenge. I can and will destroy you. As I destroyed your husband."

The queen's face paled for a brief moment before turning pink with anger. "You and I both know he died at the hands of that murderer, Kieran."

"Aye, and he was handy with a sword. Too bad he didn't have the guts to finish the job. I assure you, I will."

"The Elves and the Fae are removing the Treaty of Separation. We will be united. You will not be able to defeat us so easily."

Morrigan's dark eyes narrowed. "Well, then. How convenient for me. I shall be able to remove the Queen of the Fae and the King of the Elves. All in one fell swoop."

"Maeve and I have a new alliance," Urdithane said, jumping to his feet.

Henry didn't miss the flicker of annoyance in Maeve's eyes before she lifted her chin another notch. "Aye, 'tis true."

"How dare you threaten the Elves," the king continued.

"Oh, calm down, Elf. I'm not here to kill you. Or the queen." Her gaze swung back to Maeve. "At least not today. Today I've come to offer my congratulations to the handsome Knight of the Realm, Lord Derron, and his lovely bride."

"You've said it then. Be gone." Maeve folded her arms across her chest.

"I will. But not before…"

She paused and then lunged for the queen. The guards around her went into action. One grabbed Morrigan around the waist. Henry tried to push his way to the front to Maeve, but he couldn't move past the other Fae knights. Morrigan grabbed a handful of Maeve's hair, the strands slipping through her fingers until she had one pinched between her thumb and forefinger. She jerked, yanking out a long blonde strand.

And then she shoved off the men as though they weighed nothing more than a feather. Laughing, she disappeared in a puff of smoke. Once the goddess was gone, Henry rushed forward and made it to her side before anyone else. Her face had drained of color and her once rose-red lips were pale pink. Her hands shook. He slipped next to her and her too-bright eyes met his.

"Sir Henry."

He didn't miss the sigh of relief when she said his name and started to reach for him. But Elyne and Derron had hurried to the front of the room before he could ask if she was okay. She jerked her hand back.

"Mother! Are you all right?"

"I'm fine I think." She pressed a hand against the side of her head. "She took one of my hairs."

"We need to ward the palace walls immediately," Derron said.

"She won't do anything," Maeve replied. "She can't."

"I'm not taking any chances." He turned to his captain of the guard. "See to it the walls are secure. Place extra sentries outside the queen's chamber as well as all the exterior gates. And find the High Druid."

"Aye, my lord." He gave a quick bow before leaving the great hall.

"Let me take you back to your chamber," Derron said, turning back to Maeve.

"I'm fine, Lord Derron." She stepped away from the table. "I need a moment alone."

"But my queen—"

"I need some air, Lord Derron. That is all." And that was that, it seemed. "Continue with the celebration."

She motioned for the musicians to start playing again. She gave one last look at Henry before she headed for the door. But Derron intercepted her. Henry remained near her, overhearing the exchange.

"My queen, I'm not comfortable with you being alone now. How can you go on with the celebration as though nothing happened? Morrigan is dangerous—"

"I'm well aware, Lord Derron, how dangerous she is. Believe me I do not take her threat lightly. However, this is a day of celebration and we must continue with that to keep the masses calm. I don't want to cause any hysteria. In the morn we will discuss this more. For now, enjoy your day."

"But—"

She held up a hand. "No more. Now see to your wife."

She pushed by Lord Derron to head toward the gardens but Henry fell in step beside her without missing a beat.

"What are you doing, knight?" She nearly growled the words.

"Following you. Lord Derron was right. You shouldn't be alone right now," Henry said.

"I thought I made myself perfectly clear. I can take care of myself."

"You did make yourself clear. It's not that I don't think you can handle yourself. In fact, I'm sure you can do that." And he brazenly looked her up and down with a grin, making sure she was aware of his lascivious gaze. "But I'm going with you whether you like it or not."

"Impossible man. I order you back to your chamber."

"You can order me all you want but I'm not going."

She huffed and then looked him over with a cursory glance. "I'm almost certain I've seen you somewhere."

He didn't want to point out she'd seen him in the hallway when Eldrin escorted him to Princess Elyne. He'd been human then and he knew she didn't care for humans. He would *make* her care for them. Him, specifically. Even now, walking so close to her, the heat emanating from her wafted over him, taunting him. Teasing him.

"Mayhap a mere coincidence, your majesty," he said.

He followed her out of the room, all too aware of Lord Derron's glare and Princess Elyne's and Maggie's curious glances. Maeve headed into the drafty hallway. She went through the doors and into the evening air to the nearby gardens.

They walked in silence down a winding cobblestone path. At a fragrant rosebush, she paused and turned to face him. Moonlight spilled over her beautiful features, softening them even more than usual.

"Lord Derron was right. Morrigan is quite dangerous," she said.

"What does she want with you?" he asked.

"Besides my death?" Maeve gave a humorless laugh. "She thinks I wronged her many years ago. She wants revenge."

"By killing you? Seems a bit extreme."

"She is the Goddess of War. She is the epitome of extreme."

"Is there anything I can do to help?"

She looked him over, one eyebrow arched. "A simple Fae knight of the Queen's Guard would not put himself in harm's way for me. Only one of the Elite would do that. And you are no such knight. That speaks of more bravery than most of them possess. I have seen it from one other and he is Guardian of the Sword of Light and Knight of the Realm."

He knew she referred to Lord Derron. He'd heard the man's titles enough. Henry shifted from one foot to another, wondering how to reply. He couldn't tell her he was a human in Fae clothing, nor would he give up the princess's ruse of hiding him in Fae glamour. He moved closer to the queen.

"Maybe they wouldn't, but I would. I want to help you."

"Why?"

He shrugged. "Why does anyone do anything?"

The explanation why he wanted to help her eluded him. He couldn't bear the thought of anything happening to her.

"You seem familiar to me yet I do not know you." She still looked him over, peering at him intently. "Did someone send you to watch over me?"

"No one sent me." Though he considered Princess Elyne had nudged him toward the Otherworld with the promise of seeing his daughter. Closer still he moved. The scent of roses mingled with that of the jasmine on her skin, intoxicating him.

She shifted, aware of how close he stood. He liked how tall she was—a mere inch shorter than his six-foot frame. He liked how youthful she looked, despite the fact she was probably hundreds, perhaps thousands, of years older than him. Her skin was as smooth as porcelain. Her eyes like a blue topaz. A breath shuddered in and out of her.

"Did you know the Goddess of War was coming to attack? Are you in league with her? Did she send you to get close to me so that you may help her kill me?"

He wanted to laugh. In fact, he chuckled. "If she did, my queen, would I tell you truthfully?"

"No, I suppose not."

He took her face in her hands. He wasn't sure what made him do it. He had to touch her, to feel her skin against his palms. His eyes met hers, never looking away. He wanted those luscious lips against his.

He thought he saw a shadow flicker in his peripheral vision. He turned his head, but whatever it was had gone. As he turned his attention back to the queen, he saw movement again to his left. Releasing her, he turned to peer into the shadows.

"What is it?"

"I thought I saw something moving over there."

"I didn't see—"

Before she could finish, the shadow separated from the others. It took a shape, looking a lot like a ghostly outline.

"A Shade," she said.

It flitted back and forth for a moment before lunging toward them. Behind him, Maeve gasped as she clutched his arm.

"Come on!"

She dragged him away, back toward the castle walls, weaving in and out of the plants on the cobblestone walkway. Henry stole a glance over his shoulder. The Shade followed, closing in.

"It's getting closer," he warned.

"We need to get to inside the palace," she huffed.

But she tripped over a loose stone and stumbled. Henry snatched her by the arm and kept her on her feet. They started back down the pathway, the Shade on their tail.

"What is it? What does it do?" he asked.

"If it touches you, it will kill you," she said.

"How do we get rid of it?"

"We don't."

She zigged to the left, pulling him along behind her. They were nearly to the palace walls now. Torches burned brightly around the entrance. Glancing back, the Shade kept to the shadows as it followed them. It gave him an idea. If he could reach the torches, maybe he could get rid of it that way.

As they reached the palace walls the Shade caught up to them, hovering over his shoulder. But it wasn't interested in him. It went directly for Maeve, snaking one long translucent tendril over his shoulder. Inches from touching her.

Not knowing what else to do, he shoved her out of the way. She shrieked as she lost her footing and tumbled to the ground. She shouted something to him as he snatched a torch from its bracket.

Maeve was on her bottom, scooting away from the thing as it advanced on her. Henry waved the torch right through the shadow. It shrieked an ear-piercing, high-pitched shriek before turning on him. The flames seemed to have cut the thing in half. He waved the torch again, splitting it again. Making it shriek again.

The Shade flitted upward, pieced itself back together and then disappeared into the night sky. With shaking hands, Henry replaced the torch and turned to Maeve. He held a hand down to her to help her up.

"Are you all right?" he asked.

"I'm…fine. How did you…know to do that?" she asked, her words breathy. As if she couldn't believe he'd figured it out.

"It was a hunch. Glad it was right."

"Me, too. Thank you."

"Now aren't you glad I came with you?"

She smiled. "Aye, I am. You saved my life."

He took her hand and led her back into the garden among the roses.

"Now, where were we?"

He cupped her face in his hands again. Maeve's eyes searched his, her blood-red lips parted as if to object but he didn't allow her to speak. He took that as invitation and kissed her, their mouths fusing together. She sucked in a sharp breath through her nose. Her body stiffened but still he didn't stop.

She didn't resist him. His lips molded to hers in a way they had never molded to another. His tongue dipped into the honey recesses of her mouth, tasting her. And she tasted oh so sweet. So delectable. So wonderful. The smell of roses rushed over them, enveloping them. A moment later, her body relaxed and she melted into him. Yet one hand pressed against his chest, as though she intended to push him away. She did not.

For the first time in a long while, Henry's shaft hardened, straining against the soft curves of her body seeking her heat and dampness. Wanting her. His mouth devoured hers and now she returned the kiss, much to his delight. Her tongue was probing, needy. Her lips mashed against his, as if she'd allowed reckless abandon to overcome her.

But then, almost as suddenly as she relaxed, she shoved away and stumbled back a step. Her face was flushed, her lips damp and swollen. Her breathing was erratic, her breasts rising and falling.

Crushed pink petals of a rose were in one of her fists. She must have grasped the bud and ripped it from the stem. Her fingers opened, one by one, and the mashed petals cascaded to the ground.

"Thank you for protecting me, Sir Henry." Her voice rasped the words, as though she had trouble keeping it under control.

Maybe she did. Maybe she enjoyed the heat of the kiss as much as he did. Now he had a problem—a large problem straining against his breeches—and nothing he could do about it. And he certainly couldn't return to the party with a giant boner straining against the cloth. Oh hell no.

"I shouldn't have kissed you."

Why the sudden need to confess? He had nothing to be ashamed about. He was a grown man. Had they both been mortal, he would have guessed they were about the same age. And despite being in his late forties, he was still a strong, virile man.

Maeve gave him her best snooty look. "Why did you?"

His gaze flickered her to her lips and—damn it—she licked them. More taunting. More teasing. She knew what she was doing. He didn't buy the ice queen act. Deep down, she was desperate for loving. He was going to give it to her.

"You allowed me." *You cannot deny you liked it. You experienced the heat as I did.* Even though he wanted to say the words to her, he pushed them out of his mind and said, "I wanted to."

"See that it doesn't happen again."

She whisked by him, leaving behind the scent of crushed roses. Maeve walked away, the damaged rose petals on the ground at his feet. For whatever reason, he bent and picked up a few of them, rubbing the velvety softness between his thumb and forefinger. He placed the petals in his palm, examining them. Even smashed they were beautiful. He tucked them away in his pocket. He would cherish them simply because she had held them in her palm.

Chapter 7

Maeve hurried through the palace halls with her skirts clamped in her fists. She had to get away from him—far away. As the distance between them expanded, she slowed her gait. Yet her heart continued to pump hard and she had a difficult time catching her breath. She had nearly died. If Henry hadn't been there, she would have certainly died and no one would have been able to hear her screams. The husk of her skin would be all that remained of her.

That bitch Morrigan took her hair to send a Shade after her. That was all she wanted from her when she appeared at the celebration. Now that the goddess had something to track her, she would certainly send other things to attack.

Henry had used the torch to fend off the attack. He'd saved her.

She pressed her fingertips against her lips, which still tingled from his touch. The kiss had affected her deeply and more so than she would ever admit. She *liked* it. It had been too long since any man had kissed her and with such passion. Such need. Such wanting. Flames encased her entire body, igniting feelings she thought long dead.

She had not felt anything for another man since the untimely death of Adhamh. Six thousand years ago. Oh, she dallied with a consort here and there. But none would measure up. And most wanted her because she was queen. Not because she was a woman.

Henry's kiss, though, had done something to her. He kissed her as though he truly wanted her for *her*. Not her riches. Not her title. Not her kingdom. He looked at her as though he wanted to strip her and take her there in the gardens where anyone could happen along and see them together.

Who was this errant knight? Why did he insist on making affectionate advances? Most men who did were interested in her title or her realm. They wanted her for something other than her.

She suspected this Sir Henry was no different. Having been in his arms while dancing, she was sure she had seen him somewhere before.

Nor could she deny the reactions she had while he held her so close. She didn't want to admit how much she liked it. Nor did she want to admit her threats were indeed empty. And he knew it. How did he know? Most men would scurry away from her in fear. Most men would leave her at the first mention of torture. Not Henry.

He was a puzzle.

Maeve pressed her fingers against her lips again, suppressing the giddiness that wanted to erupt. Oh, aye, she had wanted him to do that. But she had pushed him away, afraid of her own feelings, her own desires and wants. She had spent many years putting the kingdom in front of everything else. Duty had always come first. Duty to her kingdom and her people. Even duty to her daughter.

She entered her chamber and prepared for bed with the help of her lady-in-waiting. Maeve dismissed her, still distracted by thoughts of Henry. She couldn't allow him to distract her when there was so much work to be done—not to mention the threat of the Goddess of War. She would have to keep away from him.

When Maeve entered the council chamber, the High Council had already assembled, as well as Elyne and Derron. Representing the Elves were King Urdithane, Prince Andahar and Lord Eldrin. Today would be the first day discussing the Treaty of Separation. A historic day for both races as they would finally come to an agreement to live together in peace. Gods willing.

"Good morrow," she greeted as she took her seat. "Thank you all for coming. King Urdithane, welcome once again to our kingdom."

"Thank you, Queen Maeve. My sons and I are looking forward to abolishing the Treaty." He nodded toward Andahar and Eldrin. "As promised by Princess Elyne."

"Lord Vaughan, please read the preamble of the Treaty so we may be reminded of its original purpose," Maeve said.

Vaughan cleared his throat and rose, opening a scroll as he did so. He read in his monotonous tone. The Treaty was due to the war between the Fae and the Elves shortly after the king of the Fae had been murdered. She realized now her decision to war with the Elves had been a mistake and for all the wrong reasons. But she had been a young queen and grief-stricken with Adhamh's death.

The Treaty had been enacted to separate the two races—the Woodland Elves would live in their trees and the Fae would continue their reign. It was the only way to achieve peace at the time. The Skye Elves and Fire Elves had no interest in their quarrel and were content to keep to their respective regions. If Maeve acted with her head instead of her emotions, she would have realized that, at the time, if the Elven race banded their clans together, they would have easily wiped the Fae from the Otherworld. A sobering thought to be sure.

When Vaughan finished, he returned to his seat.

"Thank you, Lord Vaughan," Maeve said. "Now shall we open the discussion? King Urdithane, I'm sure you have a few words you'd like to share with us here."

Urdithane rose to his full height. "Aye, I do. Many long years have passed since the Treaty between us Woodland Elves and the Fae has been enacted. When Princess Elyne came to me and asked for help with your Fae war, we had a reason to break the Treaty and come together again. Unified once again. My Elven warriors fought alongside your Fae knights. We fought and we defeated the evil Unseelie that spread across this land. I ask now you unite us once again. Abolish the Treaty and allow us to live as we did before."

"You have requested Princess Elyne be a part of these discussions." Maeve turned to her daughter then. "Elyne, please tell us why you believe the Treaty should be abolished."

Elyne stood, smoothed her palms down the front of her gown and cleared her throat. "What the king of the Elves said is true. I did ask for help with our war. Without the Elves, we would have never been able to defeat the Unseelie or Lord Kieran. I believe we—"

A loud explosion rocked the palace walls. Silence descended on the council chamber. Maeve got to her feet.

"Lord Derron, find out what that was and make sure the walls are secured."

"Aye, your majesty."

Derron stood to hurry from the room but another explosion rocked the walls. This time it was accompanied by screams somewhere in the palace. Pandemonium erupted in the council chamber. The men were on their feet, all talking at once.

Elyne reached her side. "Come, Mother. We should see you to safety."

"No. I'm staying. I need to know what's happening."

The doors to the council chamber burst open, a knight on the other side. Sweat trickled down his face and his eyes were wild.

"Morrigan, your majesty," he panted. "She's back."

Another explosion rocked the palace. Derron drew his sword. Moments later, an armed Prince Andahar and Lord Eldrin were by his side and ready for combat.

"Elyne, take her to safety," he ordered.

"No, I'll not sit idly by while—"

"You'll not be put in danger either, my queen," Derron said.

"She wants me, Derron," Maeve said, her voice calmer than she expected. "She doesn't want anyone else but me."

"Why?" Elyne demanded. "What does she want with you?"

"I—"

Another explosion rocked the palace walls again. Derron didn't wait for her to reply. He took off down the hall headed for the battle. Maeve followed. Elyne joined her, keeping up with her as they hurried through the corridors.

In the courtyard, the palace walls were lined with her men, firing arrows down. As the battle played out, she caught sight of the giant boulder heading from the sky. The bitch had a trebuchet and dared to use it upon her walls.

"Look out!" a man shouted.

A solid wall of muscle slammed into her, shoving her out of the way and gathering her close. Warm, strong arms wrapped around her as he pulled her into him and she knew immediately who had her. Henry saved her for a second time. Her head tucked neatly under his chin as his arms tightened on her, keeping her close as they crashed to the ground. He took the brunt of the fall and grunted when they came to a jarring halt.

"I've got you. Your majesty?"

"Unhand me."

Even as she said it, she knew it was a falsehood. She would have stayed there all day had it not been for the spectators around them. Or Elyne and Derron hurrying to her side.

She jabbed him with her elbow in the gut as she scrambled away, her gown covered in dirt. As much as she wanted to ignore the heat flashing through her at the intimate touch, she couldn't. Her skin was engulfed in swoon-worthy flames.

"Mother, are you all right?"

"Aye, thanks to Sir Henry." She gave him a quick glance, trying to keep her skin from flushing. He shoved to his feet, brushing dirt from first his palms and then the back of his pants. His hair was somewhat disheveled. "He saved my life." Again. "Who's helping Morrigan?"

"It looks like a small band of Fomorians," Elyne replied.

"More Fomorians? How did they manage to break free of their prison?" Maeve wanted to know.

"I believe the goddess had something to do with that. And also…Cormac is leading them." Disappointment laced her daughter's voice.

Another boulder slammed into the palace walls, rocking the ground. Rocks rained down around them. Henry was again at her side and tugging her to safety. Maeve didn't miss Derron's glower as the knight manhandled her.

"Wasn't he a prisoner?"

"Was, aye. He escaped," Derron said. "We should have executed him when we had the chance."

"And now he helps the goddess." Maeve sighed.

"I don't believe he helps her of his own free will." Elyne exchanged a heated glance with her husband. "He *couldn't*. He was too concerned with finding his wife and children before."

"Mayhap the goddess made him an offer he couldn't," Maeve replied. "How big is her army?"

"Not as big as Kieran's was. She apparently doesn't hold as much sway with the Unseelie as he did." As Derron spoke, he kept his eyes on the sky, watching for more raining boulders.

"Let me talk to her." Maeve fisted her skirts, ready to take off toward the goddess.

"Do you think that's a good idea?" Henry asked, joining the

conversation. "Especially after last night's attack."

"What attack?" Derron's eyes suddenly flamed bright.

"A Shade attacked me in the gardens. If Sir Henry hadn't been there…well, I'd be dead."

"I wasn't informed of this." The Knight of the Realm pinned his gaze on Henry, then back to Maeve.

The palace gates buckled and splintered into wooden shards. Men hurried to fend off the attackers, but Morrigan walked through with a confident gait, waving her hand with her dark magic. She shoved them away as though they weighed nothing more than a feather.

Her black gown billowed around her as she approached Maeve, a smile on her blood-red lips. She paused in front of her. Derron and Henry moved to flank the queen while Prince Andahar and Lord Eldrin joined them.

"Your men will not be able to protect you, Maeve. I think I've been quite generous with allowing most of them to live," Morrigan said. "When are you going to give up this resistance?"

"I'm to let you kill me so easily?" Maeve shook her head. "What is it you want?"

"I want you to suffer before I kill you. As I've suffered all these long years locked in the underworld. I want you to feel the pain that I've felt. The anguish. The loneliness."

"If you want her, you'll have to go through me." Elyne stepped between her and the goddess.

"Elyne, no." Maeve wrapped a hand around her upper arm, trying to pull her away.

"How valiant of you, princess. But I don't want to hurt you. After all, someone will need to remain behind to rule the realm," Morrigan said. "All I want is the queen. Turn her over to me and no one else gets hurt."

"No," Derron said. "You can't have her."

She sighed, annoyed. "Very well. You force my hand."

Morrigan raised her arms, ready to strike down the queen. But Henry leapt, jumping in front of Maeve as the goddess released the purple cloud. Everything seemed to move in slow motion as Henry dove and the goddess's magic hit him square in the chest. She screamed her frustration.

Henry's eyes went wide, his chest smoking as the tunic burned to his skin. He fell to the ground in a lifeless lump.

"Oh, gods!" Elyne shouted.

Fear sliced through her as Maeve fell to her knees beside him. She pulled away the smoking tunic, ripping it from his charred skin. The stink of burning flesh filled her nose. She tried hard not to gag. His breathing was shallow and he wasn't moving. Why in the Otherworld would he do such a thing?

His eyes fluttered open. "You okay?"

"You fool. Are you mad?"

"Had to…save you." And then he passed out.

Again, he saved her. Was the man a glutton for punishment? Was he trying to win her favor by being in the right place at the right time? Every time?

"Get the healer," she said to Elyne. "Eldrin, find the High Druid. Bring him, too."

She feared the worst. She dragged him to her, cradling his head in her lap, hoping he wouldn't die in her arms. Derron pulled his sword and charged but the Fomorians loyal to Morrigan under her spell moved to intercept him. Swords clashed.

"This is not over yet, queen of the Fae. I will return to finish the job."

Morrigan disappeared in a flash of light, taking her few Fomorians with her. But Maeve kept her attention on Henry. Color leeched from his skin, so white it scared her. She brushed away the locks of hair that fell over his forehead.

"Henry, can you hear me?"

How could she ever repay him for all that he'd done for her? And, more importantly, why did he keep putting himself in harm's way for her?

The healer arrived as Henry's eyes opened again. His gaze was full of pain.

"Henry…?" she whispered.

"Better me…than you." And then he passed out again.

Seamus was at his side. "What in the gods happened?"

"Morrigan, that's what," Maeve said, her voice sharp. "Can you save him?"

"We must take him some place where I can help him," he said.

"Derron, carry him to the empty chamber next to mine. He'll stay there until he's healed."

"Next to you, your majesty?"

"Aye. It's because of me he's injured. Seamus, I don't care what you have to do to save him, but he must live. Understand?"

"I will do my best, my queen."

Derron hoisted the unconscious Henry in his arms. Maeve got to her feet, her hands shaking and her heart thudding hard as they walked away.

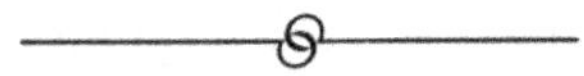

Two attacks in less than a day had unnerved Maeve. The men—Elves and Fae alike—cleaning up in the aftermath of Morrigan. They had walls to erect once again. The same walls Kieran had destroyed when he attacked the palace.

It was clear to Maeve magical wards would not keep the goddess or the Fomorians out. She would have to find another way to protect her people from them. In the meantime, she wanted to check on Henry.

He would be in good hands with Seamus. The Fae knight had managed to save her life from the Shade, the boulder and now from Morrigan herself. How could she ever thank him? And why did he want to keep her safe?

To kiss her?

Her stomach fluttered at the memory. There was something different about him, something she couldn't explain. When she thought of Henry, her heart fluttered. He made her weak in the knees. She couldn't recall anyone making her feel that way. Had Adhamh? It had been so many years since she'd felt the flutterings she had now, she wasn't sure.

She entered the chamber next to hers. Seamus stood over Henry's still-unconscious form, working his magic on the charred hole in his chest. Derron stood off to the side, one hand on the hilt of his sword as if ready to break into action. Maggie perched on the edge of the bed, holding Henry's hand. Her face was pale and she looked as though she were ready to pass out. Finn loomed behind her as the steady Scottish brick wall he was, one hand on her shoulder.

Maeve couldn't understand why the human was so concerned with the Fae knight. But then, she didn't understand humans anyway.

"How is he?" she asked.

"He will live," Derron replied. "But the goddess could have killed him."

Maggie sniffled, tears watering her eyes. "This is all my fault," she muttered.

"Nonsense, child," Maeve said. "You had nothing to do with the attack on him. He was trying to save me."

"You? Why would my—this Fae knight try to save you?"

The words stung her to the core. Maeve stiffened, straightening her back and looking down her nose at the girl. How dare she speak to her that way?

"Come, lass. Ye need rest," Finn said.

"I'll not leave his side." She gave him a sharp look over her shoulder. "He needs me."

"Under the circumstances, mayhap it would be best if you did leave. If we all did," Derron said.

Finn wrapped a gentle hand around his wife's arm and pulled her to her feet. But Maggie was resistant to leave Henry's side.

"He will be all right, lass. Come," Finn urged.

Maggie reluctantly followed Finn out of the room but not before she cut Maeve the darkest look she'd ever seen. She puzzled over this as the laird led her away. She didn't understand why the girl would be so attached to him. She knew, of course, she was friends with Elyne and they were difficult to separate. But why this Fae knight? They eyed each other until the human was gone.

"You should leave too, my queen," Derron said.

"I'm staying," she said.

"Seamus has said he'll live. Let him work his healing magic." He took her by the arm.

She jerked away. "I'm staying and that's final. The man nearly died for me. The least I could do is be here when he wakes up."

"As you wish, my queen." Derron gave her a brief bow before leaving the room.

Maeve sat in one of the vacant chairs on the opposite side of the room, remaining silent as Seamus worked. His eyes closed as his hands went over the wound back and forth, back and forth. Then he produced a jar with a milky-white substance. He dipped his fingers in and smoothed it over the charred area.

Henry groaned but never opened his eyes. When Seamus was finished, he put the jar away in his medicinal bag, wiped his hands on an old rag that had seen better days and rose.

"He will survive," he said. "He was a lucky man."

"Thank you, Seamus. But I think it is I who's the lucky one."

He quirked one eyebrow. "Indeed."

"When will he be awake?"

"Hard to say. Could be a few hours or a few days. The most important thing is he rests and heals." He reached into his bag and brought out the jar of the white substance. "I will have one of the chamber maids tend him."

"No. I will do it."

Seamus gave her a questioning glance before handing over the jar. "When that wears off, add more. A small amount will do. Cover the wound completely. If he's awake, he will resist. It is unpleasant. I'll be back in a few hours to see how he's doing. In the meantime, I have other patients to tend."

"Aye. Thank you again, Seamus."

He gave a brief nod to the queen before he, too, left the chamber.

Maeve kept a vigil by Henry's side for hours. She didn't know how long. She made sure there was fresh water in a brass ewer for when he woke up.

When the white substance had gone away, she opened the jar to sniff it. It smelled like death and she cringed. She dipped her fingers in it and smeared it over Henry's blackened skin. He stirred, grunted, but kept his eyes closed. She replaced the lid. She found a rag and wiped her hands, but her skin couldn't shake that awful smell.

At the water basin, she dipped in her hands and wished she'd thought to bring in soap. *A bath. Henry will want a bath when he wakes.*

She was about to call for a servant to bring up a washtub full of hot water when she heard him groan again. His eyes fluttered open and he struggled to sit up. Pain must have sliced through him, judging by the expression on his face.

"Careful, Sir Henry." She was at his side in an instant. "You need to rest."

"I…what happened?" he asked. He glanced around the room. "Where am I?"

"You're in the chamber next to mine. You were hit by Morrigan's magic."

"Oh…I remember." He groaned again and leaned back. "That hurt like hell."

He reached up to touch his chest but she caught his wrist. "Don't touch. You're healing."

"I thought I was dead." He looked up at her. "Are you hurt?"

"No. You took the brunt of the hit." She perched on the edge of the bed, slipping her hand in his. His concern for her touched her when he was the one who nearly died. "Why did you do it, Henry?"

"I…had to save you."

"But *why?*"

She squeezed his hand to press her point. She couldn't understand why he would sacrifice himself for her. Why was this knight willing to put himself in harm's way for her and her alone? He was nothing to her. Not a lover or even a potential lover. He was a mere knight in her army.

His gaze flicked to her face, held hers. He didn't look away.

"Because I…you are queen."

But she caught the hesitation in his voice. She wanted to ask more questions, but wasn't sure what to ask.

"Besides, if you were dead, I would never see that beautiful face again."

Her heart lurched and she was certain her cheeks heated. He sounded so sincere and the look in his eyes was so tender she nearly swooned.

"It would be even more beautiful if you smiled more," he continued.

"I smile often." She snatched her hand from his.

"If you do, I haven't seen it. You didn't even smile when your daughter married Derron," he said. "And I should know. I never took my eyes off you."

A different kind of heat flooded through her. Part of her

wanted to jump to her feet, tell him he was wrong. But deep down, she knew he was right. She hadn't smiled.

The other part of her, the feminine part, delighted in the knowledge he hadn't taken his eyes off her.

She searched her mind for an excuse but she didn't have one. One would think she would be happy her errant daughter finally made a match—and a good one at that. Derron's father, Lord Malcolm, would have been delighted. She *was* happy for them. For both of them.

She was…tired. Tired of being the one to make all the decisions. To issue all the commands. To plan everything for everyone. Her life was not her own. Her life belonged to her people, her rule, her kingdom. It always came first. And for the first time in her life, she wished things were different. Mayhap she suddenly wanted a different life—craved a different life that didn't include all her duties and schedules and decisions she had to make. A life that included someone she could love and trust and confide in. She envied her daughter had that in Derron.

"Now you look sad. Was it something I said?"

Henry spoke the truth. She was sad.

"No…I…" She heaved a sigh. "I'm glad you're all right, Henry."

She rose but he caught her by the hand. "Thank you."

"For what?"

"For taking care of me."

Her heart did a funny flip as he squeezed her hand. "I couldn't let you die, especially after you risked your life for me. I still don't understand why you did it."

"Maybe someday you will." He released her and shifted back into the pillows.

"I'll leave you to rest." She started for the door but paused, remembering something else she wanted to tell him. "You should know Maggie and Finn were here earlier while you were still unconscious. Though why the human and her husband were concerned with a Fae knight, I've no idea."

His eyes fluttered open. His face drained of color. "Maggie was here?" he asked, his voice weak.

"Aye, until I sent them away. If you'd like, I'll let her know you've awakened."

"That won't be necessary." He closed his eyes again, settling into the bed.

"What is your relationship to the human?" Maeve asked.

He cracked an eye to peer at her. "She's, ah, a friend."

Her eyebrow rose. "A friend? You've become quite social in court, haven't you?"

"I enjoy meeting people," he said.

"I see." Though she truly didn't. "I'll leave you to rest, then."

She suspected something was going on but she had no idea what. Yet. She would find out.

Chapter 8

Maeve walked out and down the hall. She knew she would need to resume talks with the Elves but she didn't want to— couldn't. She needed to think about things. Henry, for one. He had protected her from the Shade's attack and then kissed her passionately in the garden. No man had dared. No man had been so bold as to take her in his arms and kiss her like that. Because they had been intimidated by her title. By *her*.

But Henry hadn't. And when she thought back to the way he took charge…she smiled. Remembering the crushed rose, she lifted her fingers to her nose and inhaled. The gentle, faint scent of crushed roses had long since faded from her skin.

Why did he continue to save her? Why did he insist on being there for her? She didn't understand that. Or why he wanted to keep her safe. She hadn't done anything to deserve his unwavering attentions. Nor had she ever done anything to encourage his affections. Or if she had she hadn't realized it. And she certainly didn't believe in love at first sight. Though Henry certainly seemed to be attracted to her and not because she was queen.

So distracted was she by her consuming thoughts, she hadn't realized she'd ventured outside the palace walls, past the courtyard, beckoned by a fine mist swirling in the air and around her ankles. She'd managed to get through the gates and by the guards. They hadn't stopped her and in fact stood statute still.

As she spun to face the palace walls, she realized mist enveloped her and rose around the immobile guards. How could she be so stupid to leave without a guard? She had put herself into danger by stepping outside the walls. This wasn't like her. She wasn't one to be so lackadaisical about her own safety. Especially with the Goddess of War on the loose.

Hello, my queen. Oh, great ruler of the Otherworld.

The dark, guttural voice in her head startled her. She scanned the area but saw nothing through the mist.

"Show yourself."

As you command.

Red eyes blinked at her through the mist. A puff of white smoke plumed from the giant serpentine nostrils. Gossamer wings stretched behind the great beast. And suddenly the black dragon stood in front of her. She realized the mist was no ordinary mist. It was dragon's breath. That was why she was able to leave the palace walls undetected. Her guards were already under the spell.

"Nero."

He bowed his head to her feet. *Your servant.*

"Why?"

You released me from the Fomorian. I am in your debt.

Cormac. He had controlled the dragon as they fought at the Stone of Destiny. He had been defeated, breaking the magical hold the Fomorian had on Nero. And now the great dragon saw a debt that must be paid.

"That's why you followed us here," she guessed.

Aye. Nero lowered his large body to the ground with his head at her feet. The action reminded her of a puppy. And yet the beast could still look her in the eye.

It is not my wish to harm you, my queen.

"But you tried to kill my daughter. Why should I trust you?"

I did as I was commanded. You have my apologies, my queen.

Dragons were not fickle. They chose their rider and never wavered from that choice until one of them severed the link. That rarely happened. There were exceptions, though—like when Maeve put them into shadow to hide them from the hunters who were so desperate to kill them. Now it appeared Nero had chosen her. She placed her palm on his nose, the scales cool to the touch.

You are hunted by the Goddess of War, aye?

"Aye." How did the dragon know that?

She wants you dead. But she has no interest in your lands or your rule.

"I know why she wants me dead and it has nothing to do with the realm."

That is why I offer you my protection until the threat has passed. A debt owed. A debt paid.

She understood. He viewed his release from Cormac as owing

her. She would accept that but she also understood there was a price.

"What do you wish in return?"

Freedom.

She had the power to grant that to him. She could release him and let him roam free. The other three dragons—Ambrielle, Aura and Luna—hadn't been seen since the battle though Maeve knew they were still tied to their chosen riders. Luna and Aura picked Derron and Elyne, respectively. Ambrielle was hers.

"And what of Ambrielle?"

The emerald dragon cannot protect you the way I can. I will not hesitate to strike. Once the threat has passed, I will release you as you will release me. But understand this, Queen Maeve. Morrigan will return with an army of darkness that will not stop until you are dead.

Fear burned like fire in her veins and a knot formed in the pit of her stomach. She knew this. But she hadn't wanted to admit it. Morrigan proved she could bypass her palace walls with her magic and get to her. Had it not been for Henry, the goddess would have already struck her down.

"I have men here who will protect me. The Elves—"

It will not be enough. She will destroy them. She will destroy all who stand in her way. She has long harbored a deep hatred for you.

All the pieces of the puzzle finally fell into place. Maeve knew why the goddess had such hate. They had once loved the same man. She'd always suspected his murder was because Morrigan could not have him. The goddess had used the Dark Elf Kieran to kill him. Maeve hadn't thought she would go so far as to hire someone to do her dirty work. Kieran had been nothing but one of her minions. One she had convinced was powerful enough to take over the Otherworld, Seelie and Unseelie, and the human realm.

"Why does she attack now?"

The instability of the Otherworld allowed her to break free from the underworld prison in which you locked her.

Maeve wondered how long the goddess had managed to roam free before enacting her vendetta. Not long, judging by how Kieran had managed to build his army.

She had help from the Fomorians.

"The Fomorians are still alive?"

They were a race thought long extinct. A magical race that had once wreaked havoc in the realm and had been banished to an underwater prison in the Sorrow Lands long ago. Clearly, though, their banishment hadn't lasted. How had they managed to survive there?

Still, aye. And aiding her.

"I'm defenseless. I have no magic. What can I do then?"

Return to the Sacred Forest. The castle and the forest there will guard you—

"I will not run. I will *never* run. Even if I do, the goddess will find me."

He blinked his red eyes, a puff of smoke snorted out of his nose in annoyance. *The ancient castle in the Sacred Forest will guard you from the goddess. She* will *find you there and she* will *attack you there. She will not win.*

"How do you know this?"

I have seen her death in my visions. If you use the Sacred Forest, you will be able to defeat her. It is the only way to fight her without your Fae magic.

Maeve's brows drew together. He'd seen her in his visions? Was this creature—this dragon—more powerful than she realized? If she had her magic, she could tap into his consciousness.

I am more ancient than you, my queen, he said, as though reading her thoughts. And mayhap he had. *I have walked these lands longer than you have been alive. My dragon magic is more powerful than any.*

Ah, dragon magic. She underestimated Nero. She would never do so again.

"If I go—"

You will go. As will I.

"If I go," she repeated, "I intend to take my men."

He shook his head. *You will not need them. The ancient magic of the castle and Sacred Forest will help defeat the goddess. Trust me in this.*

"All right I'll go. But I need time to prepare and explain to my High Council why I'm leaving."

When you are ready, I will take you there.

After speaking with the dragon, Maeve returned to check on

Henry. She ordered a steaming tub of hot water brought to his bedchamber. He hadn't moved much and still lay on his back, the bedclothes tucked around his hips, his chest bare except for the healing salve Seamus had used.

She approached the bed and perched on the edge. His brow was damp with sweat and he was restless. Maeve pressed a hand against his forehead. His skin was hot to the touch. Rising, she went to the nearby washbasin and dipped a cloth into the cool water. She wrung it out and went back to his side, mopping his forehead with the cold cloth.

"You're going to be all right, Henry," she said, though she wasn't sure he heard her. "I'm not going to allow you to die."

His eyes fluttered open a moment and then closed. He reached for her wrist, clamped a hand around it, stilling her. She froze, but his eyes remained closed and his face impassive.

"Henry?"

He pulled her to him in one wild jerk. She lost her balance, fell forward and was able to catch herself by throwing out her other hand and bracing herself over him. She didn't want to land on his burned chest and hurt him.

They were nose to nose. His regulated breathing gave way to the subtle rise and fall of his chest. He released her wrist and then brushed his hand through her hair. Her heart pumped wildly as she waited, holding her breath, to see what he would do next. Was he aware of what he was doing? Or was this some fever-induced action he couldn't control?

Maeve remained perfectly still. His hand brushed down her neck, over her shoulder, down her arm. His fingers caressed the fist in which she clutched the dampened cloth. His eyes opened, locking onto hers. Though he looked right at her, he didn't seem to be seeing her.

A sharp knock on the door made her spring away from him.

"Come in."

The door pushed open and several servants carried in the steaming washtub for Henry. The ladies curtsied quickly before scuttling out and closing the door with a snap. Maeve pressed a hand against her fluttering heart. She spun around to face Henry but he had his eyes closed again, sleeping peacefully. Or at least pretending to be sleeping peacefully.

She couldn't carry his big form to the tub and get him in it while he was unconscious. She propped her hands on her hips.

"Henry, wake up. I've had a bath brought to you." When he made no move, she stomped to the bed. "Henry, I know you're awake."

Still nothing. Out of frustration she threw the rag at him. It smacked him in the side of the face. He still hadn't moved. Mayhap he really was asleep? She took a step toward the bed. A moment ago, his breathing had seemed so strong but now she couldn't see the regular rise and fall of his chest. Was it her imagination or did his skin look paler than it did a moment ago?

Fear lanced through her as she placed two fingers on the side of his neck. His weakened pulse fluttered under her touch. His skin was burning hot.

Maeve flew to the door and flung it open. The guards standing on either side were startled by her sudden appearance.

"Get the healer. Now!"

She went back to Henry's side and picked up the damp cloth. Her hands shook as she pressed it against his brow.

"Henry, stay with me. Don't leave me, do you hear me?"

Moments later, Seamus was there, shoving her out of the way.

"What happened?" he asked.

"He was fine…and then he wasn't."

"Damn black magic," the healer muttered as he set to work. "I thought I removed it all before."

He clapped his hands over Henry, rubbed them together until a bright white light formed between them. She stepped back, watching as he worked. When the light was nearly blinding, he pulled his palms apart and placed them ever so gently on Henry's burned chest.

Henry flinched, bucked. But Seamus pushed him down into the mattress.

"Don't hurt him!" Maeve said.

"I'm trying to save him," Seamus retorted.

Slowly, the healer drew his hands back and with them, a darkness drew out of Henry. The bright white light swallowed up the dark. Seamus flinched and his face contorted in pain before it all dissipated. The light faded. The charred skin that had been on

Henry's chest was now nothing more than new, pink skin. It still looked tender to the touch but at least the black was gone. He groaned.

Sweat beaded the healer's brow and he panted.

"Are you all right?" Maeve put a hand on Seamus' shoulder in comfort.

"The black magic was poisoning him. I've managed to remove it." He rose, a little unsteady on his feet. When Maeve tried to help him, he shrugged her off. "I will be fine."

"Thank you, Seamus."

"I'll be back later to check on him." He gave her a nod before leaving the room.

Maeve glanced back down at Henry. He looked pale. His skin was dewy with sweat. She pressed the back of her hand to his forehead. Thankfully, the fever seemed to be gone.

His eyes blinked open and he glanced around. He winced, as though still in pain. "What happened?" His voice croaked.

"You gave me a fright, that's what. I thought I'd lost you."

"I feel…I feel…tired. Weak. And my chest…" He reached up, brushed a hand over the pink skin and flinched again.

Before she could reply, he passed out once again.

Henry was in and out of sleep. Once when he awoke, the royal healer checked his wound. He rubbed on more of the disgusting white stuff that stank like road kill and looked like toothpaste.

"What is this stuff?" he asked.

"A healing salve," Seamus said. "This should be your last dose. It looks much better."

"Thanks, doc. For what you did for me."

"You're not a Fae," he said suddenly.

Henry stared at him, unsure how to respond. The healer looked him over.

"You're human, aren't you? I sensed it when I used the magic to heal the wound. I've never seen it poison a Fae the way it did you."

"I'm human," Henry croaked, admitting the truth. "But she

doesn't know."

"By 'she' you mean the queen?" Henry nodded. Seamus narrowed his eyes. "Who is concealing you with glamour?"

"The princess," he said. "I'm Maggie's father."

"Ah. That explains why the human girl was so distressed over your injury."

"You won't tell the queen, will you?"

"Not yet. I'll leave that to you. I trust you'll make the right decision and break the news to her soon."

Not a chance. Henry wasn't finished with her yet. He may never be finished with her and if that was the case, *then* he would decide what to do and if he was going to tell her the truth. He'd have to talk to Elyne about keeping his glamour. He liked it. He wasn't so sure he wanted to give it back.

The healer rose from the bed. "There's a washtub full of water but it's since gone cold. I'll have it removed and a fresh one brought to you."

"Thank you. This stuff stinks."

When Seamus left, he was all alone again with his thoughts. When Maeve mentioned that Maggie had come to visit him while he was still out cold, he was certain she was fishing for information. What if she suspected he wasn't a Fae? Then what would happen? He hadn't enough time to woo her. He needed more time.

Hours seemed to pass before the door opened and Maggie poked in her head.

"Daddy?"

Henry propped himself up on his elbows. "Mags, I'm happy to see you."

Relief flooded her face as she entered and closed the door. She hurried to the bed, throwing her arms around his neck in a giant hug. He grunted. She realized what she did and pulled back.

"I'm sorry. Did I hurt you?"

"No, no. I'm fine. Better. Doc was here earlier. I'm going to live." He gave her a winning smile.

Maggie sniffed as tears suddenly flooded her eyes. "Dad, you scared the life out of me. Why on earth did you do that?"

"You mean flinging myself in front of Maeve to save her?"

"Yeah, that." She nodded and whisked away the tears with the back of her hand.

"I…wanted to save her."

"But you don't even know her. And she hates humans."

"You and Elyne keep telling me that." He pressed his mouth into a thin line. "Maggie, have you ever felt drawn to someone? Ever looked at them and *knew* that was who you were meant to be with?"

She blinked. "Yes, with Finn. But—"

"Then you understand how I feel."

"That's impossible. She's a Fae. And a queen. And you just met her."

"Is it impossible to you, magpie, because she's Elyne's mother or because she's a Fae queen?"

She blinked again. Opened her mouth to respond, then closed it. Then opened and closed it again. He reached for her hand, squeezed it.

"I'm not marrying her, you know," he said. "We're not buying a summer home and picking out curtains or anything."

Maggie pressed her fingertips against her lips. "You mean like date her? I don't think you can exactly ask her to dinner and the movieplex."

"And I'm also a grown man with feelings and needs."

She scrunched up her face. "Ew, Dad."

"How do you think you got here? It was by good old-fashioned—"

"Dad!" She held up her hand to stop him.

"Sorry." He chuckled at the look of horror on her face. "I loved your mother very much. A part of me always will. No one could ever replace her."

"I know."

But she stuck out her lower lip in a pout. Something he knew all too well and was very familiar with. Maggie wasn't getting her way. She contemplated her next question and he didn't have to wait long for her to ask it.

"How do you see this working out anyway? I mean, you can't possibly pretend to be a Fae knight for the rest of your life. She'll figure it out eventually."

"I realize that," he said. "But right now, I want to be with her."

Maggie squeezed his hand. "I don't want to see you get hurt. Emotionally or…otherwise. I can't bear the thought of losing you, too."

"It's the same for me, magpie. You'll have to trust that everything will be all right."

"I hope so. Because…well…because I'm going to have a baby."

He knew already since Elyne had told him. Still, he loved hearing it from his daughter. He grinned. Before he could reply, she rushed on.

"It's really important to me that you accept Finn, Dad. I love him. I want to have lots of children with him. And build a life with him. Granted, I know we'll be living in the Middle Ages, but I—"

"Maggie, it's all right. I understand." He had to interrupt her to get a word in. "And I'm happy for you. Besides, I already knew you'd have children with Finn."

She blinked. "You did?"

There was no use in fighting it. Despite his determination to get Maggie home, deep down he knew it was a lost cause. She was married to Finn, whether he liked it or now, and carrying his child. There would be no parting her from the Scottish laird. He understood now. He'd experienced something similar with Maeve, though not as intense.

"Did you forget I was at McCullough Castle in our time? I saw portraits of you and the children."

"The children?" She flushed, her cheeks turning bright pink.

He laughed. "Yes. *Children*. Plural."

"How many? Boys or girls or mix?" Excitement lit her eyes. "No, no. Don't tell me. I want to be surprised. I'd rather be surprised anyway." She leaned down and pecked him on the cheek. "I'll let you rest now. Thanks, Dad. For everything."

"See you later, magpie."

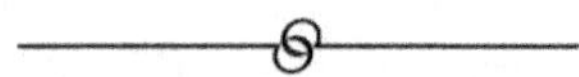

Henry slept more after his daughter left. He wasn't sure, but he thought he had another visit from the healer. He sensed feel someone in the room. But when he opened his eyes, there was no one there. He was finally well enough to sit up without being in complete and utter pain.

He glanced down at the wound still caked with the white salve. It had dried and cracked but at least the injury had healed. Whatever Seamus did to remove the black magic worked.

True to his word, Seamus had a tub full of fresh hot water ready and waiting. Henry couldn't resist the draw of the water and flung off the bedclothes. He stepped into the tub, grateful for the bath. Now that the white stuff had been washed away, all that was left was a faint scar. After a thorough cleansing, he toweled off and dressed.

He threw on a tunic, leaving it open at the throat, and pulled on a pair of breeches. Waning light filtered through the tapestries over the windows and he knew night approached. Needing fresh air, he headed out to the balcony.

When he stepped outside, he was startled to see Maeve standing on her adjoining balcony. Her white shift blew around her in the evening breeze, showing the outline of her soft curves. Nothing was left to his imagination. Her blonde hair hung the length of her back in soft waves. Her profile looked as though it had been carved by the angels themselves. She gripped the railing, deep in thought.

He stopped breathing as he drank in the sight of her. Memorizing every curve of her youthful body. She must have sensed eyes on her for her head turned, her gaze falling on him.

He couldn't speak. The words died in his throat. And anything he said would sound ridiculous anyway. A simple hello would do but he couldn't say it.

"I couldn't sleep," she said, her voice soft in the night. "You?"

"No," he said, finally finding his own. "I'm tired of sleeping. Been doing it most of the day."

"I know."

He *had* sensed someone in his room.

"Should you be out of bed?" she asked.

"I feel fine." Well, not fine exactly. His chest ached. He would never allow her to see his pain. He thanked Seamus for the bath, glad no longer reeked.

She turned back to the night, staring into darkness. He wondered what she saw, if anything. There was no moon.

"My world has turned upside down. Instead of order and peace there is chaos and turmoil. I've lost more soldiers than I can count. My people's lives have been devastated. My daughter made a promise to the Elves I now have to keep. And I still don't have my magic back."

Henry slowly inched closer. Her scent drifted on the wind. This time not roses but jasmine. Beckoning him.

"Now Morrigan. With the weakening of the veil, I should have seen it coming and prepared for it."

She huffed out a breath and her gaze met his. She blinked, surprised he had closed the distance with stealthy steps. He hadn't wanted her to stop her talking.

"How could you have known what was to come?"

"The world had been peaceful far too long. After six thousand years of silence, I should have realized it would come to an end sooner or later."

Six thousand years? *Whoa.* Was she speaking of a time when she ruled? How old was she?

Henry reached across the railing and placed his hand on top of hers. She was cold.

"What's done is done. You can't beat yourself up about what's happened. All the 'should haves' in the world won't change the past."

"What are you doing?" she asked, her gaze never leaving his face.

He didn't falter. "Attempting to comfort you."

"I don't need your comfort." Yet she made no move to take her hand away.

"How long have you ruled, Maeve?"

Her jaw tightened, an almost imperceptible action had he not been watching her so intently. Had she noticed he hadn't used the terms *your majesty* or *my queen*? Was that why her jaw ticked? "You are a Fae. You should know."

One eyebrow rose. She had him there. "Humor me."

"I was a young queen when Morrigan had my husband murdered. Elyne was but a child," she said. "That was six thousand years ago."

A young queen. But how long had she lived before then?

Hundreds of years? He didn't know and it didn't really matter all that much. All that mattered was he wanted her. She had suffered great loss when her husband died. It was in the depths of her eyes. He wondered if that was why so was so cold and distant. Was she afraid to allow herself to love again?

Another challenge.

He wanted to soothe her and crumble the walls she'd built to protect her heart. He could relate to her feelings. He had lost his beloved wife to cancer. He had also lost his eldest daughter in a car accident. He couldn't stand the thought of losing Maggie. It was why he had to follow her to Scotland when she disappeared. He couldn't think about those dreadful things. Not now. He turned his attention back to Maeve.

"Why does Morrigan want you dead?"

"She is the Goddess of War. She thrives on fear, violence and wrath."

But something told him there was more to it than that.

Henry pressed against the railing, the cold stone biting through his breeches. Her eyes dropped down to linger on the open collar of his tunic before meeting his gaze again. He couldn't help the smugness that spread through him. His hand slipped up her arm and she shivered. From cold or his touch, he didn't know.

"The…dragon told me to leave this place."

"The dragon?"

"Nero," she said. "He followed me here from the battleground. He prophesized the goddess's death."

Dragons could talk? He had a lot to learn about this place. He wasn't familiar with Nero, yet he guessed he would soon become acquainted. "Do you believe Nero?"

"He is far more ancient than I," she said. "Aye, I believe him. He wants me to go to the Sacred Forest. There is a castle there that was forged by the first Fae High King of the Otherworld. The walls are fused with magical wards and the forest is enchanted."

Enchanted forests and magical castles. Bring it on.

"Will you go?" he asked.

Did she realize he leaned toward her? That the stone railing and a mere breath of cotton separated them? Did she know she leaned toward him, her breath shuddering in and out of her? He had to have another taste. One kiss would never be enough. Perhaps if he got one more he would be satisfied. It would squelch this awful wanting inside him and kill the need to have her beneath him.

"I-I don't know."

"Why would you go into a forest and leave the safety of your palace?" He cupped her face. She licked her lips.

"Nero said I should go with him. I'm going."

"Don't you think that's dangerous?"

"Aye, but—"

"Have you thought this through?"

"If the dragon thinks I should go, then I will go."

"Shouldn't you take someone with you? Someone you can trust who can protect you?"

"Such as Lord Derron and my men? Or mayhap the Elves?"

"So many questions." His lips brushed hers. "Did the dragon say to bring them?"

"No."

"And you trust this dragon?"

She hesitated. "Aye."

"I don't think you should make a rash decision." Again, his lips brushed hers. He couldn't bear the thought of being separated from her. Not yet. He wanted her to stay here, close to him.

"I'm going. I plan to tell the High Council tomorrow at the Treaty negotiations."

"Would you like me to be there for moral support?" He flashed a grin.

She snorted. "I should think not."

"Are you certain about this plan? Your kingdom needs you."

"I won't do the kingdom any good if I'm dead."

Her voice was intoxicating. Her soft curves pressing against his body drove him mad.

"Nor will you do me any good if you're dead."

She started to reply but he smothered her mouth with his. He kissed her and much to his surprise, she leaned into him again. For the second time, they shared a soul-stealing kiss. He couldn't stop himself from touching her. His hands slipped from her face, followed the curve of her shoulders, down her arms.

She wore nothing under the shift. He'd seen the outline of her body under the opaque material. He palmed her breasts, cupping the perfection and feeling the peaks against his skin. His thumbs roved over them, teasing the pearls beneath the softness of her shift.

Heavenly. Oh, so heavenly.

Warmth cascaded through him, spreading to every extremity. His better half—the one that resided in his pants—made its presence known loud and clear. And it was all he could do to keep from vaulting the railing and dragging her to bed. She moaned in his mouth, making the situation even harder.

Henry gathered the material in his fingers, lifting it ever so gently so as not to arouse her suspicions. He wanted to arouse her pleasure. He heard her sharp intake of breath and she stilled against him. His mouth left hers, trailed kisses down her throat as a little mewl escaped her.

Hearing the sound made him nearly come undone.

At last his hand landed on her cold skin and moved across the expanse of her abdomen. The swell of her hip. He'd never felt anything so smooth. Dare he move closer to paradise?

It was worth a try.

Chapter 9

Henry's hand swept the top of Maeve's thigh and moved nearer to the apex of her legs. As his fingers brushed over her, she jumped. Maeve instantly broke apart from him and moved back, leaving him empty. Cold. Unfulfilled.

"No, Henry."

"You want me. I want you. It's simple."

He leaned in for another kiss but she pressed her hands firmly against his chest. "No."

"No, you don't want me? Your kiss could have fooled me."

Maeve dragged her lower lip through her teeth. Why did she insist on torturing him?

"When was the last time a man seduced you?" he asked when she didn't answer.

A slender, perfect blonde eyebrow rose. Her lids went half-mast and her face took on that snooty look.

"Never?" he queried. *Could it be?*

She blew out a breath.

"A travesty. A woman as beautiful as you *should* be seduced."

Finally, she shoved him back and stepped out of reach. "You are too bold, Sir Henry."

"Back to the 'sir' now? Seems a bit silly to call me that after sharing such kisses." He paused, his gaze touching over her body. "And caresses."

"And you will address me as 'your majesty'. Never use my name again without permission."

She *had* noticed and hadn't liked it. "I take it I don't have permission," he said wryly.

"Nor do you have permission to kiss me." Despite her words, she flushed. "Or put your hands on me."

"You should be kissed and often. And by someone who knows

how."

"I'm sure you're the person for that job," she retorted.

"I can come over this railing and take you in my arms before you could blink." At least he thought he could even with his injury. He was feeling rather energetic at the moment.

Maeve lifted her chin. "You wouldn't. You couldn't. Aren't you still hurt?"

Another challenge. His heart raced. His fingers twitched. "Care for me to prove it to you?"

She hesitated. "No."

A lie and he knew it. He vaulted the railing without a running start. Despite his bravado, pain lanced through him. He didn't let that sway him as he charged toward her, his blood whooshing through his veins. His heart pounded a wild beat and his adrenaline surged. She took a few steps backward in retreat, her eyes wide and round and her face flushed. Before she could react, she was in his arms.

Maeve's pulse fluttered in her throat as her breasts crushed against his chest. He locked his grip around her, refusing to let go even when she tried to shove him off. Oh, no. He wasn't letting her slip away so easily this time.

"Let me go."

"What are you afraid of?"

"Nothing. Release me." She struggled against him.

"Not yet. Not until we come to an understanding."

She stilled, fire in her gaze as she stared at him. Being almost the same height, they met eye to eye. In his world he preferred petite women he could tuck under his chin. But with her he quickly changed his mind. She was full of vibrant life and all softness in his arms. He glanced down to see her breasts against his chest. Two perfect mounds that would fill his palms.

"You're going to stop lying to me about how you feel," he said.

"How dare you demand anything of me? I am your queen." But her words lacked conviction and heat. Almost as though she didn't truly mean them.

His first thought was to retort she wasn't his queen. But then she would know he was human and he couldn't blow his cover yet. She wasn't ready for the truth.

"Aye, my queen. Ruler of my heart." He dipped in for a kiss but she jerked her head back. So that's how it was going to be, was it? It was time to pull out the big guns. "Can you deny the heat between us, *your majesty*?" He emphasized the title of address so she would know he meant business. "Can you deny you *want* me to kiss you?"

"You don't know anything about what I want." Her voice took on a razor edge.

"Oh, I know." He grinned, sure of himself. "The sounds you made when I touched you were all the evidence I needed."

"Insolent bastard." She gave him a forceful shove.

He could have locked his arms and kept her in place, but he relaxed his grip and let her go. She stumbled back a few steps, closer to the entrance to her chamber.

"I should have you apprehended. Taken to the Reformatory."

"What's stopping you then?"

She balled her fists and thinned her lips. She clearly didn't like when he challenged her. It messed with her authority and cool exterior. Maeve was a woman who needed to be in control at all times and when he touched her, kissed her, he destroyed that control. One day she would relinquish it all to him. That day would be when she was naked beneath him.

"Go back to your chamber!"

She spun away. Her bare feet were silent on the stone balcony as she disappeared into her room. A moment later the door slammed and the lock clicked.

Maeve stalked to her bed and flung back the covers with shaking hands. She broke into a cold sweat. How dare he. How dare he kiss her, touch her, whisper those words to her as though he meant it.

She climbed into bed, pulling the blankets to her chin. For a brief moment, she considered covering her head and squeezing her eyes shut. But even if she did that, she knew it wouldn't banish the image of Henry jumping over the balcony and stalking toward her with that purposeful stride. It ignited the passionate fire within her. She hadn't expected him to actually do it.

And when he took her in his arms, insisting she be honest with him about her feelings she *wanted* to slap him. Her good sense stopped her. What did he know about her? Nothing. How could he have any kind of feelings for her? An inward groan erupted at the thought of allowing him to kiss her with reckless abandon. That wasn't like her to allow someone to take such audacious liberties.

And yet, she pressed her fingertips against her lips as if she could still feel his mouth there. In all her long years, she couldn't recall another man as bold as Henry. Even her long-dead husband hadn't been as daring. Before they wed, he always as her permission before kissing or touching her. He knew his place with her as queen.

Unlike Henry who didn't seem to care one whit about her status or title.

Maeve took a long look inside, allowing honesty to come forward. Deep down, there was something unsettling about Henry's brash seduction—and she was quite aware he was seducing her. But the unsettling part wasn't that she didn't like it, rather she liked it quite a lot. She wanted him to kiss her and her traitorous body responded with the need and desire she'd craved for eons.

Maeve jerked back the covers and stood. She prowled the length of the room, pressing her palms against her temples, her eye sockets trying to press away the memory.

His words played over again in her mind. *You should be kissed and often. And by someone who knows how.*

He certainly did know how to kiss her. How she wanted him to kiss her. How she longed for his mouth to devour hers.

"No. I cannot think this way."

She halted, staring at the dying embers of the fire. She stoked them, forced the flames to reignite.

Like the flames of her heart. Henry had somehow managed to inflame long-dead feelings she had buried. After her husband had died, she vowed she would never love another as she had loved him.

But with Henry now a constant presence firmly planted in her mind, she wondered if that would change. *Could* she allow that to change in light of her current situation? Morrigan was determined to destroy her. All because of an old vendetta that stemmed from deep-seated jealousy.

Maeve had reservations about going to the Sacred Forest. It *was* enchanted and she knew all the things lurking there. The forest was almost sentient itself. It could take one's deepest fears and twist them to make one think it was reality. She disliked the thought of going alone but she knew Henry was right. Someone should go with her.

She couldn't leave the palace behind unguarded should Morrigan attack again. Nor could she take her daughter with her. If anything were to happen to her, Elyne would have to take over the rule of the kingdom. Of course, Nero would be with her. Would it be enough having the dragon to protect her from Morrigan when she came to attack?

Mayhap that was why Nero insisted she go to the Sacred Forest. The enchantment *could* keep her safe. Still, she knew someone should accompany her as her personal guard. And not Derron. He had too many duties here with Elyne. He must stay to protect her and the kingdom. And not any of the High Council members. They were practically worthless. Nothing more than bags of hot air.

Mayhap she could take one of the Fae knights… Aye, she would. And she knew who she'd take with her. She padded to the bed and slipped under the covers. How would her errant knight feel about her order to accompany her? As she drifted off to sleep, Maeve knew what her decision must be.

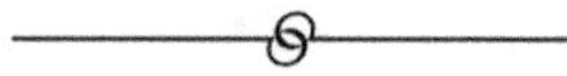

Maeve gathered her council along with Princess Elyne, Lord Derron and the Elves. Despite her restless night, she was determined to follow Nero's advice and leave the palace for the Sacred Forest. She intended to take Sir Henry with her, though he didn't know it yet.

She expected to meet some resistance to her decision from her council and Lord Derron. But her decision was final and she refused to back down no matter how much hell they gave her. As she took her place at the long oval table, she glanced around the room. Every face was expectant and waiting.

She hesitated. Instead of making her announcement to the High Council and the Elves that she would be leaving, she launched the discussion about the Treaty of Separation. Mayhap Henry was right. She shouldn't be making such a rash decision. She needed to think it through more.

"Welcome, honored guests and High Council. I hope today we can continue with the discussion of the Treaty without being interrupted this time."

A few chuckles went around the room.

"King Urdithane, would you like to open with some remarks?" she asked.

The Elven king stood, looking regal as ever in his royal dress. His sons sat on either side of him. Maeve scanned the room for the Elven princess but didn't find her.

They all listened intently as the king talked about the alliance between the Fae and Elves, how things once were and how they could be again. He droned on and on until Maeve no longer heard him. Until her thoughts turned back to Henry.

She couldn't stop the memory of his lips on hers from flooding back to her. She was certain she could still feel him kissing her, even now. She resisted the urge to press her fingertips against her lips. She'd never reacted to a kiss like this before. Or his touch. The way his fingers had trailed over her skin.

Stop it.

She wouldn't allow herself to think about that right now. She needed to focus.

"Wouldn't you agree, Queen Maeve?"

What had Urdithane been saying? To what was she supposed to agree? She bit her bottom lip. Elyne, sitting next to her, placed her hand on her arm.

"Mother, what's wrong? Your face is flushed."

She'd allowed her emotions to get the better of her. *She* knew why she was flushed but she couldn't share that information with her daughter, the entire High Council or the Elves. More heat—embarrassment—flooded her cheeks.

"I—"

Then it happened. An almost imperceptible vibration in the room. Her heart fluttered and not from the amorous thoughts she had about Henry.

"Did you feel that?" she asked. Her senses were suddenly on high alert.

"Feel what?" Derron asked. He glanced around the room. "Mother?"

The vibration happened again. This time more apparent. Maeve's heart sped up. Despite having no magic, she sensed something…felt something…knew something was about to happen. Slowly, she got to her feet. Another vibration. Louder this time. Enough to rumble the walls and rattle the pewter cups on the tables.

"Lord Derron—"

But that was as far as she got when all hell broke loose.

A shudder went through the room, the walls vibrating and undulating, almost as though some sort of wave hit the building. Maeve nearly lost her footing. Derron jumped to his feet, sword drawn at the ready. Lord Eldrin was also on his feet, making his way to Derron's side with his sword also drawn. Then everything stilled.

"What was that?" Elyne's voice was barely above a whisper.

A roar, then, like some angry beast that hovered over the palace. Another *kaboom* and the walls shook. The tables rattled. Cups toppled over and liquid spilled.

"Get the king and queen out of here and to safety," Derron barked to Andahar.

The Elven prince had climbed to his feet, wobbling on them as the room continued to shift with the quaking ground. Elyne was at Maeve's side, wrapping her hand around her wrist.

"Come, Mother."

"No. Running isn't the answer."

"Your majesty, it's not safe for you here." Andahar had reached her side and took her by the arm. "Or you, princess."

Derron and Eldrin ran past, out the doors and into the hallway. Maeve caught sight of Henry and her heart—stupid heart— skipped a happy beat. Before he could make a move, another boom rocked the palace. This time so violent that it knocked everyone off their feet. Maeve found herself on the floor, looking through the stars in her eyes at the cracked ceiling. A groan next to her was Andahar. The back of her head throbbed and she realized she must have cracked it on the floor when she landed. She blinked, trying to focus.

"She's injured! Get the healer."

That was Elyne, panic in her voice. Maeve rolled to her side and curled into a ball. She reached back, touched her head gently. The tips of her fingers brushed a large lump that had suddenly formed.

I must have hit my head harder than I thought.

"Henry! Thank the gods. Help her." Elyne again. But her voice sounded far away. As if she were in a tunnel.

Maeve wanted to search for Henry. She was weightless as she was lifted off the floor.

"I've got you."

A deep voice rumbled next to her and she realized Henry held her. He cradled her next to his chest and she tucked her head under his chin. She sighed his name.

"We've got to find Seamus," Elyne said. And then Maeve heard her daughter gasp with a sharp intake of breath.

"What is it?" Maeve muttered.

A loud roar was her answer. What was happening? She couldn't open her eyes to see. She didn't *want* to open her eyes. It hurt too much. Her stomach clenched and for a horrifying moment, she thought she might vomit all over Henry.

"We've got to get her out of here." Elyne again but this time her voice was a tight whisper.

"Where?" Henry's clipped tone.

"I don't—"

A roar. A boom. A crash. Men shouting. Women screaming. What the bloody hell was happening? Maeve forced her eyes open. Above her was the blue expanse of sky, dark smoke curling upward from somewhere. The stench of blood and burned earth. As she stared upward, a great red dragon flew across the sky. The rider's long dark hair fluttered behind her. *Morrigan.*

The red dragon? It was a beast long known to be hidden in the realm. Once put into shadow like the others. Morrigan must have found it and released it, like Maeve had released the others. The red dragon would never leave survivors once it was released to attack. That bitch was riding it and probably had it under a dark spell.

"We're doomed," Maeve muttered.

A moment later, Nero passed by, burping fire at the red dragon. That must have been all the noise. The red dragon attacked and

Nero fought back to protect her and the palace.

"Daughter," she croaked. "Use your magic."

"How?" Elyne asked. She moved into her line of vision. Her face was lined with worry. "What do I need to do?"

"Cast it out. Use a banish spell." It hurt to speak. Thank the gods Henry still held her in his arms. *Such strong arms.* "Go. Before it kills everyone."

Elyne turned and ran toward the battle, her blonde hair bouncing behind her and her skirts flying.

"Henry…"

"Shh. Don't talk anymore. You're hurt and I'm going to find Seamus."

"What…happened?"

"That red dragon blew up the palace. If your black dragon hadn't been around…"

She knew. If Nero hadn't been there to protect them, they would have all been killed allowing Morrigan to win.

Maeve bounced in his arms. She knew he resumed walking again at a clipped speed. What had happened to King Urdithane? Prince Andahar? Were they all right?

Henry moved farther and farther away from the battle. She wanted to ask more questions, to find out where they were going and what was happening. She was too tired, though. Couldn't keep her eyes open and then, mercifully, she passed out.

Maeve's head pounded as she cracked open her eyes. She was in her bed, propped up on several pillows. Elyne sat on the end of her oversized bed while Seamus stood over her.

"She's awake," he said.

"Thank goodness. Mother, how are you feeling?"

"What happened? Does the palace still stand? How many dead? What about the Elves?"

"Calm." Seamus put a hand on her shoulder and pressed her into the pillows. "You hit your head quite hard on the stone floor."

Remembering, she touched the back of her head, sickened by the large lump there. Seamus had already mended her, thank goodness. Her head was still tender and she had a raging headache but at least she wasn't dead.

"We were worried about you," Elyne said.

"Aside from a tremendous headache, I'm fine."

"I suspect you'll have that for a few days. I'll get you something for it."

"No, no." Maeve waved it away. "No more herbs, Seamus. I'm all right."

"Are you certain, your majesty?"

"Aye, I am. I need a clear head. Not muddied with more of your potions. I seem to have to thank you once again for saving my life."

"'Tis becoming a habit," Seamus said with a nod. "A habit I'm starting to dislike."

"Me as well."

"I'll be back later to check on you." He patted her shoulder and left her alone with Elyne.

"Tell me what happened," Maeve demanded once the healer was gone.

"Morrigan and the red dragon attacked the palace," Elyne said. "She's awakened the red dragon. If it hadn't been for Nero, I'm not sure what would have happened. I didn't realize he had followed you from the Hill of Tara."

"Aye, he did. His protection is his way of thanking me for releasing him from the dark spell he was under with the Unseelie."

"He told me," she said. "He also told me he…wants you to go to the Sacred Forest."

"Did he? I'd intended to speak to the High Council about that today after the negotiations."

"You intend to go then?"

"I think for the safety of all here, I should."

"No, Mother." Elyne moved to sit beside her on the bed. She gripped her hand. "It's too dangerous. No Fae has stepped in the Sacred Forest in thousands of years."

"I'm well aware of that, daughter. However, under the circumstances, I believe it may be for the best."

"You sound like you've already made up your mind."

"Did King Urdithane and Prince Andahar survive the attack?"

Maeve asked, changing the subject.

"They did. They're uninjured. I used the banish spell, like you told me. I was able to send away the red dragon and Morrigan. For now. I fear she will return, though."

"Aye, she will. That's why I have to leave this place."

"The palace sustained a lot of damage," Elyne said, carefully ignoring Maeve's last statement.

"Which sets us back once again." Maeve sighed. She closed her eyes and leaned her head back into the pillows. Her head throbbed. "We will have to begin rebuilding all over again."

"Mother, don't worry about any of that. I'll take care of it."

"I know you will. Send me Henry, daughter. I wish to speak with him."

"Henry? Why?"

"Because I wish to speak to him. Now send him to me."

"Aye, Mother."

A few moments after Elyne left, Henry entered. He approached the bed, stood beside it and gazed down at her. The relief was evident in his eyes.

"Thank god you're all right," he said.

"Thanks to you." She smiled up at him and reached for his hand. Their fingers intertwined. His skin was warm, comforting. "I'm glad you were there."

"The goddess will be back."

"I've no doubt about that." She motioned to the bed. "Sit. I wish to speak with you."

He eased down next to her. "How's your head?" He reached out, brushed a lock of hair from her face and tucked it behind her ear.

The simple motion sent her heart into a fluttering. How could this man affect her so? She didn't understand it.

"It hurts but I will heal. I've been thinking about what Nero told me and I've made up my mind."

"You're going to the Sacred Forest?" When she nodded, he added, "Are you certain?"

"This last attack made up my mind. The dragon thinks there is something there that will help me defeat the goddess. And since I have no magic, I'm inclined to believe him."

His hand squeezed hers. "I hope Nero is right about that."

"As do I. Sir Henry...I do not wish to go alone. I hoped that mayhap you would accompany me."

Disbelief briefly washed over his handsome features before he got his reaction under control. He stared at her, silence stretching between them. Mayhap he was considering all his options and deciding whether or not to agree to go with her. She could command him to but she didn't want to force him.

"You were there for me for all three attacks," she said. "You put yourself into danger to protect me. I cannot forget that. That's why I'm asking you to go with me. Will you go, Sir Henry?"

Henry smiled slowly, his face softening. "I should be honored."

"Good." She settled back into the pillows, aware he still held her hand. "I intend to tell the High Council in the morning and then Nero will fly us to the Sacred Forest."

"What about the kingdom?"

"Worry not, Sir Henry. I have a plan. I want you there tomorrow when I make the announcement to the High Council."

"As you wish."

Though he agreed, Maeve didn't miss the look of discomfort on his face and how he shifted on the bed.

"Are you up for the challenge?" she asked.

He lifted her hand and kissed her fingertips. "Where you go, I will follow. No matter the danger."

For a moment she lost all thought. Her stomach did a flip and spirals of desire curled down her abdomen. He said it with such conviction she knew he meant it. He reached for her and brushed away her hair again. He ran his fingers through it and those tendrils of desire increased.

"You should rest. I'll stay here and watch over you. It's my turn to take care of you."

She knew he would be true to his word, too. With an inward sigh, Maeve drifted into blissful sleep.

Chapter 10

The following morning Maeve entered the council chamber to see the entire High Council had gathered. She'd sent word to Elyne she didn't want the Elves present yet for a private High Council meeting about the state of the kingdom. Thankfully, her daughter was able to convince them not to come. Maeve didn't want to discuss her leaving in front of them for fear it would cause problems for Elyne. She would let Elyne or Derron break the news to them later.

She took a deep breath and exhaled slowly. Henry must have sensed her apprehension for he kissed her on the cheek and whispered, "Good luck." He took a seat near her at the table. Having him there boosted her confidence. However, Maeve didn't miss the look of disdain Derron gave him as he took his seat.

Well, he'll have to get over that.

Nor did she miss the curious glances the other councilmembers gave Henry. There would be questions about why he was there.

She knew the council—especially Lord Derron—wouldn't agree to let her go so easily. They would fight to keep her here. She could admit it *did* sound crazy leaving the safety of the palace walls to go to the Sacred Forest alone with one knight and a dragon. But then the palace walls weren't so safe these days, were they? Morrigan had managed to breach the walls on more than one occasion. She couldn't take any more chances.

"Good morrow. Thank you all for coming. Instead of discussing the Treaty, I have called this special High Council meeting. With the threat of Morrigan, I have come to a decision." She paused, her gaze touching on the expectant faces around the table and halting on Elyne's. Maeve knew someone would have to remain in power when she left. She was resigned to that. Accepted it. And hoped her daughter was up for the task. "The Goddess of War is only interested in me. I will not put this kingdom at any more unnecessary risk. At dusk, Nero will fly me to the Sacred

Forest where I will remain in Conn's castle. I will deal with Morrigan there."

Elyne's face remained impassive as she'd already heard the news. The men burst into arguments, talking over one another.

Maeve calmly held up a hand. "My decision is final and I will not change my mind."

"Your majesty, this is madness." Lord Roderick pounded the shiny table with his fist to press his point. "We simply cannot allow you to do this."

"My queen, I agree with Lord Roderick. What you're proposing to do puts the entire kingdom at risk," Derron said. "You cannot go alone without adequate protection."

"I will not be alone. Sir Henry has agreed to go with me."

Elyne gasped. Derron's face flushed. Murmurs went through the room as the men shifted in their chairs.

"Your majesty," Derron began, "you cannot take one knight. He alone cannot possibly protect you."

"And why not? He was there when the Shade nearly killed me. He was also there the two times Morrigan attacked. He saved me from the boulder that nearly crushed me and he put himself in between me and Morrigan's magic."

"He lacks the experience to serve as your personal guard," Derron said. His gaze flickered to Henry then back to the queen.

"He has all the experience he needs to protect me." She lifted her head, staring down her nose in her trademark glare.

Elyne cleared her throat. "Mother, are you certain about this?"

"Aye, I am."

Worry lines creased her daughter's face. The men of her High Council all looked at her as though she'd lost her mind and, mayhap, she had. Following the advice of the dragon and taking along one Fae knight as protection did seem like folly.

"How do you know you can trust the black dragon?" Lord Vaughan asked. He was the calm one. The voice of reason.

"He has given me no reason not to trust him," Maeve said. "I believe what he says is true and I intend to follow his advice. If it hadn't been for him, the red dragon and Morrigan would have destroyed this palace. Or do you all forget this?"

"You put yourself at risk by leaving here with that monstrosity,"

Roderick said.

"I put myself at risk as well as the rest of you if I stay." Maeve had never seen him so angry or so vehemently opposed to any of her decisions as this one. "Nero is not a monster. He was controlled by evil before. He is not evil. I have spoken to the dragon myself."

More murmurs spread through the room.

"What if he isn't?" Derron asked, his tone demanding. "What if he's trying to lure you away from the palace so Morrigan can kill you?"

"I will not allow anything to happen to her." Henry spoke then, his voice quiet confidence.

"Stay out of this, hum—knight," Derron warned.

"Derron, please." Elyne placed a hand on his arm to calm him. "I believe Sir Henry will protect her as he says. And my mother has specifically requested him as her personal guard."

Derron pursed his lips, mayhap to keep from retorting.

"Mother, I'm not sure this is the best idea but if this is your decision then I will support you."

Elyne had never sounded so much like a ruler as she did then. It made her proud. Proud her daughter had come so far in so short amount of time. "Thank you, Elyne. In my absence, I leave the realm in your care and hereby appoint you Queen Regent."

Silence descended and everyone stilled. Maeve was aware of all the shocked stares and the way Elyne's face paled. She clutched Derron's arm, her nails digging into the cloth of his tunic.

"Queen Regent?" Elyne's voice quavered. "Are you certain?"

"I am," Maeve said with a nod.

Elyne bowed her head. "Thank you, Mother."

But Derron looked far from pleased at the prospect. "We are supposed to negotiate the abolition of the Treaty of Separation with the Elves. How are we to do that with you gone?" Derron asked.

"I have confidence my daughter can handle the negotiations on her own. As does King Urdithane."

Now Elyne flushed, her cheeks turning pink. Maeve stood, council members following as well as Henry and Elyne.

"If there is nothing else, I take my leave of you. There are preparations to be made. Sir Henry and I leave at dusk."

"We have not voted on this decision," Roderick said, almost sounding like a challenge.

"I don't believe I requested a vote, Lord Roderick."

"You would leave here without our approval?"

"I am still *queen*, am I not? My first duty is to the realm. My decision to leave will keep you safe in my absence. Morrigan's quarrel is with me and me alone."

Without waiting for a response, Maeve walked out of the room with her head held high. She had expected more resistance, more arguing. Mayhap that was to come. She hadn't left yet, after all.

"Mother, wait."

Maeve paused in the corridor and waited for Elyne to catch up. Her cheeks were still flushed and sweat beaded her brow.

"I'm honored with your decision to put me in charge of the realm, but…are you certain about this?"

Ah, here it was. The men must have sent her to talk sense into her. "I am."

Elyne bit her lower lip.

"Where is your self-confidence, girl? I thought I taught you better than that," Maeve chided.

"You did, but I…I didn't expect this."

"You made a promise to King Urdithane. Now it is up to you to keep it. After everything that's happened, I leave things in your capable hands. And you'll have Derron and the High Council to help you."

"The High Council is nothing but old cronies," Elyne said with a sour look.

Maeve struggled not to laugh. The men were frustrating and pushy and thought they could do a better job simply because they were men. It was a struggle with which her daughter would soon become familiar. Maeve's hope was that Derron would be there to give her the support she needed. Much like her husband had been before he was killed.

"I couldn't agree more. In time, you'll learn how to get your way with them as I did."

"Are you sure about this, Mother? Are you not afraid of what lurks in the Sacred Forest?"

"No."

"Well, I am. Father told me tales. The spirits there can destroy you," Elyne said.

Maeve smiled and patted her daughter's shoulder for reassurance. "Those were nothing more than bedtime stories. Your father enjoyed making them up. That's all. I will be safe. I promise."

"Let me send a few men with you. It would make me feel better," Elyne said. "As it will the High Council and Derron."

"No, daughter. I leave with Nero and Sir Henry. No one else."

"Why Sir Henry?" she asked. "I don't understand this sudden loyalty to him."

"He saved my life from Morrigan," Maeve said. "I've no doubt he can do it again."

"But Sir Henry is…not experienced. He's…untested. And he…hasn't been in the Queen's Guard for that long. I'm not sure—"

"It will be fine. I trust him. As you should." Maeve wasn't sure why her daughter acted strange about the knight. Mayhap because her mother was leaving with no other guards.

Elyne shifted from one foot to the other, her cheeks flushing. "Mother, there's something I should tell you."

"No more talk, Elyne. My decision is made. I'm leaving with Sir Henry."

She started walking again, expecting Elyne to follow her. She didn't, much to her surprise. Mayhap she had accepted her decision and didn't want to fight her anymore. Why would she? She had all the power and now she had the realm. And, strangely, Maeve trusted her with every bit of it.

Henry waited until Maeve disappeared down the corridor before speaking to the princess. In fact, he'd been standing there the entire time Elyne tried to talk her out of going with him. A sense of pride and honor flooded him at the confidence Maeve had in him. And also fear of failing. Maeve thought he could protect her and protect her was what he intended to do.

Despite all his bravado, he couldn't shake the trepidation that went over him. What if he couldn't keep her safe? He couldn't allow the fear and worry to consume him. He had to be strong for the queen.

"Princess Elyne, a word?"

Elyne spun to face him, her face still flushed and her hands curled into fists.

"Henry, you can't go," she said before he could get a word out. "What if you can't protect her and she dies?"

"I'm not going to let that happen," Henry said with conviction.

"But—"

"You have to trust me."

She pressed her lips together in frustration. Then whispered, "She'll know you're human."

That was exactly what he wanted to talk to her about. "Then you'll have to make sure this glamour you cast on me will stay in place because I *am* going."

"But she doesn't like humans. If she finds out—"

"You'll have to make sure she doesn't," he said. "Tell me everything I need to know about her and the Sacred Forest."

"She's stubborn and controlling," she said.

"I know that much. What else?"

"She always has to be right."

"I know that, too. Anything else?"

"I-I don't know. She's changed since the battle with the Unseelie. She's…not the same. The mother I knew would never follow the advice of a dragon, least of all run and hide in a castle in a haunted forest. She'd stay and fight with everything she had."

"What do you think changed her?"

"Mayhap her near-death experience on the Hill of Tara with Lord Kieran. She told me she thought she was going to die that day. That's why she gave me all her magic."

Elyne scrubbed a hand down her face. She looked tired already and she just assumed the position of Queen Regent.

"You will promise to keep her safe?" Elyne asked.

"I swear to you I will."

"Can you? Morrigan is the Goddess of War, Henry. She's not someone to be trifled with. She's dangerous and powerful and—"

"I know that," he said softly, his words enunciated with precision. "Believe me, I know."

"Then why are you doing this?"

Why? Because Maeve asked him. Because Maeve needed him. Because Maeve wanted him.

"Because I have to," he said. "Now tell me. Is the forest truly haunted?"

"I've heard the stories since I was a child," she said.

"How is it haunted? How do I protect Maeve?"

She heaved a heavy sigh. "There are spirits there. Evil ones. They haven't allowed anyone to come out of there alive in centuries. Eons. For as long as I've been alive. This isn't a good idea."

"I know, but she's going and I'm not going to let her go alone. How can we defeat Morrigan when she comes?"

"How should I know? This is Nero's big idea. I think it's crazy. She should be here where we can protect her. Not out there in some wicked forest waiting to be murdered."

"Yet you supported her decision to leave," he said. "Why?"

"Because she was going whether I did or didn't. I figured it would be less trouble if I supported her and let her go. There's no stopping her. Derron isn't happy about it nor is the High Council."

"But that's your problem now that you're Queen Regent."

Her face drained of color. "Aye. Lucky me."

"Can you keep the glamour in place?" he asked, shifting the subject back to the matter at hand.

"Aye, I can. Until the spell is released your glamour will remain."

"Good. Where can I find Maggie?"

"Oh. You'd want to tell her, of course. She's in her chamber with Finn, I would imagine."

"Thank you. And, Elyne, one more thing. If I don't make it back—"

"If you don't, then my mother won't and that's unacceptable." She folded her arms to press her point. "I do not wish to be queen forever, you know. Well, at least not yet."

"Right. But if I don't…promise me Maggie will be well cared for when her time comes." He didn't like the idea of missing the birth of his first grandchild, but he would worry about that later. His priority now was to protect the queen.

She softened and gave him a small smile. "I will. You have my word."

He gave her a nod of approval before he left her. He knew he had to say goodbye to Maggie. He didn't want to leave her so soon. But Maeve needed him more than she did. Maggie had Finn, after all. He found his way to their chamber door and rapped twice. When the door opened Finn filled up the space.

Henry had met him one time. He had to look up at the man. He wore no shirt and a pair of breeches loosely tied at the waist. Henry shifted from one foot to the other, uncomfortable and realizing he must have interrupted the newlyweds. Finally, he cleared his throat and straightened his back.

"I've come to see Maggie."

Finn stepped aside and opened the door wider, allowing him to enter. The bed was rumpled and a fire blazed in the nearby hearth. Maggie emerged from the inner room, her hair a tangled mess around her face. She pulled a robe tight over her shift and folded her arms. Surprise flickered in her face when she saw him.

"Dad? What are you doing here?"

"I need to talk to you, Mags."

"I dinna think ye need me here. I'll see ye after." Finn kissed the top of her head. He snagged his tunic and tugged it on as he shuffled out the door, closing it behind him.

"You okay, Dad?"

"I'm fine. Listen, Mags, I'm going away for a while."

"Away where? Back home?"

"The queen is leaving for the Sacred Forest tonight. She's taking me with her."

Maggie stared at him in disbelief. "Why would she take you?"

"I'm her personal guard now. She thinks since I've managed to protect her from Morrigan, I can keep her safe. What she doesn't know is I happened to be in the right place at the right time."

"Is she taking anyone else? The Queen's Guard? Derron? Princess Elyne?"

"No. Me and the dragon, Nero."

Maggie shook her head. "I don't think that's a good idea."

"I'm going. I wanted to see you before I left. To tell you goodbye."

"I don't like this. Why isn't she taking anyone else?"

He knew the story sounded crazy. Would Maggie think so, too? Who took orders from a dragon? Apparently, the queen thought it wasn't weird at all.

"The dragon told her to go alone and Morrigan would find her there. He said the Sacred Forest would help defeat the Goddess of War."

Maggie scowled. "The dragon told her."

"Yes."

"Dad, you do realize how insane that sounds, right?"

"Yes."

"And you also realize she thinks you're a Fae knight?"

"I do."

"You're going anyway?"

"I am."

"Dad! You can't go with her. You're not…I mean, you don't… She'll figure out you're human," she said, twisting her hands together.

He knew what she was getting at and suppressed a grin. "Maybe not. I've spoken to Elyne. She says the glamour will remain in place until the spell is released."

"I don't like this. You don't know anything about being a knight. How are you going to protect her? Do you even know how to use that sword?" She pointed to it.

"Well…no. But I plan to learn."

"How? There aren't any 'How to Use a Sword' manuals lying around." Now she propped her hands on her hips.

"Trust me." He quirked a grin.

"Dad! You are not Indiana Jones. Have you lost your mind?"

"Maybe I have, Mags. Maybe I'll end up getting myself killed and maybe I won't. All I know is I have to go. I have to protect her. Something is drawing me to her. She wants me with her and I'm going."

Maggie dropped her hands and stared at him. "I knew it. You like her."

His heart rammed hard in his chest. Was he that transparent?

Could his daughter see right through him? "Don't be ridiculous."

"You do. You like her. And it's more than a little. You *like her* like her."

"Maggie…"

"You don't have to pretend with me. I get it." She smiled. "She's beautiful and she's the queen. Who wouldn't want her?"

"I don't want her like that." Lie. "I'm trying to do my duty to her."

"You don't have a duty to her because *you are human.*"

"Oh, you had to remind me." He rolled his eyes.

"Are you sure this is the best idea, though, Dad?" She clasped her hands together again. The worry lines creased her forehead.

"Honestly, no," he said and it felt good to admit it. "But I have to try."

"I think it's sweet. And I love you're being so…chivalrous. Plus, I'm really glad to see you like someone again. Even if it is Elyne's mom."

He knew what she meant. He was lost without his beloved wife after she died. He hadn't known what to do with himself. It had taken months to clean out her clothes. Maggie had helped. Which was hard for both of them.

Could be why he was so hell-bent on protecting Maeve and why he wanted her so much. Not that he could have protected his wife from the cancer that killed her. But he wouldn't sit idly by when he could actually *do* something to protect Maeve. There was also a part of him that was afraid another woman would never desire him again. As if he'd lost his touch. He would do whatever he could to win Maeve's heart.

"Please be careful," Maggie said then. "I don't think I could bear it if I lost you, too."

"Ah, Mags. I'll be fine."

Henry pulled her into a bear hug, squeezing her tight. He didn't want to see the tears shimmering in her eyes and didn't want to acknowledge he may not come back. Determination surged through him. He *would* make it back. He *would* bring the queen back alive with him. He *would* see the birth of his first grandchild.

"I promise I'll come back in one piece."

"Good. Because you'll want to meet your grandchild." She

patted her belly, which had yet to start showing.

"I guess I have no choice but to approve of your man."

"Really?"

"Really." He held her at arm's length. "If he ever hurts you, I will make sure he suffers terribly."

"Oh, Dad."

"Take care of yourself, Maggie. I'll see you soon."

Maeve decided against taking anything with her other than a few gowns. She was uncertain how long she and Henry would be in the Sacred Forest. It occurred to her as she pondered over her gowns that she and Henry would be totally and utterly…alone.

When the realization hit her, she sank to the edge of her bed. What had she been thinking? That Nero would be along for the ride. And while Nero was a sentient being and could speak to her with his mind, she wasn't so sure he would be the best conversationalist. Nor would he keep her safe from Henry's seduction.

And she had no doubt Henry would seduce her. Or try to. She wasn't sure how much longer she would be able to resist his charms.

She flung the gowns to the side. She would take none of them. At any rate, the castle would give them whatever they needed. Why was she trying to impress him? It wasn't as though they would have a future together. Mayhap a fling.

Would that be so terrible?

She shoved away the thoughts as she yanked open her door. What was wrong with her? She was as giddy as a young Fae on the eve of her first royal ball. Times were different then and she was older now. Much older. And there were no more balls. She wished things could be as they were in the era before the Elves and Fae were at war with each other. Before her husband had been taken from her. The Beforetime, they called it.

But then…I wouldn't be in this predicament and there would be no Sir Henry.

It had never occurred to her to turn back time and save her true love like Elyne had for Derron. Elyne's father had filled her head with romantic stories. No one had done that with Maeve.

She arrived in the courtyard, ready to take flight with Nero and Henry. Her knight was already waiting, the afternoon sunlight on his face. Making him even more handsome if that were possible. He granted her a knee-melting smile as she approached.

"You pack light," he said.

She suppressed a scowl. She'd tormented herself deciding what to bring but now she was glad she'd made the decision to bring nothing. "The castle will provide us with what we need."

He looked perplexed. "Really?"

Why was he surprised? Hadn't he heard of the Sacred Forest? Didn't he know about the castle there?

"Aye. Shall we?"

He followed her through the courtyard toward the gates. They were greeted by Lord Vaughan, Lord Roderick and Lord Derron.

"Looks like we have a bon voyage party," Henry said.

"Bon voyage?"

"They must want to send us off in style."

In style didn't exactly describe the men's stance. They looked like a wall of muscle ready to keep her from leaving the gates. She would have none of that.

"Stand aside, men," she said.

"No. We're not letting you leave." Derron rested a hand on the hilt of his sword. His gaze flickered from her to Henry and back again.

"You don't have a choice. And I'm not asking for your permission."

"My queen, we cannot allow you to put yourself in such a precarious position." Vaughan didn't have an aggressive tone. He merely stood with his hands clasped in front of him.

"Leaving with that beast is a mistake," Roderick said.

"But I am leaving. Henry is coming with me. And you three will stand aside."

"I'm afraid we can't do that, your majesty," Derron said.

She took a deep breath and exhaled it slowly. If they were going to be forceful, she would have to push back. "Fine, then."

Nero. Come to me.

"Then you'll stay?" Derron asked.

"I don't think so."

"We aren't letting you pass." Roderick sounded as though he'd won.

As if they had a choice. Maeve allowed the *whomp* of wings to be her reply to the men. Nero was so black he looked like a moving shadow across the sky. He swooped into the courtyard, landing so hard the ground reverberated. The men went from aggressive to stepping back away from the dragon as his nose lowered to the ground. He snorted hot steam at them.

"We're leaving. Come, Henry."

Henry mounted the dragon first and then held a hand down to help her. She accepted it, marveled at the strength of his hands as he pulled her up. She settled in front of him, acutely aware of his heat washing over her.

Let's go, Nero.

As you wish, my queen.

As Nero lifted off, Maeve gave the men a jaunty victorious wave.

Chapter 11

Maeve smelled faintly of roses. He couldn't get the scent out of his nose. It was amplified as she scooted closer to him on Nero's back. Her body was soft as he imagined it would be pressing against him. Her hair was like golden silk, the fine strands tickling his face.

He wished he had a snapshot to remember the three faces of the men as they lifted off and flew away. He loved that she waved. It was almost as good as giving them the finger, something he knew the dignified queen would never do. Still, he chuckled imagining it.

"What's so funny?" she asked.

"Remembering those looks they gave you as we left. It was priceless."

She turned her head to look at him over her shoulder. He wasn't sure, but he thought he spied a faint smile on her luscious lips. "They should not have tried to stop me."

Her tone boasted authority and she stiffened her back as she said it, as though to press her point. She turned forward, her hands pressing against the shiny scales of Nero. The great beast banked to the left, careful with his passengers.

The orange orb of the sun balanced on the pink horizon, ready to plunge under it and thrust the Otherworld into darkness. The last rays of light played upon the lush green landscape, sparkled on the cool waters of lochs and bounced off stone circles. Even though this land was much like the human realm—how strange he thought of it that way—it still boasted something unique. Ethereal.

Maeve belonged here. She was part of this land.

How he wanted to touch her. He wanted to slide his hands over her shoulders, down her arms, slip his arms around her waist. He was content inhaling the sweet scent of her hair.

"How far is this Sacred Forest?" He couldn't stop from

fingering those silky strands.

If she noticed she didn't react. "A short ride. We will be there by nightfall. I should warn you the Sacred Forest is haunted."

"Haunted, huh?" Elyne had told him it was but he wasn't sure he believed in such things. Though he probably should since he was walking among Faeries and Elves. And riding a dragon. "How is it haunted?"

"Long ago, many wars were fought there. It was a bloody battleground. Conn of the Hundred Wars eventually defeated all those who opposed him and proclaimed himself High King, the first High King of the Otherworld. He chose to build his castle in the Scared Forest on the battlefield where he defeated his enemies as a reminder of what he went through to gain his lands. He reinforced his castle with wards and magical protections."

Henry loved listening to her smooth voice as she told the story. He continued to finger her hair. When she didn't stop him, he ran his fingers through the strands, relishing the way it felt against his skin. Wanting so much more.

"Those who had died fighting for the king, though, did not rest. Nor did those who had died fighting against him. What Conn did not know was the Sacred Forest had its own magic. And it was not pleased he killed so many and he was bold enough to build his home there.

"The spirits still reside there along with the Shades and shadow beings that can touch your mind. They know your deepest fears, your darkest thoughts and they will never hesitate to use them against you."

"Sounds like a fun place," Henry said dryly.

"Conn eventually went mad," she continued as though he hadn't spoken. "He killed himself in the castle. His men deserted him. His people abandoned him. And no Fae has stepped into the Sacred Forest or Conn's Castle since. That was thousands of years ago."

"And you want to go there now?" Henry asked.

"Nero believes I can defeat Morrigan from there," she said.

"Are you sure this is a place you *want* to go?"

"If I can defeat Morrigan, then aye."

Henry had his doubts. Haunted forests, Shades and a magical castle didn't sound like a picnic. But then, what did he know?

Maybe Nero was right and they could defeat the Goddess of War there.

"But what about us? Won't the spirits and shadow beings affect us?"

"Aye, they will. We must be cautious."

He wanted to ask how they were supposed to be cautious but Nero began his descent. Darkness had settled over the land. Inky-black treetops was all that was visible as they approached. There was a definite beginning and end to this forest of the Fae. The closer they got the more apprehension flickered through Henry.

When they landed, Maeve slid off the back of the beast. Henry followed. She paused a moment, her hand on the dragon's snout. It appeared as though she spoke to him. She patted him affectionately. Nero took to the skies once again.

"Where's he going? I thought he was going to stay with us."

"Even the great Nero is afraid of the forest."

"That's not reassuring at all."

Maeve looked back at the densely packed trees. A breeze fluttered her gown and lifted strands of her hair. Even in the darkness, he could see the gooseflesh rising on her arms. He stepped closer, caught her faint scent.

"Now what?" he asked.

"We walk from here."

Henry wasn't too keen on walking through there at night with nothing to protect them but a sword—a sword he really didn't know how to use effectively. They had no flashlight, no torch, no source of light whatsoever. For all he knew it was the Fire Swamp complete with Rodents of Unusual Size and lightning sand. Everything about this was a bad idea. He wasn't Mr. Survivalist, either. Oh sure, he'd seen those survivor shows a couple of times, but that was about the extent of his training. As he stared into the woods, he thought he saw shadows dancing back and forth at the edge of the tree line. Hungry shadows. Waiting to sink their hungry shadowy teeth into them.

"We're not going in there." And he meant it. There was no way they were walking through that place at night.

"We have to." She sounded determined. Even straightened her back, ready to take a step.

He snatched her arm, pulled her closer. "Hell no, we don't have to. We're staying right here until sunrise." He pointed to the ground to press his point.

"Here?"

Maeve lifted an eyebrow and looked at him as though he'd lost his mind. Maybe he had. Even these conditions weren't exactly ideal. They had no shelter. They had no water. They had no fire. And he knew from watching that show there would be a definite need for all three.

"We can't stay here," she added.

"Then summon your dragon and have him take us somewhere safe until dawn."

"What difference does it make if we go now or go at dawn?"

"Light, that's the difference. At least with the sun up—"

"No." She folded her arms, defiant. "Light does not touch the Sacred Forest. Whether we go now or at dawn does not matter. It's dark either way."

Henry's shoulders drooped, deflated. "Oh."

She motioned to the forest. "Shall we?"

There really was no choice. Henry fell in step beside the queen. "I would feel better if we had a torch or a lantern."

Almost as soon as the words were out of his mouth, he banged his head on something overhead. He cursed, took a step back, and was blinded by the light from a lantern swinging from a low-hanging tree branch. Beams slanted across them to and fro until he reached up and caught it, stopping the motion. With his head throbbing from the impact, he gently took down the lantern.

"Careful what you ask for," Maeve warned. "And guard your thoughts well, Sir Henry. The forest will pluck them from your mind and use them against you."

"Understood. Lead the way, your majesty."

Maeve moved closer to him as she brushed aside limbs and headed deeper into the forest. He suppressed a smile as her hand brushed his and he wondered if she intended to take it. Not waiting for permission, Henry took the initiative and laced his fingers with hers, pulling her even closer to him. The lantern illuminated the queen's delicate features, her blue eyes nothing more than dark orbs.

He was grateful for the light as it seemed to keep the Shades at bay. They skittered away from the shafts of light, hovering on the edges as though they were ready to dive. He wasn't sure what they would do if they landed on them. He wasn't keen on finding out.

"We will be safe once we reach the castle walls," she said.

"You mean *if* we reach the castle walls."

"Quiet your fears," she said. "Or we won't make it."

As they walked, Henry was certain he heard the skittering of creatures, great and small, through the underbrush. Leaves crunched and twigs snapped. He couldn't stop the thoughts of bloodsucking creatures from entering his mind. Nor could he stop the thoughts of giant hairy beasts playing through his imagination. He clutched the lantern tighter and Maeve moved closer.

The ground vibrated beneath his feet. The hair on the back of his neck rose and dread washed over him. Thinking it was part of his overactive imagination, he shoved away the fear. But then the ground vibrated again. This time he was certain he felt it.

"Henry…?" Maeve's tone held question and uncertainty.

She had to know he'd imagined something horrible. At least it wasn't a giant Stay Puft Marshmallow man, à la *Ghostbusters*, that would explode all over them.

The vibration happened again. This time he was certain it was right behind them.

"Henry!"

He drew his sword. To do what, he had no clue. The hilt bit into his palm, the weight pulled his arm muscles. He didn't even know how to fight. What the hell was he thinking? He must have lost his mind to come here with her. Unprepared. Unskilled.

Maeve reached for him, her hand clamping around his arm. Her sharp nails dug into his forearm. Her eyes were wide and round and tinged with fear. He turned to see what held her attention and nearly dropped the sword. Sweat popped out on his forehead, in his armpits and on his palms. Fear washed over his entire body, the heat prickling every nerve ending.

The giant horned beast towered over them by three or four feet. It was ugly. And it smelled like death and rot. It had two curved horns like a ram's but a snout like a pig's, complete with protruding tusks. It stood on two hoofed feet. Its upper body was covered in coarse hair—again like a pig. But it had two human-looking arms that ended in long bearlike claws. Several tree branches were all that stood between them. He was fairly certain the beast looked at them as though they were a tasty morsel, judging by the thick drool that slipped down its chin.

"You thought about the giant beast, didn't you?" she asked, her voice breathy with fear.

"I couldn't help it. I tried hard *not* to think about it but then it was all I *could* think about." He hated the confession. Hated his weakness. "What do we do now?"

"Now? We run."

They turned in unison, both bolting through the trees. Behind him, the damned grotesque beast crashed through branches following them. Each footstep shook the ground. All the while he clutched his useless sword in one hand and the lantern in the other. What was he going to do? He had to think fast. He'd promised her he would keep her safe and so far, he was failing miserably.

A little help would be great right about now.

But what would come in the form of help, he had no idea.

Branches slapped them in the face. He heard her yelp and glanced over. She had a cut on her cheek where a limb had smacked her. That was his fault, too. If he had kept his thoughts buried, they wouldn't be chased.

Help didn't appear, so Henry tried a different tactic. If the forest could produce the lantern, maybe it could produce something to help him defeat the ugly thing.

Give me a sword that will kill the monster.

Henry looked at the sword in his hand. Nothing happened. It still felt the same. He tripped and fell face first into a pile of leaves. Maeve yelled at him to get up, even grabbed his arm and helped haul him up. The beast was right behind them, hot on their heels. With its bigger steps, they probably didn't have a chance.

Curse the sword. Maybe he hadn't asked the forest the right question. He tried again.

Give me the strength to kill the beast. Enchant my sword.

Suddenly, his body halted as though he had no control over it. He dropped the lantern at his feet and spun to face the monster.

"Henry?"

He clasped the sword in both hands, his muscles quivering. He widened his feet and prepared for battle. As though he could take on the world. As though he had the strength of ten thousand men.

"What are you doing?" she shouted.

"Get behind me. Stay behind me."

He had no idea what was happening but he had to trust in the sword.

It charged him. Both legs lumbering with every labored step. Henry hunched down, ready to lunge. But the thing head-butted him. Well, not exactly. Its giant head punched him as if he were nothing more than a balloon. Pain exploded and he literally saw stars. He flew backward, his vision gone. Maeve must have stepped out of the way, because he didn't run into her. He landed flat on his back, looking up at the canopy of dark leaves, trying to catch his breath. He gasped and blinked. His vision was blurry. Inhale, exhale. Then he realized he'd lost his sword.

"Get up, get up, get up!"

Maeve was shouting at him again. He rolled to his side with a groan, crawled to his hands and knees and pushed to a standing position. He searched the ground, looking for his sword. He didn't find it. She was at his side then, dragging him as she hurried backward. The beast was ready to charge again.

"Your sword! Where is your sword?"

He didn't know. He searched. Maeve screamed an ear-piercing scream. The thing was nearly upon them again. He gave her a shove out of the way and ran toward it. He had no idea what he was going to do, what his plan of attack was. He ran between the thing's legs. It grunted, turned around and growled at him.

Henry frantically searched for something to throw at it. His hand fell on a thick tree branch. He snatched it up and lobbed it at the thing's head. He missed. It growled again. Then grabbed a tree as though it were nothing more than a twig and jerked it out of the ground. The tree with roots and all hurled toward him.

"Damn it!"

He ducked and the tree went sailing over his head. It crashed a few feet away with a loud roar. Good thing the stupid beast wasn't a good throw or he'd be in real trouble. Like dead trouble.

"Henry! There's your sword!"

He saw it then, gleaming against a carpet of leaves. He dove for it as the thing took a swipe at him. The claws scraped across his shoulder to his back. He cried out with the sudden searing pain, heard Maeve shout something else but couldn't make it out. He was too intent on getting that sword.

He landed on the ground with a thump and a grunt. His hand was on the hilt as he snatched it. His shoulder burned with the heat of the wound and he could smell his own blood, knew his shirt was ripped. Before he could move, the beast wrapped its clawed hand around his ankle, started to drag him. Maeve still shouted something but he couldn't hear. He was losing his grip on the sword because his palm was sweaty. Plus, he was dragged backward through the underbrush. Limbs scratched him in the face. He could smell the scent of damp earth and leaves, heard Maeve's voice fading with every inch he was dragged.

He had to do something before he ended up as dinner.

Before he could think of a plan, the beast released him and he came to a sudden halt. The thing emitted a loud howl. Henry looked back and saw the whites of its eyes as they rolled back in its head. It held those clawed hands to the side of its face where several arrows were sticking out of its cheek. Blood spurted through the fingers.

Fighting through his pain, Henry scrambled to his feet and ran through its legs again, this time holding aloft his sword. He sliced through the creature's testicles. It emitted another howl, this one so high-pitched it nearly burst his eardrums. It stumbled to the side, lost its balance and then crashed to the ground with a loud boom. Birds scattered.

Beat-up and tired, Henry hobbled toward the thing and stabbed it in the side over and over and over again. It finally stopped wailing. He didn't know if it was dead or unconscious and he didn't care.

Maeve hobbled to him holding a bow limply in her hand. Her cheek was bleeding from the cut and her hair was full of leaves and twigs. She tried to catch her breath.

"Did you do that?" he asked, pointing to the arrows still buried in the thing's face.

She nodded, her chest heaving as she caught her breath. He noticed then the bodice of her dress was ripped, dipping dangerously low but still covering her beautiful breasts.

"Nice work."

"Someone…had to…help you," she panted. She gulped in a deep breath and held up the bow for him to see, waving it in the air as if in triumph.

"Where'd you get that?"

"The forest gave it to me."

"The forest gave it to you?" he repeated. "How is that possible?"

"I conjured it by thinking of what I wanted. That's what you did with the beast. You conjured it by thinking of it."

"Well…I'll try to keep that down from now on."

She seemed less than amused by his comment. She held up the bow to look at it again, running fingertips over the smooth wood. "It's been many years since I've had my hands on a bow and arrows. I was but a girl the last time I used one."

"Sorry about conjuring that thing. Is it dead?"

"Don't know. But I don't want to stay to find out."

He cupped her chin in his hand and turned her face to get a good look at the cut. It wasn't deep but it needed to be cleaned.

"I'm all right," she said tersely and jerked her chin out of his hand. "Promise me no more thoughts about giants."

He didn't have to be told twice. "You got it, your majesty. Let's get to the castle before something else attacks us. You need doctoring." And his shoulder hurt like a son of a bitch.

"I'm fine," she repeated, as though trying to convince herself.

He sheathed his sword and they started walking again. They passed the lantern he'd discarded and picked it up. The light gave him a sense of safety, though he knew if he didn't watch what he imagined, they would be attacked again. Wanting reassurance, the beast wouldn't be following, he turned back to look. It was completely covered in Shades.

"What was that thing?" he asked.

"I don't know. I've never seen one before." She slanted a look at him. "Something from the dark recesses of your mind, mayhap?"

He cleared his throat. "Could be."

He found it difficult to believe *he* had anything to do with that. Yet he *was* thinking of ugly, hairy beasts. He flushed. He would definitely have to keep his thoughts in check for the rest of the trek through the forest.

They walked in silence for a while through the never-ending leaves and trees and underbrush. All the while Henry was very aware of the Shades skirting the shadows close to them. He couldn't shake the feeling they were being watched. He peered around the trees, looking for signs of something or someone. But he saw nothing.

"The forest is restless," Maeve said.

"You sense it?" he asked.

"Aye. Mayhap the beast disturbed the spirits."

"Is that why I feel as though we're being watched?"

"Aye. They are close. Keeping a watchful eye on us."

"For what purpose?" he asked.

"This is their domain. Their home. They haven't seen a Fae enter the forest in thousands of years. They are curious. And they are willing to attack if they think we're a threat," she said.

"Are we?"

"For our sake, I hope not, Sir Henry."

Funny how she went back to calling him Sir Henry when before, during the whole Beast About to Kill Them episode she shouted his name over and over.

Maeve halted and her back stiffened. She stared at something ahead of them. But it was something Henry couldn't see. He peered into the shadows, straining his eyes. Then squinted as if that would help him see better.

"What is it?" he asked.

"Do you not see him?"

He followed the line of her gaze and searched. He saw no one. "No. Who?"

"Conn of the Hundred Wars. He stands there." She pointed ahead of them.

He looked again. Again, he saw no one. "Are you sure?"

She stepped closer to him. "He approaches."

Perhaps it because he was human, he couldn't see the ghostly man. Or perhaps it was because there was nothing there. Maeve straightened her back, her eyes wide and not blinking. Then she bowed her head, gave a slight curtsey.

Why she was curtseying to a dead man, he didn't know. The guy had been gone for thousands of years.

"To the castle," she said.

She must be answering a question he couldn't hear. He wondered if he should draw his sword or merely stand there and wait for her direction. He rested his hand on the hilt.

"I was told to come here." Pause. "My dragon." Pause. "My life is in danger and he said I would be safe here." Pause. Pause. Pause. "We want no trouble."

She shifted from one foot to the other and gave Henry a glance before looking back at nothing. "My apologies, your majesty. He didn't realize what his thoughts could do." Pause. Then she sucked in a sharp breath. "I don't...are you certain?" Another pause. "Farewell."

And then she relaxed. The specter must be gone.

"That was...interesting," Henry said. "You talked to Conn?"

"I did." She wouldn't look at him and suddenly everything got weird between them. "He rules this forest. He is going to grant us safe passage to the castle."

"That's a relief to know we won't be attacked again. What else did he say?"

"Nothing of importance."

He knew it was a lie. She wasn't telling him everything. What did the ghostly king tell her? Clearly, he was in trouble for causing that beast to appear and attack. He frowned, trying to reason why she would suck in a sharp breath like that. What did that mean?

"Sorry about the beast," he muttered. He couldn't feel more like an impudent child.

"'Tis all right. The forest can be overwhelming to...those who do not guard their thoughts."

Was she insulting him? Insinuating he had a weak mind and couldn't control it? The glow of defeating the beast faded and Henry had the distinct feeling he would have to be better at hiding his emotions and his thoughts if he were to convince her he was a true Fae knight.

Chapter 12

The castle gates were a welcome sight. Maeve expelled a sigh of relief. The spirit of High King Conn told her many things, including that the castle was still haunted and enchanted. He'd also told her a little something about Henry. Something she had begun to suspect when Maggie fretted over his injury and again in the forest when he fumbled with the sword. The king said he wasn't a knight. Maeve suspected he wasn't even a Fae. How she would prove that, she didn't know. He looked like any of her kind with the pointed ears and the angled features.

"Thought we'd never make it." Henry blew out a breath, his voice quavering.

The sheen of sweat on his brow and his upper chest was apparent even in the shadowy darkness. His face paled and his lips were chalky. He'd been favoring his arm where the beast slashed him and now held it against his body.

"Are you all right?"

"Fine," he said tightly.

She gave him a quizzical look. He didn't seem fine. She quirked an eyebrow. He avoided her gaze and cleared his throat. She spotted the blood seeping through the torn fabric of his shirt. Why hadn't she noticed before? Had she been too wrapped up in her own well-being to notice?

"Let me see your shoulder," she demanded.

"No. I'm fine, really. Is the gate locked?" He held the lantern closer to get a better look at the gate, trying to change the subject. "Can we get inside?"

There was a deep festering slash wound on his shoulder. The beast had gotten him. "You need medical attention." She put a hand on his forehead. "Gods, you're burning up."

Maeve gave the gate a gentle push and it swung open on creaky hinges. She stepped through and he followed closely, stumbling behind her. She knew he struggled to walk, probably from the poison leaking through his blood from the beast. She shouldered his weight and helped him walk. He gave her a sheepish grin.

"Thanks," he muttered.

"I'll take care of you as soon as we get there."

Worry gnawed at her but she was thankful the castle loomed ahead. Nothing but the outline of a dark shadow. Maeve had never seen Conn's castle but she'd heard the stories as she grew and then even as a young queen. She failed to see how the enchanted castle and haunted forest would defeat Morrigan.

But Maeve couldn't think about Morrigan now. She was more concerned with Henry. His skin was so hot it burned right through her clothes and seemed to sear her flesh. He stumbled once but she managed to keep him on his feet, keeping most of his weight on her.

"A little farther," she said.

"I'm…so tired. I…need to rest." His teeth chattered.

"No rest. Not yet, Henry. We need to get you inside. We can't stay out here. It's too dangerous."

The rustle of creatures was nearby. Mayhap smelling the tang of his blood and knowing he was close to passing out. Waiting to pounce and kill. The Shades danced dangerously close to them as though salivating at the thought of sinking their wispy teeth into him.

They approached the castle walls at last. Vines grew up the stone walls covering the windows. The door, though, seemed free of obstruction. They were almost there.

As she took another step, a hellhound jumped in front of her. It blocked the path to the castle door. Snarling and snapping. It had razor-sharp spikes along its spine, its coarse gray fur stood at attention and its red eyes peered at her.

Where had it come from? She hadn't been thinking of anything—

"Sorry," Henry said.

She sighed. "Control yourself, will you?"

"I…couldn't stop the image."

"Do you *want* us to die in this forest?"

"Not exactly. I haven't…kissed you again."

Bloody man. How could he think about kissing at a time like this? They were feet away from safety. Frustration boiled through her. What could she do? She had a sick, injured man and no magic. No way to defend herself or him. Except...she had one thing.

"Nero, come!"

Oh, please. Please come, Nero.

It was all she could think of that could get rid of the hellhound. Make that hellhounds. In the distance, the howl of more echoed on the wind as they moved closer and closer. Red eyes peered at them from deep inside the forest.

"Henry!"

"Couldn't...help it."

It snarled again and snapped its long teeth. Maeve took a step backward to put more distance between it and them. It advanced. The others came out of the trees and now they were surrounded.

"Nero, now would be great!"

"My fault."

"Indeed, it is," Maeve said tightly.

She tried not to be angry with him. He was injured, after all. But couldn't he keep his thoughts away from ugly beasts and snarling hellhounds? She took another step backward but all the hellhounds advanced closer and closer. The one in front of her snarled again. Drool cascaded from its mouth.

Overhead was the *whomp whomp* of Nero's wings. She prayed he was close. But how he would get to them she had no idea. The treetops blocked his flight path.

Come on, Nero!

The trees rattled together like sticks and then another second later the hellhound leapt.

Maeve cringed and squeezed her eyes shut. She felt the burst of fire on her face and then smelled burning fur and flesh.

"Gross," Henry said.

When she opened her eyes there wasn't much left of the hellhound or some of the trees. They were broken and charred. Nero sat to their left and puffed another flame at the remaining hounds. They whined and scattered.

Thank you, Nero, she said.

By your command, my queen. He bowed his massive head.

"I don't…feel so good."

"We're nearly there, Henry." She started toward the castle once more, still shouldering his weight. Her arms were numb from carrying him. Her back ached. He wasn't so light but she knew he had trouble walking on his own.

"I need…to sleep."

"Stay awake!"

If he passed out, she had no idea how she'd get him inside. She made it to the door and kicked it open with what strength she had left. She dragged Henry inside. The lantern he'd been carrying slipped from his fingers and crashed to the floor, extinguishing what little light they had.

"I'm going to put you down here." Gently, she lowered him to the stone floor and propped him against the wall. She pressed her hand against his cheek. It was so hot it nearly burned her. "I need to find supplies. I'll be right back."

But as she straightened in the great hall, she realized she had no idea what to do, where to go. The rumor was the castle was enchanted. If it truly was then mayhap it was as simple as a voice command.

"I could use some lit torches," she said.

Seconds later, every torch in the place lit up, blazing brightly. The place was dirty and musty. Cobwebs hung from every available corner. Thick dust covered the floor and she regretted leaving Henry there. But she hadn't much of a choice, had she? To her left, a long table where there was probably many a banquet. To her right, a massive fireplace.

"Give me a fire," she ordered.

Immediately, a fire sprang up. It sent warmth throughout the entire drafty hall. Now she needed medicine and a bed for Henry. But how? It couldn't hurt to ask.

"I need a healer for my friend."

Silence for a heartbeat, then a knock on one of the doors.

"Hello!" a high-pitched singsong voice called.

Maeve spun to face a short, hunchbacked woman with long stringy white hair. She had a hooked nose, a deep cleft in her chin and dark-brown eyes. She wore nothing more than rags.

"Who are you?"

"Ye asked for a healer, did ye not?"

"I did." *Ask, and ye shall receive.* Apparently, that was the way of the castle.

"Well, where is the patient?"

"There." She pointed to Henry who was completely passed out. His face was pasty, his clothes damp from sweat.

"Move away, dearie. Let me get to work." The gnarled old woman waved Maeve away. "Go make use of yeself."

"Will he die?" Maeve asked, worry gnawing at her.

"I can't say yet, dearie. Be gone and let me work me magic." When Maeve still refused to move, she turned her dark gaze on her, her fists on her hips. "Did ye hear me? Be gone! I can't work with ye hovering. Shoo!"

"I'll…see about things upstairs."

"Aye, see about things upstairs."

But, she thought, she would be back soon. She wasn't sure she trusted this woman with Henry. Healer or no.

Henry peeled his eyes open. He blinked, trying to get his surroundings into focus. He couldn't remember for the life of him where he was. He didn't recognize the room he was in. Or the bed. He didn't remember falling asleep in this giant four-poster bed draped in opaque material. It smelled musty and was dark. He shoved upright and his body objected to the sudden movement.

Pain burned through his shoulder. Wincing, he reached up and touched the bandage. It all flooded back to him then. The forest, the beast that tried to kill him, the wolves. Or were they really wolves? He wasn't sure. He remembered seeing them, feeling sick to his stomach. Sweating. Hot. And the queen…

"I see you're awake."

Maeve's voice filtered through the darkness, caressed his ears. She'd gotten them out of the mess he caused. She'd called Nero and the dragon had come. The last thing he remembered was her lowering him to the floor.

Glancing down, he saw he wore his tattered breeches. A sheet covered him to his waist. How did he get here? Had she managed to drag him to the bed? He was no lightweight and she wasn't exactly muscular.

"You gave me a fright," she said. "Are you feeling better?"

"I don't feel like I'm going to die, so I suppose that's an improvement."

"Good. Glad to hear that."

She rose from her chair. Her skirts swished as she moved throughout the room. She shoved open the tapestries covering the window. First one. Then another. Pale sunlight filtered through the room. Beyond the windows, the thick forest dark and foreboding. Maeve was right. It was always dark here. She walked to the edge of his bed. The scent of roses followed her, wafting over him. He inhaled it deeply, loving the way she smelled.

When he first met her, she smelled of jasmine. Now of roses. He wondered if that was a direct result of their first kiss in the rose garden. He recalled the crushed petals he still carried in his pocket. A keepsake from the woman he couldn't keep his eyes off.

Her golden hair cascaded over her shoulders. She wore a pale-pink gown with a scooped neckline trimmed in gold braid. The cut on her cheek faded, nearly healed, and was relieved she wasn't injured worse than she was. All his fault.

"Do you remember what happened?" she asked.

"We were attacked."

"Aye, because of you, you dolt. I warned you about the forest."

He flushed, the heat burning through him. "You did. I'm sorry."

"And the hellhounds? Do you remember that?"

Ah, hellhounds. He'd conjured that? He hadn't been thinking of hellhounds. In fact, he'd been thinking of feral dogs. Maybe hellhounds were what the forest equated to feral dogs. He would have to be careful to keep his thoughts to himself when they were in the forest.

Maeve perched on the edge of the bed, peering at him with ice-blue eyes. "Who are you?"

Fear tingled through him. Had he lost his glamour? Could she see his true appearance? Or was she merely guessing? He peered at her intently. Judging by the way she looked at him, she seemed suspicious. As if she might know he was human. And that worried him.

"What do you mean, my queen?" Maybe if he said "my queen" every now and then, he could throw her off course.

"You know what I mean. Any Fae knows the dangers of the Sacred Forest. Yet you allowed your mind to run wild. That tells me either you're stupid or you aren't who you appear to be." She folded her arms over her chest. "I really don't believe you're stupid. Who are you?"

He had to think fast. He suspected she could still see his glamour, which was good. However, she thought he was someone else. That was bad. What was he going to do?

"All right," he said. "Here's the truth." He paused, trying to come up with a plausible story she would believe.

"The truth," she repeated, though her voice held a note of suspicion.

"I'm, um…not a knight."

"That much I figured out," she said. Her lips thinned into a straight line. "How did you come to be in the palace? And, furthermore, how did you come to be part of the palace guards?"

"I snuck in," he said. "I stole one of the uniforms and dressed as a knight."

"Why?" She narrowed her eyes.

"I'd heard of the Fae queen of surpassing beauty and had to see her for myself." Oh, *geez*, did that sound believable? It sounded ridiculous to him. Would she buy it?

She shook her head. "Not good enough. Did Morrigan send you to infiltrate the palace and get close to me?"

"No!" Hell no. He raked his hand through his hair. He needed to tell her the truth. Or as close to the truth as he could get. "My daughter…she's in your palace. I snuck in to see her. And that's the truth."

"Who is she?" She relaxed a little, though was still guarded.

"Nothing more than a scullery maid, your majesty." He banked on Maeve not knowing every maid or servant in her palace walls. If she did, though, he'd be royally screwed.

But Maeve dropped her arms. "That I believe. Why did you save me from Morrigan?"

At last a question he could answer honestly. "I couldn't allow her to hurt you. Not before I'd had a chance to get to know you. What's with all the questions?"

He wanted her from the first moment he saw her.

She stiffened. "High King Conn told me you were not what you appeared."

"The dead guy? And you believed him?" No wonder she was suspicious.

"I have no reason not to."

"Sure, you do. He's a dead guy."

She flashed him a look of annoyance. "Don't make me regret bringing you along, Sir Henry."

Again, with the *sir*. She hadn't called him that when he was nearly dying. And he remembered that clearly. She called him Henry. She was worried about him but was too proud to admit that now. Fine. He could play that game, too. He would make sure Maeve didn't regret bringing him along.

"You won't regret it."

His strength surged and he sat up. They were close, almost nose to nose. He could smell her lovely scent and see the pupils in her eyes expand and then contract. He reached for her, but she put a hand on his chest.

"Don't, Henry."

"Don't what?"

"Kiss me."

"But you want me to kiss you."

"No." Yet she licked her lips.

"Oh, yes you do. You really want me to kiss you." Daring, he tipped his head, his mouth a breath from hers. "You also want me to do more than kiss you."

"No, I don't." This time she dragged her lower lip through her teeth.

She was killing him in a slow, painful death.

"Why do you resist me?" His lips brushed hers, taking a sip of her.

Sweet heaven.

Her breathing increased. She pushed harder on his chest, though it was a weak attempt.

"This is…inappropriate," she said.

"I'm a nice man. You're a beautiful woman. What's inappropriate about that? There is no one here to chaperone us." They were alone. Totally irrevocably alone.

"You are…and I am…"

She struggled with the words. He knew what she was trying to say. She was royalty and he wasn't. As if that mattered to him. He didn't care. She could be a pauper for all he cared.

"I want you."

A mewl escaped her. It was nothing more than a little sound but it sent his senses reeling. His mouth landed on hers as he tasted her. She didn't fight him. She leaned into him, their bodies melding together. His hand tangled in the length of her hair, his fingers slicing through the silky strands.

Oh, she was divine. She let him kiss her. Then she kissed him back, her tongue dancing with his. Her arms slid around his neck and she actually pulled him closer. Deeper. Her scent was in his nose, in his mouth, on his skin. He couldn't get enough of her. He didn't want enough of her. He wanted more. And more. *And more.*

His mouth trailed down her neck. Her pulse raced as she threw her head back for his kissed to dance over the column of her neck. He flicked his tongue over her earlobe and she whimpered.

He was a shaking mess. His raw nerves were on high alert. He needed more of her, had to touch her, had to feel her curves in his palms. He'd gotten so close before and she'd stopped him.

With his mouth at the hollow of her throat, he slipped his hands over her soft curves. It was as though she were made for him. He caressed her, the heat washing over him as he realized how good she felt. He could imagine the rest of her.

"Oh no, Henry. Stop." With a violent shove, she pushed him away and scampered off the bed. "No."

Her breath see-sawed, her chest rose and fell with her rapid breathing. She pressed a hand against her abdomen and took a step back. His gaze never left her face. Her lips were damp from his kisses and her cheeks were rosy.

She wanted him. Even if she couldn't admit it.

"Why did you ask me to come with you, Maeve?" His voice was harsh, demanding. He wanted the truth.

"I told you why. To protect—"

"No. That's not it. Tell me the truth."

Maeve balled her fists. "That is the truth."

"You wanted me to come because of the way you feel about me. Isn't that it?"

Now her expression changed to one of anger. Her face flushed hot. "And how do I feel about you, Sir Henry?"

That was it. He could stand it no more. He yanked off the sheet and swung his legs over the bed. Her eyes widened as he stood but that was as far as he got. The dizziness overtook him and he fell back to the mattress, his stomach in a sickly knot.

Perhaps moving so soon after his injury hadn't been the best idea. Maeve was at his side in an instant, easing him back to the pillows.

"You shouldn't have done that."

"You shouldn't make me crazy."

Maeve tucked the sheet around him, making sure he was comfortable. Her face softened as she kissed him on the temple. But her lips stayed there as she whispered against his skin.

"I do feel something for you." When he started to reply, she put two fingers on his lips. "But it can never be. I think we both know why. I'll leave you to rest."

He grasped her hand, kissed the tips of her fingers before releasing her. She turned, started to walk away but he grabbed her wrist and held her in place. Not that she couldn't leave. She could. But she didn't. Their eyes met, gazes holding. And for a moment he saw the spark of desire hidden there. Desire and then sadness.

She wouldn't allow herself to have feelings, to let go, to fall in love. Even a little. Maybe it was because she was queen and was nobody. Falling for him would be beneath her. It was like a knife in his already tattered heart.

"Thank you for saving my life, Maeve."

She slipped her wrist out of his grasp. "Don't thank me. Thank the old hag who came to heal you." She lingered there a moment longer, her gaze still on his face. "When you're feeling up to it, there's food in the great hall."

Lying alone in the bed was torture. He was in pain, yes, but it was a different kind of torture. Knowing Maeve was down the stairs and within the same walls as he and they were virtually alone was killing him. He'd come so close to having her he wasn't sure if he could live another day without her. Her taste was still in his mouth, her scent still lingering on his skin.

Damn her.

He wasn't sure how much time had passed when hunger finally drove him to fling off the blankets and crawl out of bed. He found a clean tunic and pulled it on, along with his boots. He needed to get away from this bedroom.

In the hallway, numerous torches lighting the corridor did their best to chase away the shadows. But even so, there seemed to be a bit of gloom hanging in the air.

He made his way downstairs to the great hall. There, he saw the long wooden table lined with more food than he'd seen at his family's Thanksgiving feast. In the center was some type of roasted bird, stuffed and steaming. Fresh loaves of bread lined one end along with wheels of cheese. A variety of fruits were piled high on a platter in a colorful arrangement.

Maeve sat alone at one end, her hair gleaming in the candlelight like a halo.

"Welcome, Sir Henry. I'm glad you could join me."

Totally different demeanor than earlier. She was relaxed. Her cheeks were rosy. A glass pitcher of wine sat on the table in front of her, half empty. How much of that stuff had she drunk?

"We're not on a first-name basis yet? Especially after everything that's happened?" he asked, approaching the table.

The queen poured two tankards of wine and passed one to him. "Do you wish me to call you Henry, then?"

"Can I call you Maeve instead of my queen or your majesty?"

She gave him a long look as she contemplated. "Aye. You can."

Shock rolled through him. She'd agreed? She was clearly drunk.

He accepted the tankard of wine and took a sip. "Nice spread. Did you cook all this up yourself?"

"Don't be ridiculous," she said and she slurred a little. "The castle did."

"The castle cooks?" He quirked a grin.

"It's enchanted." She said it as though he were an idiot and he should know that already.

A servant appeared, sliced several slabs of the meat and placed them on a metal plate.

"We have servants now?"

"Enchanted, remember? I had to make some additions."

"How long have I been out?"

"A couple of days."

That surprised him. She made no mention of that when she woke him earlier. "I thought the castle was deserted."

"You don't catch on very fast, do you?" She sliced through her meat, then took a delicate bite. "They're part of the enchantment. The castle can give me whatever I ask for. Even servants."

"Fascinating."

"I believe there are weapons High King Conn left behind in the weapons room. However, we can simply ask for what we need to fight Morrigan should we find nothing." She popped a grape in her mouth.

"Won't they be old and useless?"

"Possibly. Hence the reason we ask for what we need."

He'd let her condescending tone slide since she was the one in charge and he was nothing but a lowly knight/human. "Any sign of the goddess?"

"Nay. Nor do I expect her to arrive yet."

"Why not?"

"Conn told me that."

"Conn again?" The dead guy really was chock-full of information, wasn't he? "He told you a lot of things, didn't he?"

"Indeed."

He was beginning to wonder if the queen imagined him or if he really was a ghost.

"What else did he tell you?" he asked.

"That you are not what you appear." She said it casually. As though talking about the weather.

"Oh, I thought we covered that already." This dead king was going to ruin his chances of shagging the gorgeous queen.

"Oh, that's right. I forgot." She covered her mouth with her hand as she giggled. Giggled! She really was drunk.

A smile drew up her red lips. She rose, walked the length of the table, her fingertips dragging the tabletop as she approached. Her hips swayed in a *come-hither* invitation and her mouth still held that grin. What is she up to?

Before he could react, she slipped her fingers through the hair at his temples, gazing down at him with such adoration it made his stomach bottom out. And that smile. She was going to kill him with it.

"I find you very attractive, Henry."

He could smell a hint of wine on her breath. Then she plopped down on his lap, her bottom scooting over his legs as she snuggled up to him. She slipped her arms around his neck.

"Maeve, what are you—"

"Shh. You'll ruin everything with talking. So much talking."

"You've been drinking."

"A teensy bit."

He had never seen her this way. Odds were no one else had either. She leaned in close. Her lips brushed his.

"Don't you want to kiss me some more?" She whispered the question against his mouth.

Sure, he did. But not like this. He needed to take evasive action. "I always want to kiss you."

"Do you still want me?" She nuzzled his neck, his earlobe. Before he could answer, she said, "You were right about one thing. I do want you."

Well, wasn't that an interesting turn of events? Too bad he couldn't do anything about it. He wouldn't take advantage of her. Not now when she was drunk. He wanted her sober and clearheaded. He wanted her to know *he* was the one with her in her bed.

But it was hard to turn her down when she was kissing his neck. And sucking on his earlobe.

"Maeve…"

With a gentle hand, he grasped her arms and pushed her away as easy as he could.

"Did you change your mind?" She frowned.

Oh, no. He would never change his mind. Her hand slipped

down his chest, diving toward his lap. He clamped his fingers around her wrist.

"Maeve," he started again.

But his brain was fried. He couldn't think straight with her doing things to him. Especially the way her cheeks turned rosy and the way her lips were ripe for kissing. So pink. So plump. So…perfect. He couldn't stop looking at them. She knew it, too, by the way she swiped her tongue over them.

"Take me, Henry. I'm giving myself to you."

He groaned his frustration. Instead of taking her, he lifted her off his lap and put her on her feet. Her dismay was evident by the disappointment on her face.

"Maeve, I cannot."

"Why not?"

"You know why." He gripped her wrists to keep her hands still. If she touched him again, he might lose his nerve. He wasn't going to lose his nerve.

She swayed, nearly falling into him. "No, I do not."

"You're drunk," he said.

She grinned and leaned toward him, her lips a scant inch from his. "I know. Something I haven't done in a very, very long time."

She wiggled her hand free and her fingers walked up his chest to his collarbone where she slipped her hand over his shoulder. She pressed her curvy body against his.

She really was going to bloody kill him before he could ever bed her. He sent a silent prayer of strength skyward. Maybe she wasn't really drunk and she was testing him to see how much of a gentleman he truly was.

He'd prove to her he was worthy.

"As much as I want you, Maeve, I think you'll regret it if we do it like this."

She blinked and took a step back. Her hands slipped over her breasts. He stifled the groan that wanted to erupt. Now what was she planning? There was a twinkle of mirth in her eyes. And then she tugged at the laces of her gown, releasing the tie.

Oh no. No, no, no. He wouldn't allow that. Henry stilled her hands. He cupped her fingers in his.

"Maeve, stop."

Her gaze met his. Pain flickered through her eyes. It cut him to the core. He didn't want to turn her down. He had to make her understand *this* wasn't going to happen under these circumstances.

"Let me help you to bed," he said.

She flushed, her cheeks turning bright red. She realized what she'd done. She shoved his hands away and then pushed a hand through her hair.

"No. I'm fine. I'll take myself to bed," she said. "Alone."

She flung around, her hair and skirts bouncing in her wake. Before he could say anything more, she hurried away, leaving him with disappointment.

Damn.

Chapter 13

Maeve knew she'd had too much to drink. Her friendly buzz had worn off about the time she'd run her hands down her body. About the time she'd started to unlace her bodice, ready to drop it right there in front of him. She flushed at the memory, her face hot with embarrassment.

Mayhap Henry didn't want her and he was trying to be kind to her. He was trying to help her save face yet she continued on and on and on. Like a fool.

She'd hurried to her chamber and climbed into her bed, pulling the covers over her head. She replayed the horrible memory until she finally fell asleep. But when she awoke sometime later, she was accosted once again with the image of her flinging herself at Henry. When she threw off the bedclothes, she stared at the ceiling, wondering what the bloody hell had come over her. She flung herself at Henry as though she were nothing more than a tavern wench. Even now the shame of it all washed over her.

She rolled to her side and groaned as she stared into the darkness, unable to sleep. He *did* want her. She was sure of it. He'd told her as much, by the gods. And *she* had told *him* it could never be. Even though she wanted nothing more than to fall into his arms. She wanted to feel again. She wanted that tenderness with someone who adored and cherished her. Whether he was Fae or not.

Frustrated, she climbed from the oversized bed and paced. What did he think of her? He'd turned her down, that much she remembered. He'd told her no. Refused her advances, drunken fool that she was. She had never expected Henry to make an appearance. She had simply wanted to drown her regret, her sorrows, her frustrations.

Not like this, he'd said.

And yet she'd tried again. The humiliation of him pushing her away swam through her mind. She rubbed her temples, trying to make the image go away. Not like that because he was a proper gentleman. Because he wouldn't take advantage of her. Because he had feelings for her.

"Ridiculous," she said to the empty room.

She reached for her gown and tugged it over her head. She needed some fresh air.

When she flung open the door, Henry stood on the other side, hand poised ready to knock. She forgot to breathe. She forgot everything but her humiliation.

"Henry."

He dropped his hand. "I came to check on you. See how you were feeling after your, uh, splurge."

Her cheeks warmed. "I'm better."

They stared at each other. An awkward silence stretched between them. He didn't say anything. She didn't either. What could she say? The damage had been done.

"Well, good night." She started to close the door but he stopped her, his hand fisted on the door.

"Where were you going?" he demanded.

"I needed some air."

"You're not leaving these walls without me. It's too dangerous."

"You're wounded and I'll be fine." She could still see the outline of his bandage under his tunic. The last thing she wanted was to reinjure him. He needed to recover and heal.

"You're not leaving *without me*. Is that clear?"

"But you need your rest."

"I've rested enough." He shoved open the door and stepped inside.

She took one step then two backward. "Henry, you—"

"Want you. That is if you're sober enough for me yet." He kicked the door closed with the heel of his foot.

Maeve stiffened as the heat of desire warmed her. He was serious despite the imbecile she'd made of herself the night before. Her nerve-endings tingled, making her body respond in a way she hadn't felt in far too long.

"You intend to—"

"Kiss you. Seduce you." He advanced toward her, closing the

gap between them. His warmth radiated around her, delighting her.

Could she give into her passion, her need, her desire and be with Henry? His jaw had a determined set to it as he clenched it. Underneath the surface of his eyes, yearning simmered there. It mirrored her own. Her heart throbbed quickened tattoo.

"Henry, I'm not sure we should—"

"I do. You think I don't know why you brought me here? We're alone in this place, Maeve. No one can interrupt us here." His hand slid around her waist as he gently pulled her to him. "I think deep down you wanted to be alone with me. You want this as much as I do."

It had never crossed her mind until he'd put it that way. Her determination to have Henry with her stemmed from his gallant efforts to keep her safe at the palace. But mayhap deep down she *did* want him all to herself. Hearing the truth was a hard pill to swallow.

"I know under that icy exterior lies the heart of a warm woman dying to claw her way out. I was with you when you were drunk. I know your true feelings for me." His lips brushed hers.

Her heart pounded so hard she thought it would pump out of her chest. What had she said to him? Oh, gods. She remembered all of it now.

But he refused her because he was an honorable man who wouldn't take advantage of a woman. She flushed. The tingling sensation swept up the back of her neck and across her face. How had he managed to unlock her heart and soul in so short a time? He'd seen right past her frosty façade. It hadn't deterred him. If anything, it encouraged him. As though she were a challenge he needed to conquer.

Her sober admission was she *did* want him. Despite the fact he was probably human. She'd grown suspicious when they made their way through the Sacred Forest and when Conn warned he was not what he appeared. All Fae could see the spirit. Henry could not. She'd tried to suppress her feelings and make them go away. But try as she might they wouldn't. They persisted. She could no longer deny them.

"I don't want to make your injury worse." Her voice was but a faint whisper.

That wasn't what she'd meant to say. She'd meant to tell him to go away. Go back to his room. To fend him off. But the fire within her burned deep and hot.

"You won't." To prove it to her, he stripped off his tunic and tossed it aside.

The bandage dominated most of his upper body. Her fingers itched to touch him.

"Undress for me."

A demanding request. No one dared speak to her like that. She'd been with men who would placate her, follow her lead, do as she command even between the sheets.

Not Henry. He was in charge and he knew it.

A breath shuddered out of her as the air between them crackled, each one craving the other in a fervid ache of longing. Her mind was frazzled. Reason and clarity abandoned her. With shaking fingers, she tugged at the laces of her gown.

She *wanted* this. She *wanted* him. Human or not. She didn't care at that moment. The Fae queen part of her faded away, leaving only the woman inside who wanted the pleasures she'd long desired.

At last the laces came free and the material pooled at her feet. Only the thin material of her shift separated the two of them.

"Now the rest," he said, his voice deep and dark and hoarse.

At the base of her throat, her pulse pounded a furious beat as though her heart had swelled from its usual place. She tilted her head back and looked him over him.

"You first." She hardly recognized her ragged voice.

Henry's eyes were full of desire. She'd never felt more alive than at that moment. He seemed more amused than anything when he kicked off his boots and then went about with the same slow, methodical unlacing that nearly tore her asunder. When he finally pushed down his breeches, he shoved away the clothing with a foot.

Her heart gave an erratic thump at the sight of his long lean body.

"Now it's my queen's turn."

A shiver of delight ran through her. Maeve was all too happy to comply and pushed the shift off her shoulders. The material landed at her feet with her gown. His admiring gaze moved off her as he closed the gap between them. Only a breath of air separated them.

"Perfection. As I knew you would be."

He swept her into his arms and, despite his bravado, she caught the slight wince when he picked her up. She knew the injury still bothered him even though he insisted he was fine. He carried her to the bed and eased her down to the feather mattress, then lowered next to her.

"Are you sure you're not in pain?" Maeve brushed her fingers over his cheek.

"I'm fine." He turned his head, kissed her fingertips.

"I don't want to hurt you."

"Shh." His mouth covered hers in a kiss.

She knew, at that moment, she had come undone. He had torn down the walls she'd so carefully constructed. He had unraveled all her secrets. And still he was not afraid of her, who she was or her title. When they joined, their bodies were a perfect fit for one another. She'd never felt anything like it before in all her long years. They came together in a sweet, sensual moment she would not soon forget.

When it was over, he moved to lie next to her. She curled into the curve of him and he held her close, bushing hair from her face. He held her as though he might never let her go.

"Did I please you?" His tone was teasing, playful.

"Oh, you pleased me very well." Suddenly she remembered his wound. "Did I hurt you?"

"Not at all." He nuzzled her neck. His tongue flicked over her earlobe. "You can never hurt me."

Oh, but she could. And mayhap would. Especially because she had to send him back to the human realm. He would never forgive her, but he couldn't stay here as queen. She couldn't allow it.

The thought of going back to life as it was with her magic returned and ruling the kingdom sent a pang of sorrow through her. When the time came, could she give him up?

"Tired?" he asked.

"Aye."

"Then rest now."

She remained in his arms listening as his breathing deepened and he slept. For now, she would bask in the afterglow. But she

knew it was not enough. It would never be enough.

Henry was human.

Deep down, she knew. Her suspicions had been confirmed with their lovemaking. She wanted to be angry. She wanted to banish him from her realm back to where he belonged—and would have before they ended up in bed together. *If* she'd had her magic. Which she didn't and which still vexed her to the core.

When she discovered the truth, the anger boiled inside her but she managed to mask it well. She buried her emotions behind those walls she'd so carefully constructed over the years because deep down, she liked being with him. Mayhap she even *wanted* to be with him despite her objections.

She tried to push him away. Tried to keep him at arm's length. But the damn man had saved her life numerous times and he didn't seem to take no for an answer. He'd managed to crumble those walls one stone at a time. Slowly, methodically. Not rushing toward her like a battering ram. Until she had no choice but to yield to him. To surrender to his charms and his kisses and his advances. She'd let her guard down. She'd let him in. She had no regrets.

Only Elyne could have hid his true appearance behind that glamour. But why? Why put them in danger? Morrigan would happily kill them both.

Who was he really? Why was this human in her realm? She thought back on the day he was injured, when Maggie had been inconsolable and Maeve couldn't understand why. She thought of Maggie and how some of her mannerisms were similar to Henry's. How the inflection in their tones were similar. And, when she looked closely at Henry, how even under the glamour there was a hint of resemblance. Then it hit her. Maggie was his daughter.

He must have come looking for her and stumbled into the Otherworld through one of the open portals. And he'd found Maggie, she was sure, with Elyne's help. Curse her daughter. She would share her displeasure with Elyne the next time she saw her.

So why come with her? When he knew he didn't have the skills to save her or keep her safe? Mayhap he'd come on this mission to prove something to his daughter. Or to prove something to himself. Whatever the explanation, she could not allow Henry to stand in the way of danger.

Maeve needed to get away from him. She needed to be alone with her thoughts and decide what she was going to do about him. She slipped off the bed and reached for her ruined gown. She used the magic wardrobe to conjure another one and quickly dressed. She took one last look at Henry before she left, watching him sleep. His eyes were still firmly closed as he snored softly.

Dawn neared. They'd been together most of the night. They'd made love more times than she could count. And for the first time in her very long life every muscle she possessed was sore. Henry was passionate. A man who knew what he wanted from her. A man who twisted her ancient body into positions she didn't even know it was capable of. A man who took making love to her as serious business.

She needed to leave the room before she lost her nerve and climbed back into bed with him. The door closed with a soft click behind her as she slipped from the room. She stood a moment with her back against the door. She was an utter mess.

Henry had somehow managed to destroy her cool control. He'd gotten under her skin and planted his tenterhooks so deep she wasn't sure if she could ever be free of them. Shaking off her thoughts, she decided to take a tour through the castle walls to see what she could find.

It hadn't taken her long to find the armory. Or what was left of it. There were blades of all shapes and sizes. Longbows. Arrows. Shields.

"Hello, Queen Maeve."

She knew the voice belonged to the dead high king. He shimmered in front of her and gave her a nod in greeting.

"Conn," she said.

"You have at last found my weapons." He smiled. "I'm glad."

"Will they help me defeat Morrigan?"

"Most assuredly. And if they don't meet your needs, you know you can ask for anything."

"Aye." She picked up an ax, felt the weight of it in her hands. She'd never wielded a weapon like this before. She wasn't even sure how to hold it and returned it to its resting place. It would never do. The only weapon she was comfortable with was the bow.

"Have you discovered the truth of your traveling companion for yourself at last?" he asked.

"I know Henry is human. He lied to me by hiding his true form." She clenched her fists, her emotions warring inside her.

"I believe he can help you defeat the war goddess, your majesty."

"How?"

"By fighting by your side."

"Fight alongside a human?" she scoffed.

"He is not as weak as you think."

"He nearly got us killed in the forest," she said.

The ghost king chuckled. "Aye, he did. He did not know how to guard his thoughts. But he cares greatly for you and he will make sure you do not perish at the hands of the goddess. Shouldn't that account for something?"

She supposed so. But still… She had allowed her feelings to take over. She had allowed herself to… *No. I won't think of that. Not now. Now when there is a battle to be fought.*

But could she really deny those feelings she harbored for him? A human? She couldn't and she knew she couldn't.

I'll think about that tomorrow.

"I know you're right but I do not wish a human to be involved in this fight."

"You cannot send him through the forest alone. His imagination will get him killed," he said.

Then what would she do with him? An idea formed. She hated the thought of chaining up Henry, but she knew she would have to do it. For his own safety.

It was time for Elyne, Queen Regent, to preside over her first negotiation session with the Elves and the High Council…without her mother. She hated the thought and her stomach was twisted in knots. She smoothed her skirt for the hundredth time.

"You'll do fine."

Behind her, Derron wrapped his arms around her. She looked at his reflection in the mirror. He kissed the top of her head.

"Are you sure?"

"Aye. You know King Urdithane. He wants this abolished as much as you do. I will be by your side every step of the way."

It warmed her knowing he would be there. She turned to face him, slipping her arms around his neck. "I'm glad. I couldn't do this without you, Derron."

"But you're worried about your mother," he said.

"You know I am. And Henry. What if she discovered the truth about him?"

"Well…there's not much she can do about it. She has no magic, after all. Despite the fact she has no love for humans she won't hurt him. It's against her nature."

"I know. I still worry."

Guilt swept through her. Not that it was her fault her mother had no magic. Maeve had been the one to give it to her in the first place. The High Druid couldn't figure out how to return it to the queen. And while Elyne didn't want to be Queen Regent forever, she knew that was her duty until her mother returned and she could get rid of the magic that didn't belong to her.

If that wasn't enough, what if Maeve didn't make it back alive? What if Morrigan was successful and killed her? If her mother died, would Henry survive?

"Don't fret, my princess." He kissed her forehead. "I can see the worry in your eyes. I know what you're thinking. She won't die."

"How can you be so sure?"

"She survived the Stone of Destiny, didn't she? She's a strong woman, Elyne. She will be fine. And I don't think Henry will allow anything to happen to her."

"Still, it would make me feel better to send troops to the forest. To make sure."

He smiled. "All right. If it will make my princess feel better, I will send a small garrison straightaway."

She blew out a sigh of relief. "That would make me feel better. Thank you, my darling."

He took her hand. "Now come. We have negotiations."

They gathered in the High Council Chamber. Elyne took her seat—her mother's seat. King Urdithane, Prince Andahar, Lord Eldrin along with the Fae High Council had all resumed their positions at the table. Ready to speak, to negotiate.

"Good morrow, gentlemen. The last few days have been difficult with the continued disruptions. You have my heartfelt apologies. It is my hope that we can avoid additional delays and finally get these negotiations underway today," Elyne said.

"May I first say, congratulations to you on your recent appointment as Queen Regent," Urdithane said.

"Thank you, your majesty," Elyne said.

"And I would like to add my congratulations as well," Andahar said. He smiled and gave her a nod.

It did nothing to calm her churning stomach. She didn't want their congratulations. She wanted to get this done and over with so she could go back to her normal life. She longed for the days when she would follow Derron though the human realm, watching him as he jousted. She longed for that freedom again. How she wished she could do that again. Sift away where she wouldn't have to worry about any of these ruler things.

"I appreciate your well wishes. Now let's discuss the Treaty of Separation and how we can come to new terms of the agreement."

Before they could begin a knock sounded. Startled by the interruption, Elyne froze, unsure what to do. King Urdithane groaned his frustration. Before she could command someone to open it, the door flew open and Morrigan, Goddess of War, strode in. Cormac followed closely on her heels.

"Cormac," Derron growled.

Morrigan came to a halt, her gaze landing on everyone and stopping on Elyne. Her black hair cascaded over her shoulders and she flipped it back.

"Not again," Urdithane grumbled. He scrubbed both hands down his face. "Interrupted yet again."

"Princess Elyne, how nice to see you."

"What are you doing here, Morrigan?" She didn't want to give anything up, to let the woman know Maeve wasn't there.

"If I didn't know any better, I would think you planned these interruptions, your majesty," Urdithane said. "You and this woman are working together to foil the attempts to break the Treaty."

"No, King Urdithane. I can assure you that is not the case," Elyne said.

"Oh, a tiff. I do so love a good fight," Morrigan said. "It does my heart good to see it."

"There is no fight," Elyne said. "What is your business here?"

"My business is with your mother. My Shade did not work. Even when I came for her myself, I was robbed of her death. I will no longer be cheated of that pleasure. I know she's not in the palace. That is why I spared your pitiful walls from yet another attack. Where is she?"

Elyne pressed her lips together, refusing to answer.

"She's somewhere safe. Where you won't find her," Derron replied.

"Oh, is that so? We'll see about that. Cormac, do your magic."

"No!" Elyne jumped to her feet. "You will not use dark magic here."

Morrigan laughed. "And who will stop me? You?"

Elyne wasn't sure what she intended to do. She knew Cormac was under the goddess' spell. His eyes were completely black. She walked around the table.

"Elyne—" Derron said.

She held up her hand to silence him as she paused in front of Cormac. At the end of their war, he was the prisoner she deemed to save because she wanted to find his missing family. She had failed him. But she also knew he wasn't evil. He couldn't be. He'd spared her life and for that she owed him.

"You're better than this, Cormac. Fight her. Fight her magic."

"What do you think you're doing, girl?" Morrigan growled.

"I've seen your magic. You have more power than her. Fight her hold," Elyne continued, ignoring the goddess.

"Don't listen to her. She's nothing to you. Remember who owns you, Cormac." Morrigan slipped a hand over his shoulder and leaned down to say the words in his ear. "She doesn't. I do. And do not forget what will happen if you disobey me."

Cormac, though, never broke eye contact with Elyne. Was she getting through to him somehow? Could she break through

Morrigan's dark spell?

"I know I promised to find your family, Cormac. And I still will. I gave you my word."

"Elyne, what are you doing?" Derron's words were sharp and low.

She never took her gaze off Cormac. "Did she promise you she would find them? Give them to you?"

Morrigan released a scream of frustration. And suddenly Cormac was forgotten. The goddess launched toward Elyne and had her hands around the princess's throat before anyone could react. Elyne tumbled to the ground, the woman on top of her. She couldn't breathe as Morrigan's thumbs pressed into her throat.

Elyne heard Derron unsheathe his sword, followed by shouts. Were they trying to pull the goddess off? She couldn't tell. All she knew was she gasped for breath. Darkness crept into the edges of her vision and any minute she was going to pass out.

"You will pay for that, princess!"

And then, suddenly, they were gone from the council chamber. They were in a wilderness. Something sharp pressed into her back and she realized she'd landed on a rock or two. Pain shot through her body as she tried to fight the chokehold the woman had on her. The goddess had transported them from the palace to here. But still Elyne gasped for breath.

"I will kill you."

Elyne flailed her arms, her hands fumbling at her sides. Her fingers finally landed on something solid. A stick? A rock? Did it matter? With her last bit of strength, she smashed the object against Morrigan's temple. It was enough to knock her off Elyne. She fell to the ground and rolled but immediately climbed to her feet and came after her again.

Elyne rolled to her side, reaching for a small log. But Morrigan snatched her by the hair and yanked her back. Now she held a blade to her throat, pressing the sharp edge into her skin.

"Move and you die," she warned.

Elyne froze, fear creeping into her. She had no weapon. No way to defend herself. What now?

"Where is the queen?" Morrigan asked. "Tell me true or I slit your throat."

Use your magic, idiot.

Elyne reached for the tendrils of magic inside her and used it to shove Morrigan off. The woman released her and went flying backward. Smiling, Elyne climbed to her feet. Morrigan caught her breath, shook her head and got back on her feet.

"You think that will stop me? Stupid girl."

She raised her arms and threw a bolt of bright white light at Elyne. She dodged, the power barely missing her. A tree exploded behind her. She realized the target was not her, but the tree. Which was now falling toward her. Gasping, Elyne dove, landing on the ground and rolling out of the way.

Elyne tried another tactic. She sent a blight spell toward the goddess, hoping to defuse her temper and mar her beauty. But the goddess sensed her next move and put up a shield, breaking the spell as it tried to attack her.

"Bitch. Tell me where Maeve is."

"No," Elyne said.

Before she could react, Morrigan sent another bolt of magic toward her. This one hit her in the shoulder. The powerful jolt knocked her back a few steps and she stumbled. She smacked into another tree so hard, the air pushed from her lungs.

In a flash, the goddess was in front of her again, the knife at her throat once more.

"No more playing with magic. Tell me where your mother is or I slit your throat."

"If you kill me you will never find her."

"There are others who know her location. And you are expendable."

Gods, she hated this woman. "She's…waiting for you." To tell or not? Nero had said Maeve would defeat the goddess in the forest.

"Waiting for me where?"

Elyne decided withholding the information would delay the inevitable. Morrigan could kill her here and now and then use Cormac and his dark magic to find Maeve anyway. And she was right—there were others who knew the location of the queen. She couldn't risk Derron or the others.

"In the Sacred Forest."

Morrigan removed the knife and stepped back. "The Sacred Forest?"

Elyne rubbed the tender skin at her throat. "I don't think I stuttered when I said it."

"Then that's where I'll go. Say goodbye to Mommy. She'll be dead by morning."

And *poof* the goddess was gone.

Leaving Elyne to wonder where in the Otherworld she was.

Chapter 14

It took her a few minutes to get her bearings but Elyne finally realized the goddess hadn't sifted her far. She was a mere stone's throw from the palace walls. She walked out of the trees, relief washing over her at the sight of her home. Derron would be worried, wondering where she'd gone. She quickly sifted herself to the council chamber.

"Princess! Thank the gods you're all right," Lord Roderick said.

"Elyne, what happened?" Derron was at her side in an instant, looking her over. "Did she hurt you?"

"No, but Morrigan is heading to the Sacred Forest now to find my mother. She's going to kill her."

"Then we'll follow her to stop her."

"But Nero said she would confront my mother there. Shouldn't we—"

"We're going," Derron said with finality in his tone. "I'll gather the men. We'll leave as soon as we can."

"I'm coming with you."

"No. If anything happened to you—"

"Derron, she's my mother. I'm going." It was her turn to give him the tone of finality.

"I suppose I won't be able to talk you out of it?" he asked.

"No."

"All right. I will have your horse readied then."

"Forget the horses," Elyne said. "I'm calling the dragons. Luna, Aura and Ambrielle are our best chance of defeating the goddess. And then I will use my power to sift us all to the edge of the Sacred Forest."

Derron gaped at her a long moment before finally nodding. "If that's your wish, your majesty, then I will follow your command."

"It is my wish. And if we're lucky, we'll beat Morrigan and her dark army there. Go, Lord Derron. I will follow once I finish business here with King Urdithane."

He glanced from the king and back to her, question in his eyes. He didn't know what she was planning to do and, truthfully, she hadn't made up her mind yet either. For when her mother discovered what she'd done, there would be hell to pay.

But wouldn't it be worth it? Her mother would be safe, the Elves would be happy and all would be right with the Otherworld once again.

When Derron hadn't moved she gave him a little nudge. "I won't be long."

"I'll be waiting." He gave her a look that told her not to tarry.

She wouldn't. What she had planned would only take a moment. Derron and a few of the other councilors left the council chamber. Prince Andahar and the king of the Elves approached her then. She could read the anger on the king's face. The way his nose scrunched up. They had yet to negotiate anything thanks to Morrigan's constant interruptions.

"The Treaty," King Urdithane said. "You once again manage to keep the negotiations from happening." He folded his arms over his chest.

As she looked at the king, who so clearly despised everything about the Fae, she decided she would go ahead with her snap decision. She took a deep breath.

"I know what it looks like, your majesty. I assure you that is not the case."

"Then what is the case?" he demanded. "How will we ever move forward?"

"I do apologize for everything that's happened. I know you arrived here in good faith to negotiate the terms of the Treaty of Separation."

"I did," he said with a nod. The anger was still evident on his face.

"And there have been nothing but interruptions beyond our control. My mother would not approve of my decision but I make it now as Queen Regent." The Treaty lay at her place on the table. She snatched it and held it in front of the two Elves. "I hereby proclaim it null and void." She ripped it in half.

Shock registered on the king's face as the two halves fluttered to the floor.

"Your majesty…I don't know what to say."

"Say thank you and then join us in the fight against Morrigan," Elyne said. She looked at Prince Andahar. "Both of you."

Urdithane closed his mouth with a clink of teeth to hide his disbelief. "Aye, thank you. We would be honored." Then he grinned so broad his eyes crinkled with delight. "You are much like your father. I knew I saw him in you."

"I'm glad to know that. Now…shall we? We have a battle to fight and my mother to save."

And she motioned toward the door.

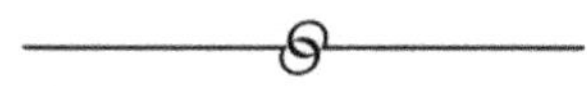

Maeve had never felt so much like a traitor than she did now. She knew what she had to do. She couldn't let any of her feelings get in the way of it. She paused outside the door with a heavy heart. Closing her eyes, she took a deep breath. Knowing what she had to do nearly destroyed her. Her hands shaking, she pushed open the door.

Henry flung aside the bedclothes and stood when she entered. Happy to see her. His tunic still lay in a heap on the floor. He took her in his arms and planted a fervent kiss on her lips.

"Where have you been?" he asked.

"I found the weapons."

"Good. Then we can arm ourselves against the goddess." He released her and bent to pick up his discarded tunic.

A pang went through her. She didn't want him anywhere near the goddess and their fight. The ruse had gone on long enough. And yet she admired the strength of his back, his arms, the curve of his chest into solid muscle. Despite whatever feelings she might have for him, she couldn't allow him to continue this charade.

"Henry, I know who you are."

He froze. His fists clenched so hard on his tunic his knuckles turned white. His lips formed a thin, straight line.

"What do you mean by that?"

"I know you are human. Who cast the glamour on you?" As if she didn't already know but she wanted to hear it from his lips.

"I don't know what you're talking about." He tugged the material over his head and reached for his boots.

"Let us not play such games," she said.

"All right then. Have it your way." He pulled on a boot. "If you know who I am, why did you allow me to bed you?"

Before she could stop the reaction, her cheeks flamed. She knew he saw it, too. She took a step back. How could he use that against her?

She liked it. He knew she liked it. If it weren't for the fact he was a human, mayhap she would allow it to happen again.

And yet, she never experienced such passion as she did with Henry. She realized the truth of his identity. She also realized they could never be together. It hurt her to know that. What would happen if her people knew she had accepted a human into her heart? If she had allowed him to stay in her kingdom and her bed? She would lose her people's respect and loyalty. Her kingdom would suffer and her people would hate her. Her duty was and always had been kingdom first.

Sometimes she hated her duties as queen.

"I didn't know what you were until then," she said.

"Oh? Did you have your suspicions before?"

"I suspected, aye. You don't know how to use a sword. And no true Fae knight would be as bold as you are."

Anger burned in his eyes. She didn't like making him angry. She didn't like telling him she knew the truth. But he had to know the truth and she had to get him out of the way before Morrigan decided to make an appearance. Because she couldn't have him getting hurt. Despite what High King Conn said, she didn't want him anywhere near the fight. Even if he could help.

"Bold because I'm not afraid to take what I want?" His gaze raked over her.

She shuddered from the scorching look but still held her ground. "Any other knight would be beheaded for such actions."

He stared at her a moment longer, never breaking eye contact. Until, finally, he could no longer look at her. "The glamour is courtesy of your daughter, Elyne. Don't even think to punish her for it. I asked her to do it." He pulled on his other boot and stood.

"Why? Why did you hide in my realm? And why weren't you

put with the other humans?"

"I should think it rather obvious."

Because of her? She stared at him as though she could read the answer on his face. He raked a hand through his hair.

"Have you ever had a connection to someone, Maeve? Have you ever looked at someone and knew that person was the one, the only one, for you? Have you ever had such strong feelings they drove you toward that person? The one perfect person who could complete your soul?"

Gods, why did he have to put it that way? Did he know her so well? It was as if he saw into her heart. Aye, she had those feelings with Henry. That connection that meant it was something more than mere physical attraction. She didn't want to acknowledge the deep-seated feelings she had for this man. This *human*. Mostly because she'd never felt that way before. Her marriage to her husband had been one of arrangement. She'd grown to love him over the years of their betrothal and marriage. But there hadn't been passion between them. There was no fire. No flame that would burn forever inside her.

Henry, though, was different. The spark burned long and hot for him. She could not deny that. Long, hot, ardent passion. Even now she ached for his touch.

But she was Fae and he was human. And the idea of a relationship with him was completely out of the question. When all of this was over, she would go back to her world and he to his. They would part ways. She would never forget him, though, for the rest of her long days. It would pain her to live without him. She had no choice. She had to.

"I think you have," he continued, unaware of her internal debate. "And I think you're too afraid to admit it to yourself."

He softened then, the anger dissipating. He stepped toward her, took her face in his hands. "You are beautiful when you blush."

Maeve shoved his hands away. "Stop it."

"Stop what? Telling you the truth? Telling you how beautiful you are? How much I desire you? How much I want to kiss you and make love to you?"

"Stop it, I say!"

"I can deny it no longer, Maeve. I love you. Even though you may not love me back, I'm willing to wait for you. For however long it takes. I'm willing to give you the chance to discover how you feel about me on your own."

Her fists clenched in frustration. "Don't you understand? A life with me is not possible. I am Fae. Queen of the Otherworld. I am—"

"Blah, blah, blah. Technicalities. We can overcome anything as long as we're together." He reached for her again and slipped his hands up her arms. "I know you are immortal and I'm not. I *know* that. But it doesn't stop how I feel and sometimes…sometimes you can't help who you love."

It made what she meant to do to him all the more painful. All the more difficult. Why couldn't he go quietly? Why couldn't he keep those love words to himself? Bottled up? Like she did. She never allowed her stoic façade to crack. Never allowed anyone inside.

But Henry got in.

That she knew. And she hated it. Hated herself for allowing him to seep under her skin and to break down those walls she so carefully constructed.

"Come," she said at last. "I will show you the weapons."

Maeve led him from the bedchamber down the curving stone staircase and into the foyer. But she didn't take him to the weapons room. She took him into the depths of the castle. Down to the place where many a Fae had been tortured and killed. And with every step her heart grew heavier.

How could she do this to him? *It's for his own protection.*

Despite the fact he'd managed to save her on numerous occasions from the Goddess of War, she still did not want him anywhere near the battle. *Acknowledge your feelings for him. You love him. Yet you cannot tell him. To tell him is to admit weakness.*

"The weapons are down here?" he asked.

"Aye, I will show you." The lie scalded her. Burned her to the core.

They'd reached the level where she needed a torch. An unlit one perched in a bracket and immediately sprang to life when she placed her hand on it. Her heart did a wild patter in her chest, nearly bursting through the rib cage and skin. Could she really do this? Could she go through with it? Oh, aye, she had to.

They stepped into the dungeon and Maeve moved aside to

allow him to enter first. He stood in front of an open cell. Her heart lurched in her chest. Her stomach twisted in a knot.

"I don't see any weapons here," he said.

"That's because there aren't any."

She shoved him so violently he stumbled into the cell. Her eyes filled with tears when she slammed the door behind him and twisted the key in the lock.

"Maeve, what are you doing?"

"I'm truly sorry, Henry. But this is for your own good."

She put the torch in the bracket by his cell door then pocketed the key. He peered out through the bars, the glow from the firelight casting eerie shadows on his face.

"You can't leave me here," he said. "Damn it, Maeve! I have to help you."

"You'll be safe here. I can handle Morrigan myself."

"No, you can't. She's tried to kill you already. I can't protect you from her if I'm in here."

"I am sorry," she said again.

And before he could answer she spun and fled the dungeon, tears stinging her eyes.

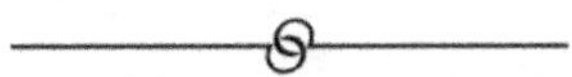

Elyne led King Urdithane and Prince Andahar to the palace gates where Derron, Lord Eldrin and the men waited along with the three dragons. To her surprise, Maggie, Finn, Sir Drake and Princess Allanna were there as well.

"I'm going, too," Maggie said. But Finn was already shaking his head.

"I don't think that's a good idea," Elyne said. "Ye should stay here and rest, Maggie."

"I'm tired of resting. All I've been doing is resting. I'm pregnant. Not an invalid. I need to *do* something before I go stir crazy."

"Riding into battle is not something I want ye to do. Ye canna go, lass. Think of the wee bairn ye carry."

"He's my father, Finn. I have to go!"

Elyne recognized the fright in her voice. She felt it for her mother when they fought at the Stone of Destiny. And now again when her mother's life was threatened by Goddess of War. All the worry and fear exhausted her.

"No, Maggie," Derron said, his voice gentle. He stepped next to Finn, his hand on the hilt of his sword. "I have to agree with your husband. It's too dangerous." He turned to Finn. "I'm leaving the protection of the castle in your and Sir Drake's charge."

There was her man, taking charge. Elyne smiled, happy he'd come to the rescue.

"With Morrigan busy, though, I doubt she'll return," Sir Drake said.

"Aye, 'tis my thinking as well," Finn said. "Good luck." Finn extended his hand to Derron and they shook.

Maggie muscled her way between them and clasped Derron by the arms. "Derron, you have to promise me you'll bring him back safely."

"I will do my best, my lady."

"No. Promise me," she begged.

He exchanged a glance with Elyne. She understood. It was the same for her mother. She wanted to make sure Maeve would come home in one piece.

"I promise."

Maggie expelled a sigh of relief and hugged him hard. Derron gave Finn an *it wasn't my fault* look before she released him and stepped back next to Finn. The Scotsman put an arm around her shoulders and held her close.

"'Twill be all right, lass."

Allanna hugged her brother then her father. "Be careful. I shall worry about you both until your safe return."

"We will be well, daughter," Urdithane said. He patted her cheek and gave her a small smile.

Allanna stepped back beside Drake. He took her hand in his for comfort. Elyne detected it did not go unnoticed by the king by the sour look on his face.

"We'll be back soon," Elyne said. "Take care of her, Finn."

She mounted Aura, patting her scaly sapphire neck. Derron took Luna, the one that was the color of moonlight and the Elven king and prince rode with Ambrielle, the emerald dragon.

Holding the reins in her hands, Elyne closed her eyes and with a mere thought, she flashed the entire army to the edge of the Sacred Forest. She heard the sharp intake of breath next to her from the king.

"You…sifted them?" Urdithane asked.

"I did," she said. "Now let's fly."

Hopefully, they would get there in time to stop Morrigan.

As Maeve locked Henry away, guilt flooded her. She ran back up the stairs away from the dungeon with tears streaking down her face and Henry's shouts in her ears. "For your own safety, Henry," she whispered, speaking mostly to herself, and whisked away the tears.

As she entered the great hall, she saw them. The wraith-like beings clustered around the entire area. All looking at her with those ghostly expectant gazes. All waiting for her. Conn stepped to the front of the group.

"The Goddess of War has arrived, your majesty," he said.

"Where is she?"

"She has entered the Sacred Forest with her Fomorian army."

Good. Now she would make sure the woman paid for everything she'd done to her.

"What would you have us do, your majesty?" Conn asked.

She spun to face him. "The time for battle has come. If you help me defeat her and her army, will you still haunt this forest and this fortress?"

Conn bowed his head. "No, your majesty. We will finally have one final victory to allow us to rest. Once this duty is fulfilled, we will be gone from this place forever."

Provided they were victorious. Taking a deep breath, Maeve opened the door to the Sacred Forest where the darkness pressed all around.

"Then let the goddess come."

Maeve wasn't about to let Conn and his army fight her battle for her. She was grateful for the help but disposing of the Goddess of War was up to her. She didn't know how she would defeat her with no magic. She wasn't good with a sword either. But there was a weapon of choice she could use.

"Wait for me outside," she instructed Conn. "I will join you in a moment."

He gave her a silent nod as she took off for the weapons room. She recalled seeing a bow and arrows there. The one there was far too ancient and brittle. She needed something better. The enchanted castle could give it to her with a mere thought. She closed her eyes and envisioned the bow she had as a young princess. The weight of it. The feel of it. It had been made from the strongest Elven wood. The roughhewn material had been sanded smooth and lacquered, making it shiny. She loved that bow.

She held her hand out, palm up and imagined it. She could almost feel it in her hands. No, that wasn't right. She *could* feel it in her hands. When she opened her eyes, she held the bow. The same one she remembered having when she was younger. A quiver of arrows sat at her feet.

She slipped one of the arrows from the quiver to examine the tip. It had been forged by the Elves and stamped with their sigil on the arrowhead. These were also the arrows she recalled she'd had so long ago. Remembering how to shoot was as natural as breathing.

With a smile she slipped the arrow back into place and snatched up the quiver, slinging it over her shoulder. She joined Conn and his men, holding the bow at the ready. Now she was prepared for the goddess.

She stood rigid, waiting. The forest had gone eerily silent. Nothing stirred. No birds or creatures. But she knew Morrigan's army was in the forest. What she didn't understand was how they were making their way so quietly and why the forest wasn't working against them. Mayhap she had prepared them for the dangers of the forest. She could have put some sort of spell on them to keep them from thinking of anything but the task at hand.

Fomorians were powerful in their own right. With Morrigan in charge, though, Maeve feared what they could do. What they would be capable of.

"Why is the Sacred Forest so silent?" she asked.

"The Goddess of War has arrived," Conn said. "No creature wishes to be in her path."

She disliked waiting to be attacked. What other choice did she have, though? She heard the distinctive flap of wings overhead and glanced up. Through the treetops she could make out Nero circling overhead. It gave her some comfort to know he was there.

"Do you intend to stand here and wait for them to come to you, Conn?" she asked.

"They will be here soon enough."

Silence still pressed around them and then it was as though all the oxygen had been sucked away from them. Maeve held her breath as she nocked an arrow in the bow.

The first of the Fomorians broke through the line and charged toward the castle. Maeve pulled back the arrow, ready to release it. But Conn stepped in front of her. As he prepared to fight, something strange happened. Once a wraith, he took the form for a man once again. She glanced around at the others and noticed the same thing. They were no longer ghosts but instead men. Men to fight with her against the Goddess of War.

Her confidence soared. Victory didn't seem so impossible now. She stepped around Conn and released her arrow. It embedded in the torso of a Fomorian. She fired off several more shots as the men went into action to battle them.

A crash above made her look up and she saw the red dragon bearing down on them. It released a fireball and set the treetops afire. Tree trunks turned into charred sticks. It was immediately followed by a squawk. The goddess rode on the back of the red dragon. It cleared a path so it could land near the army as it attacked.

Morrigan, dressed in her signature black, alighted from the dragon. Her gaze fixed on Maeve. The queen leveled an arrow at her and immediately fired. The goddess brushed it away as though it were nothing more than a gnat. Then she released a ball of bright white magic.

Maeve couldn't get out of the way fast enough. She dove but the magic fireball slammed into her right shoulder. The searing pain exploded through her body as she landed on the ground in a heap. She reached for the wound, her fingertips grazing it. They came away smeared with blood.

"My queen!" Conn knelt at her side and grasped her by the arm. "I couldn't stop her."

"It's all right, Conn."

He helped her to her feet. "You're wounded. We must find the healer."

"There's no time for that—"

Another blast of magic turned the tree next to her into slivers of wood. Instinctively she ducked but shards rained down along with singed leaves and limbs.

"Where is your human?" Conn asked.

"I locked him in the dungeon."

"Why?"

"Because he's a liability! Let me go, Conn. I have to fight her myself."

"If you do you will die." He said it matter-of-factly.

A squawk rent the air. Maeve saw the red dragon lumbering through burning forest, swiping men out of the way. Morrigan walked next to it with a purposeful stride. She never let her gaze leave Maeve.

It sent the queen's heart into a tailspin. Mayhap she had been wrong to lock up Henry. Mayhap she really did need him here. The Goddess of War warmed up another magic fireball to send her way. It blazed brightly as she released it. Conn shoved her behind him, intending to take the full blast of it himself.

"Conn, no!"

The next thing Maeve knew there was a crash, trees falling and a burst of bright orange light. Nero had dropped down from the sky and breathed fire into the magic ball, making it disintegrate into the air.

"By the gods…I never thought to see the black dragon again," Conn said.

"Nero. His name is Nero."

And he'd saved her life.

The red dragon charged toward Nero but he took flight. The red dragon followed, bursting through the tops of the trees. Leaves fluttered down and branches fell all around them. The squawking from each of the dragons shattered through the air. Every now and then she would catch a glimpse of their firelight as they battled one another.

The queen had been so distracted by the dragons she hadn't

realized Morrigan had advanced on her and now stood a few feet away. She released an arrow but the goddess merely stepped out of the way. Conn charged her but Morrigan waved him away with ease. Conn's body flew and landed like a rag doll on the forest floor. Maeve tried another arrow but it was completely useless.

All she could do was turn and run. As she did, she tripped over her skirts and tumbled to the ground. The bow flew from her grip. Before she could scramble to get a hand on it, Morrigan had her by the hair. She jerked her backward, the strands straining against her scalp.

"Now you are mine." Morrigan breathed the words in her ear.

She was paralyzed with fear as the goddess placed a dagger at her throat. Maeve squeezed her eyes shut, waiting for the final slash that never came.

Morrigan screamed and jerked and released her. Maeve fell forward, catching herself on her palms. She rolled over in time to see Morrigan yanking an arrow out of her shoulder and throwing it to the ground in a rage. Beyond her, Lord Eldrin lowered his bow.

Thank gods for the Elven ranger. If Eldrin was here then her daughter and Lord Derron must be nearby. Hope swelled within her. Help had come in the form of the Fae and Elves.

"Well, well. Will I get to kill an Elven prince *and* the queen of the Fae today? How wonderful for me."

"Not today."

Eldrin released another arrow. She batted it away with her magic. But he was not to be dissuaded. He fired off another and another and another in rapid succession. Until one slammed into her other shoulder and she shrieked. Eldrin rushed past her to Maeve's side and helped her to her feet.

"Come, Maeve. We must get you to safety," he said.

"There is no safe place from her," Maeve said.

But she didn't argue as he led her away in a hurry. Behind them, Morrigan called for her red dragon. Maeve stole a glance over her shoulder to see the goddess look toward the sky and then mount. The red dragon burst upward through the trees, disappearing, the goddess clearly interested in something—or someone—overhead.

Good. It would give Maeve time to regroup.

By the time Elyne and Derron arrived at the edge of the Sacred Forest, the Elves and Fae were already battling the Fomorians. The ground was littered with corpses. The goddess's men disappeared into the forest, leaving a path of destruction behind.

The red dragon and the goddess flew toward the castle. The dragon released a fireball, setting the forest ablaze. Then it landed not far from the fires.

That must be where her mother was.

A moment later, a bright flash of light. The goddess used her magic to attack her mother. A knot of fear gripped Elyne.

Aura, take me to Morrigan.

As you wish.

As they flew toward the flames, Nero made a sudden appearance from behind the castle. He then dove into the trees. A moment later everything was on fire.

Take me there, Aura.

The dragon wasted no time as she flapped her great wings and headed toward the blaze. Elyne feared her mother was injured or dead. But as they made their way there, the red dragon burst upward from the forest floor, Morrigan on her back. The two of them made eye contact. The dark look on the goddess's face was enough to tell Elyne her mother still lived. Thank the gods.

Despite the look of hate Morrigan gave her, the princess held fast. She would not be intimidated. Morrigan's face darkened. One instant she sat on the back of the beast, the next she disappeared in a puff of smoke.

The goddess appeared in front of her, her black gossamer gown flowing in the breeze around her lithe form. Elyne's grip tightened on the reins. Aura reared back at the appearance of the goddess so suddenly she nearly dumped her passenger.

Morrigan reached for her and before Elyne could veer out of the way, she clamped an icy hand around her throat. Elyne gasped for breath and jerked the reins, trying to loosen the goddess's grip. Aura puffed out a heated breath but remained in the air.

Bank, Aura. Let me fall.

No, princess.

Do it!

Another puff of smoke from the dragon before she banked hard to the right. Elyne slid in the saddle. She went limp and allowed gravity to take over, all the while gasping for breath. A moment later there was a flash of light, a wretched scream and Morrigan was gone. Aura righted herself immediately. Elyne pulled herself back into the saddle and gripped the reins. Next to her Derron rode Luna. Behind him was Andahar and Urdithane on Ambrielle.

Andahar lowered his bow. She knew he must have shot the goddess to make her release Elyne. He'd saved her life.

"Don't scare me like that," Derron admonished. "I thought I was going to lose you."

"So did I." Elyne's voice was raspy. She glanced down at the battle raging below. "Let's get that bitch."

But as they flew a little farther, they could see the devastation. Most of the Sacred Forest was on fire. There were more dead Fomorians. But there was no sign of her mother. Worry gnawed at her.

Charred land had formed a clearing in front of the ancient castle. Elyne pointed to it.

Land there, Aura.

She complied and a moment later Elyne slid off Aura's back. The others followed suit. Derron wielded the Sword of Light. Andahar and Urdithane readied their bows.

"I have to find my mother." Elyne worried her bottom lip.

"We'll search out here." Andahar motioned toward the forest.

"Derron and I will take the castle," Elyne said.

Andahar and the other Elves headed off through the burning forest. Elyne and Derron charged inside, not knowing what they would find.

Chapter 15

The respite didn't last long. Maeve and Eldrin had made it a few feet away when Morrigan returned in a flash of light. Her dragon had destroyed half the Sacred Forest. Most of it was on fire as she charged through, looking for the queen. She killed anyone and everyone in her path. Even those who were supposed to be fighting for her.

"She's coming back," Eldrin said.

Morrigan had several oozing wounds. One on each shoulder where Eldrin had managed to hit her. Another in her side. Her black gown was damp with blood and her face was contorted into an angry mask. Behind her the battle raged. Fomorian against Elf and Fae.

"You will pay," Morrigan said.

It all happened so fast neither of them had time to react. Morrigan fired off several balls of white magic, each one hitting Eldrin. Maeve watched, helpless, as he tumbled to the ground.

"Eldrin!"

She fell to her knees at his side. Her hand landed on the hilt of his sword as she pushed him to his back. His chest still rose and fell so he was alive but injured.

"Oh, he'll live. But you won't," Morrigan said.

She clasped his sword and jumped to her feet, ready to do battle. But Morrigan wasn't impressed with her sword-wielding skills. Before Maeve could make a move, Morrigan backhanded her so hard her back teeth rattled. The sword hung like a wet rag in her hands.

She didn't even have time to react to the hit when something hard crashed into the side of her head. Maeve's knees turned to water as she fell into blackness.

In the dungeon, Henry gripped the bars of his cell and peered into the darkness. The torch managed to flicker away some of the shadows. Mostly, though, it was dark. Outside, the rumblings of the raged on. How was he going to get out of this godforsaken cell? Maeve had pocketed the key. He needed to get out there. He needed to help her. He needed to protect his woman, damn it.

Another explosion. This one so close, the walls shook. Rocks crumbled in his ancient prison. Somewhere in the darkness he heard the unmistakable squeak of a mouse and knew he'd have visitors soon enough. Visitors he had no interest in greeting.

He looked out the cell door again. *Think, think, think.* How could he get out of here? He was going to need help from an outside source. The problem was there weren't a lot of passersby.

But wait…wasn't this an enchanted castle? If he asked for a key to his cell, would the castle give it to him? Could it be as simple as that?

"Henry!"

He knew that voice. He froze, listening. Footsteps echoed down the stairs.

"Henry!" Princess Elyne called.

"In here!"

Flickering torchlight preceded her approach. Hopefully with reinforcements. Standing in the shadows was Elyne and Lord Derron.

"Henry, thank goodness you're all right. Why are you locked in here?" Elyne asked.

"Ask your mother. She put me here. Can you get me out of here?"

Elyne gave a quick nod and closed her eyes. A key appeared in the lock.

"Let's find the queen and get out of here." Derron gripped his sword tighter in his hand and turned toward the exit.

"You don't know where she is?" A horror-chill rushed into Henry's heart and his stomach cramped.

"We couldn't find her." Worry lines creased Elyne's forehead.

They ran up the stairs and out of the dank dungeon. Henry was relieved to be out of the cell but he was worried about Maeve. If they couldn't find her then he was troubled as to what was happening to her at the hands of Morrigan.

But Maeve could not be found in the castle. As they headed through the great hall, Prince Andahar entered. He had a panicked look on his face and blood splattered across his clothes. One sleeve of his tunic was ripped at the shoulder, the material hanging down in tatters.

"Princess…your mother…"

"Where is she, Andahar?" Elyne asked.

"Lord Eldrin tried to protect her but Morrigan struck. He's injured but he'll be all right. But the goddess hit Maeve in the head and knocked her out. My father and I tried to stop Morrigan but it was no use. My father…Eldrin…"

"What about my mother, Andahar?" Elyne couldn't hide the fear in her voice. And if she'd heard him mention his father and Lord Eldrin, she ignored it. Something terrible must have happened to them.

"She took her."

"What do you mean she took her? Took her where?" Henry demanded. He feared the worst. If the goddess had Maeve and they couldn't find her she would certainly be dead.

"The goddess took Maeve to the underworld."

"Shit," Henry said under his breath.

"Gods!" Derron raked a hand through his dark hair.

"We have to get my mother back."

"How?" Henry asked. "Do you know how to get to the underworld?"

"There are ways, Henry. I can use my mother's magic to get us there."

"You're not going without me." Derron gripped her arm to press his point.

"Or me," Henry said.

"You, human?" Derron shook his head. "The underworld is no place for you."

"Look, your lordship, Maeve brought me here to protect her. That's what I'm going to do." He thumbed as his chest.

"You mean protect her by being locked up in the dungeon?" Derron asked. "A lot of good you did."

"*She* locked me up. She tricked me. It wasn't my choice."

"You're staying here."

"The hell I am! I'm going." Henry turned to Elyne. "Princess, take me with you."

"Elyne, you cannot allow that," Derron said.

Henry shot him a heated glare. Elyne's head bobbed back and forth between the two of them like a spectator at a tennis match.

She shrugged off Derron and threw her hands up. "Enough bickering, you two. You're giving me a headache." Then to Henry, "Derron may be right—"

"I will give my life for hers if I have to."

A brittle silence descended between them. Henry's gaze never left Elyne's face, which paled at his sudden declaration. Beside her Derron stood still, unmoving. The princess dragged her bottom lip through her teeth.

"Maggie would never forgive me," Elyne said at last. He started to protest but she cut him off with a wave of her hand. "But…there I believe you can help us. My mother believed you could protect her. You can come with us."

"I hope you're not making a mistake," Derron growled.

"Until my mother is returned safely, I am still queen. If I say he's coming, then he's coming." She gave Derron a pointed look. "Prince Andahar?"

"I cannot. My father and brother were injured by the goddess. I must stay behind to tend them."

"Of course. The castle is enchanted. It will give you whatever you need to help. Even a healer."

"Thank you, princess."

Elyne turned back to Derron and Henry. "Let's get to the underworld and save my mother. Give me your hands."

She extended both hands to them. Derron took hers immediately. Henry followed after some hesitation. He slipped his fingers in hers and she closed her hand. He was desperate to get to Maeve.

The princess took a deep breath. "Here we go, gentlemen."

She closed her eyes. Henry wasn't sure what to do or how to act. Derron also closed his eyes. With a shrug, he did the same. For a moment it seemed as though everything around them stilled.

There was no air to breathe. No sounds beyond the castle walls. Everything was gone.

A *whoosh* and it was as though the floor fell out from under him. His heart lurched. His stomach somehow ended up in his throat before twisting in a sickly knot. He thought he might vomit. He heard Elyne emit a squeak, a gasp and then everything stopped.

Heat pressed all around him. It took him several seconds to find the courage to open his eyes. They stood on the edge of a cavern. Beyond them a river of lava flowed. Nothing grew here.

"Welcome to the underworld." Elyne sounded less than enthusiastic. And then she sucked in a sharp breath and bent over.

"What is it? What's wrong?" Derron was immediately at her side.

"Not sure." Elyne gulped in a breath and righted herself but her face was bright red. "As soon as we got here, I think something may have happened to my magic."

"Do you still have it?" Derron asked.

"I can still feel it but it's not nearly as strong. Morrigan's dark power must be subduing mine."

"Can you get us home?" Concern creased Derron's brow. It was the same question Henry had.

"I believe so, aye. But it's going to make it difficult to find her and rescue her."

"Where do we find her?" Henry asked, wanting to cut to the chase.

A scream ripped through the air.

"That sounded like my mother." Elyne's breath hitched in her throat.

Derron drew his sword. "We must be cautious."

"Screw that. We have to find her," Henry said. He started to take a step in the direction of the scream but Elyne clasped a hand on his arm to stop him.

"Derron is right. We *must* be cautious. There are dangers here no Fae or human knows."

"I don't care about the dangers. I have to save her."

He jerked his arm free and took off. If the princess and Derron followed so be it. All thoughts were of Maeve. Finding her. Making sure she was all right. Injured he could deal with. Dead he couldn't.

Maeve dead. It was a quick and disturbing thought that made his heart go cold and still. He couldn't imagine her life snuffed out by the goddess. His hands fisted. The mere thought Morrigan had harmed her sent him into a rage. He would kill the goddess himself. If he could figure out how.

He was distinctly aware of the footfalls behind him and he knew Derron and Elyne followed. He hurried along the bank of the lava river, hoping he was going in the right direction. Another scream. This time closer and he knew he neared Maeve.

"Henry, wait." Elyne caught up to him and pulled him to a stop. "I sense her. She's around the bend."

"Then what are we waiting for?"

"We need to see what we're walking into," Derron said.

Henry consented despite wanting to charge in with guns blazing. Except he didn't have any guns. What he wouldn't give for some sort of weapon right about now. He cursed for not thinking of it while back at the enchanted castle.

Derron took the lead and edged toward the bend. The smell of sulfur was strong here. Stronger than when they first entered the underworld. With his sword in his hand, he leaned against the rock wall and peered around the corner. His survey didn't last long as he turned back and faced the two of them.

His face paled. He looked as though he might be sick.

"What? What is it?" Elyne demanded in a roughened whisper.

"Morrigan intends to burn her alive. She's tied to a stake."

"No." Elyne shook her head. "Are we…too late?"

"Not yet."

"What's the plan?" Henry asked. "Surely you have one?"

Derron gave him a sour look. "What do you suggest, human? That we charge in there? Morrigan has her little minions helping her." His gaze landed on Elyne then. "Cormac is with her."

"God's teeth," Elyne said. "Will we ever be rid of him?"

"Who's Cormac?" Henry asked.

"Long story that," Elyne said. "Now is not the time. We have to get to my mother."

"What are we doing? The longer we stand here and chat the more time we waste," Henry said. He raked a hand through his hair, aggravated.

"Aye, we do," Elyne agreed. "We need a diversion. One I can create. You two get to my mother and release her while I keep the goddess occupied."

"That's a terrible plan," Derron said sourly.

"You have a better one, your lordship?" Henry retorted.

"No, he doesn't." Elyne cut off Derron's reply. "Wait here until I have Morrigan's full attention. Then get my mother."

"Then what?" Henry asked.

"Then…we get out of here." Elyne took a deep breath.

"Good luck," Henry said.

"Elyne, this is crazy. I can't let you do this." Derron clutched her by the arms and held her in place.

"You can. You have to. She's my mother, Derron. I have to save her."

The two lovers stared at each other for what seemed an eternity but in reality, it was a few seconds. Derron pulled her to him and kissed her hard, fervently. As though it could be the last time.

"Be careful," he said when he released her.

"I will." She put her hand on the side of his cheek, smiled. And then turned toward Maeve.

The simple gesture reminded Henry so much of the queen. It was almost painful to watch.

Another deep breath and Elyne prepared to step around the corner. Pain exploded in the back of Henry's head. Elyne yelped and Derron growled something. Stars exploded through Henry's vision. Someone grasped him by the arms and gave him a rough shove. He stumbled forward. The next thing he knew he had a rope around his neck and someone tugged him.

"Well, well. What have we here? Knights and a princess come to the rescue of their dying queen?"

Someone shoved him to his knees. He landed so hard it rattled his bones. More pain exploded through his body as his arms were jerked behind his back and his wrists tied. Henry was able to lift his head enough to see Maeve. He had been prepared to see Maeve tied up and ready to be burned alive. He had not been prepared to see the skin flayed from her back.

The bitch had whipped his precious queen. She looked as though she'd lost the fight. As though she had given up and was ready to die. Her head hung low, her chin on her chest. Her hair was damp with blood and sweat and plastered to her head.

"Let my mother go, Morrigan."

Elyne's voice was weak. Henry turned his head to see she was in the same position, with a rope around her neck. Derron was on her other side, also on his knees and roped. Bloody minions managed to capture them before they could act.

At the sound of Elyne's voice, Maeve lifted her head. She had a black eye and a cut on the side of her head. Blood oozed down her cheek. Seeing Maeve like that sent pain slashing through his heart. Anger at the sight of her boiled inside him. He wanted revenge. He wanted the goddess's head on a pike.

Morrigan laughed. "Oh, isn't that sweet? The errant daughter has come to save her mommy." Her face darkened. "You think I'm going to release her because you say so?"

"She doesn't deserve to die. Not like this."

"Then how? Shall I slash her throat?" She produced a blade in one hand and placed it against Maeve's throat.

"Elyne…" the queen croaked. And then her gaze met Henry's. Tears spilled down her cheeks. She gave him a look that pleaded with him to get her out of there.

He would even if he had to die trying.

"Shut up, you harlot. This is a great day. Not only do I get to kill the queen but I also get the daughter, the Protector of the Otherworld, and a Fae knight. How wonderful."

"Let…them…go." Maeve's voice was a gravely whisper.

"Not a chance. How sad the kingdom will be when they learn you and the crown princess have perished. I shall have to make sure they are consoled and then I will take the throne for myself."

"Why do you want her dead?" Elyne asked.

Next to him, Elyne fidgeted with the ropes at her wrists. He realized she was stalling. But all three of them were weaponless.

"Oh, you don't know?" Morrigan looked back at Maeve. "You never told her? How precious. Your mother and I shared affections for the same man. She stole him from me. Used her feminine wiles to make him fall in love with her."

"That's not true and you know it," Maeve croaked.

"Silence." She pressed the knife into her throat. "That man

became your father and king."

Elyne stiffened. She still worked the ropes, her skin slick with sweat and blood. She was making some progress. Whoever tied them hadn't done a very good job. Henry went to work on his own ropes. Whatever the princess was planning, he wanted to be ready.

"My parents were betrothed," Elyne said through clenched teeth. "I don't believe you."

"Believe it. And now I'm done talking. Time to light the fires."

"No," Elyne said. "Please don't do this, Morrigan. Haven't you had enough revenge? Can't you let her go?"

Morrigan halted and stared at her. "Let her go? *Let her go?* After six thousand years of pain and anguish and being locked away in this godsforsaken prison? I don't think so. She will pay with her life."

"Not today."

Elyne shouted the words and in the next instant she had her hands free. What happened next was a blur of motion that Henry had a hard time comprehending. Elyne threw her hands out, palms out. A bolt of bright white light flashed from her and hit Morrigan square in the chest. The goddess fell backward, crashing to the ground and releasing the dagger. Derron shouted something incoherent. The next thing he knew the lord was on his feet, punching the minion behind him. He retrieved his sword as more minions converged on him. He slashed at them, killing them instantly.

And all the while Henry sat there, dumbstruck.

Morrigan regained her footing and unfolded her long form to a standing position. She had a scorch mark in the center of her gown and a look of pure hate on her face.

"You bloody bitch." Her fingers turned into claws as she stood there seething at Elyne, Maeve suddenly forgotten. "I will have your head for that."

"Henry!" Elyne shrieked.

And it was the signal he needed to get his feet moving. He still fidgeted with the damn ropes, unable to get free of them. The minion behind him grabbed the noose around his neck and gave a swift yank. He choked and gasped for breath.

"Derron, give Henry the Sword!"

Henry couldn't see what was happening. All he heard was Elyne shouting. More flashes of light. Apparently Elyne and Morrigan were locked in some sort of heated magical battle. He needed to get free to release Maeve. Now was his best chance with the goddess busy.

But the light was fading and dark shadows crept around the edges of his eyes. He was losing his battle. He couldn't breathe and any minute now he was going to pass out. Whoever held his rope was not going to let go or even relax his grip.

There was a commotion beside him and in the next second the rope loosened from around his throat. Henry pitched forward and broke his fall with the side of his face. When his cheek slammed into the hard rock, the impact sent vibrations of pain through his head. He thought for an instant he saw stars. His jaw ached. But he didn't have time to catalog his injuries as Derron slashed through the ropes at his wrists. He hauled him to his feet and slapped a sword in his hand.

"Get the queen," he said. And then he was gone.

Henry whirled around. Elyne was locked in her own battle with Morrigan, magic fighting against magic. At least Elyne was trying. Elyne's magic was the weaker of the two. He couldn't see much except the outline of each of them in a blur of whiteness. He blinked several times to try to focus on it but it was useless. Derron was busy fending off attackers. Morrigan's minions. Little hellion demons who were determined to get to the princess.

And then Maeve. Her head had fallen again, her chin against her chest. Minions clambered around her, looking for a way to light the sticks and peat at her feet. She was oblivious to all that was going on around her and he feared the worst—that she was already dead.

She couldn't be.

Steeling his nerves, Henry charged toward her to save his ladylove. But the minions, little shits that they were, caught sight of him. And *they* charged *him*. He gripped the handle of the Sword of Light and held his breath. He hoped this would go better than what happened in the Sacred Forest with the big hairy beast. He swiped the Sword from side to side, swinging it in a wide arc.

Much to his surprise he managed to sweep several of them out of the way. They squealed a high-pitched sound that grated on his nerves and put his back teeth on edge. But they kept coming. And he kept swinging, clearing a path to Maeve.

"No! You can't have her!" Morrigan screamed.

Something searing hot slammed into his back and he sprawled forward. The Sword flew from his hands and clattered on the ground. Heat enveloped him and his skin felt as though it might be on fire. He groaned and clawed his way to his hands and knees.

"Henry?"

Maeve's voice. So quiet and soft and tortured. He lifted his head and met her gaze. Her blue eyes were full of pain and anguish and worry.

"You came for me," she said.

But he couldn't really hear her. She'd mouthed the words. Of course, he came for her. How could he *not* come for her? He needed her like he needed air to breathe. She was everything to him.

The sword was out of reach. He mustered the strength to crawl to it.

Behind him Morrigan laughed. "How wonderful it is to see you not give up...*human.*"

He flashed her a look of surprise.

"Oh, I figured it out. You are no Fae knight, are you? You are nothing more than a pitiful, pathetic human."

Another blast smacked him in the back and he tumbled to the ground again. The pain was almost unbearable but he had to fight through it. He had to save Maeve. He managed to get back up and crawl once again toward his sword. But he stole a glance over his shoulder.

Elyne was passed out cold in Derron's lap. They were surrounded by Morrigan's minions. The goddess stood between him and Maeve, a dark look of death and hate on her face.

"What I don't understand is what *she* is doing with *you.*" Morrigan nodded toward Maeve. "She has no love for humans."

Henry knew, deep down, Maeve was in love with him. She hadn't admitted it to herself yet. He was confident she would after he saved her life, proving he was her hero. Her knight in...well, no armor. But definitely her knight.

"Did you think that by defeating me and saving her life she would fall into your arms and proclaim her undying love for you?"

Actually, yes, that's exactly what he thought but now he was rethinking that.

Morrigan laughed her hideous laugh. The kind of laugh that made any sane individual want to drive a spike through the culprit's heart.

"No one can defeat me. Not a Fae. Not a human. Not even the great and powerful Maeve. Imagine my delight when I discovered she no longer possessed any magic. What a fool she was to give it to her inexperienced, insignificant daughter. Her daughter, who is now incapacitated."

Henry inched closer to the sword. He had nearly reached it. And as he slowly crept forward, his eyes on it, he realized this was no ordinary sword. This was Lord Derron's sword. What had he called it? The Sword of Light?

He shot a questioning glace at the knight who gave him a slight imperceptible nod. Henry knew what he must do. But why didn't Derron kill her himself? Why leave it to Henry? He didn't understand.

His fingers landed on the pommel and then his hand slid over the hilt, wrapping around the handle, and at last the sword was back in his grasp.

"Give up, you sad little human."

No. He would never give up. No matter how much pain he was in. Determination renewed in him and gave him strength.

He heard something crackle like an electrical charge. Despite his pain, despite feeling as though he would die any moment, he snatched up the sword and spun toward Morrigan, holding it aloft in front of him. Her magic hit the blade and went around him. It totally missed him. The blade came to life, glowing a pale blue. And Morrigan's ball of death bounced back toward her.

She shrieked. Something totally inhuman and ear piercing. He thought his ears might bleed. And if glass were anywhere in the vicinity it certainly would shatter. When she realized what happened, she ducked, missing the bolt of light by mere inches.

That pissed her off.

Never a good idea to piss off the Goddess of War.

Henry pushed to his feet, still holding the sword. He gripped it with both hands and wielded it in front of him. He'd never before felt so powerful. So in control. And he wasn't sure why that was.

He didn't understand it. Maybe it was because he was so damn determined to save Maeve and destroy Morrigan. Maybe adrenaline had finally kicked in, giving him the strength he needed. Whatever it was he was certainly glad it decided to make an appearance.

Morrigan took a step backward and held her hands a few inches apart, her fingers curved in an arch. The ball of light formed between them. Crackling to life. Making that sound he'd heard moments ago. He wondered then why he hadn't heard it before. Not that it actually mattered.

"Cormac! Take him," she ordered.

Cormac. The man Elyne had mentioned previously. He stood off to the side, a sword dangling in his hand as though he were totally uninterested in the battle in front of him. He hadn't made a move to help anyone, least of all his mistress. He'd been nothing but a spectator during the entire ordeal.

"No," he said in a flat, defeated monotone. The man looked as though his spirit was crushed and it probably was. She'd been using him to do her evil and who knew what else.

"What do you mean no?" Her voice was nothing more than a high-pitched squeal. Like fingernails on a chalkboard. "You are my servant!"

"I don't serve you anymore. I serve no one. Ever. Again." And with that he dropped the sword with a clatter.

"Then your precious family is dead," she snarled.

"I know they're dead. You killed them."

A satanic smile spread across her thin lips. "Ah, so you discovered the truth, do you? How did you find out?"

"You forget we are in the underworld. I saw them here. You lied to me, you sadistic whore, and I'm going to let them kill you."

She screamed her frustration and instead of releasing the ball of power toward Henry she released it toward Cormac. He didn't flinch. He didn't even try to duck or step out of the way. He took the full force of the hit square in the chest and stumbled backward. He clutched his chest and his hand came away covered in charred blood. And then his eyes rolled back into his head and he dropped to the ground.

Cormac was dead.

"Now for you, human. And then I will do away with the queen."

"Why don't you kill her now?" he asked.

She glanced at Maeve and then sneered. "I like watching her suffer."

Henry clutched the sword in his sweaty palm. Morrigan was already forming another ball of power. But he had the sword and he wasn't about to let the ball hit him the way it hit Cormac.

With Cormac's murder, Morrigan's minions scuttled away like cockroaches hiding from a burst of light. They wanted nothing to do with her. Henry couldn't help but smirk at that. She'd lost her right-hand man *and* her cronies. Things were looking up.

No more standing around. He needed to take action. He bolted into a dead run, holding the sword aloft and emitting a guttural war cry befitting any knight of the realm. Morrigan gasped.

Maeve's head lifted. He thought he saw her eyes wide with fear and concern but he wasn't going to stop and take notice. All he had in mind was driving the sword through Morrigan's heart.

The goddess's gasp of surprise lasted a split second and then she was flinging the ball of light toward him. Instinct and adrenaline took over and he managed to block it, the powerful blast doing nothing but going around him, useless.

She disliked not getting her way. Her fists balled and she flung bolt after bolt toward him. He was a breath away from her. She took a step backward, suddenly realizing he meant business and refused to stop his charge. Her hands flew up in defense and her eyes were wide.

"Please, don't! Don't hurt me!"

He stumbled to a halt with the sword point an inch from her throat.

"Don't hurt you?" Henry repeated.

"Don't listen to her, Henry," Derron said, his voice echoing through the massive cavern. "Kill her."

"No. Please. I-I'll let her go. I swear." Tears brimmed in her eyes.

"She won't. She's lying. Kill her!" Derron urged.

Henry wavered. The tip of the sword trembled. He'd never killed another person before. He didn't know if he wanted to start now.

"You'll let her go?" he asked.

"I-I will. I swear it."

"She's lying! She'll never let Maeve go," Derron said. "Destroy her."

Morrigan shook her head as tears spilled down her pale cheeks. "Please, Henry."

"If I allow you to live…do I have your solemn oath that you will release Queen Maeve?"

She nodded as her chin quivered. Something deep in her black eyes gave him pause. Something that told him she might do as he requested if he let her live. If he removed the sword from her throat and stepped aside. It was probably the worst thing he could do but he wanted to believe her. He wanted to trust her.

"She's the Goddess of War, Henry," Derron said. "She doesn't give solemn oaths. Don't let her get away."

Henry lowered the sword. He wasn't sure who to trust—Morrigan or Derron. But she seemed to be telling him the truth. That she would release Maeve if he released her. Morrigan dropped her arms, whimpering.

"Thank you. Oh, thank you," she whispered.

"Henry, you idiot. She's not going to let Maeve go."

He still clutched Derron's sword as he turned toward him. "She gave me her word."

And then behind him, her devious laughter. "You should have listened to Lord Derron. He was right. I'm not going to release her."

The crackling returned and he spun around as Morrigan formed another, larger ball of light. Was that the one trick this bitch knew? She gave Henry a smug smile as she opened her hands and released the ball toward Maeve.

"Use the Sword of Light!" Derron shouted.

Henry forced his feet to move and bolted into a run. Maeve was conscious and well aware of what was about to happen. Henry didn't want to see her fried to a crisp. Not today. Not any day. He dove, holding the Sword aloft and outstretched as far as he could reach.

The glowing blade intercepted the glowing ball of light a few feet from Maeve. It reflected the powerful magic back toward Morrigan and away from Maeve.

"No. NO!"

She threw her hands up in defense but it was too late. The ball had doubled in size and hit her. It enveloped her entire body. Morrigan shrieked as she died by her own hand. Her own magic consumed her. Her skin burst into flame and she fluttered to the ground in a heap of ash. She had been incinerated. Steam rose from the ash, forming what was left of her.

Silence descended. Henry's chest rose and fell with exertion. He'd done it. He'd killed the Goddess of War.

"You did it, Henry."

That voice. So soft. So sweet. He turned toward Maeve. She still stood tied to the stake, her hands behind her back and blood now dried on the side of her face. She didn't bother to stop the tears that ran down her cheeks.

He dropped the sword and hurried to her. It took him several fumbling minutes before he finally had her untied and she literally fell into his arms. He held her slight weight, cradling her body next to his. He was grateful…so grateful she was still alive and looking up at him with those beautiful blue eyes.

She placed her hand on the side of his face. "You saved me."

"You expected anything less?" He grinned.

"Thank you, Sir Henry."

"It was my sincere pleasure, my queen."

She smiled through the tears. "Take me home."

It was the last thing she said before burying her face in his chest and passing out from the sheer exhaustion of the entire ordeal. He scooped her up more securely in his arms and turned toward Derron.

Elyne had regained consciousness finally. She had a nasty gash on her forehead but other than that she seemed unscathed. Derron retrieved his Sword of Light and met Henry's gaze.

"I told you not to trust her," he said.

"You did," Henry agreed.

"So why did you?"

"I thought I saw something in her eyes. I thought she was telling me the truth. Why did you give me your sword?" he asked.

It was Elyne who answered. "I remembered a piece of lore. Part of a fable my father used to tell me. He said the one able to defeat the Goddess of War would be a man wielding the Sword of Light. And as we all know the Sword of Light makes the wielder undefeatable in battle. I knew if you had the Sword, Henry, you would be able to defeat her."

"A piece of pertinent information you might have shared with me at the beginning," he groused.

"Sorry. I remembered it after we were captured. And anyway, you defeated her, didn't you?"

"I did. Are you all right, princess?"

"I'm fine. Though I'm not sure poor Cormac fared all that well."

She walked to him and knelt by his side. Both Henry and Derron looked on with interested curiosity as she brushed away a lock of hair from his face.

"All he wanted was to find his family. I failed him."

"Don't blame yourself for his death, Elyne," Derron said. "There was nothing you could have done to prevent it. And now he has been reunited in death with them."

"Right." She rose and heaved a heavy sigh. "I think we've all had enough of this place. Let's get out of here."

"I couldn't agree more," Henry said.

"Your magic is working again?" Derron asked.

"Aye. Mayhap because the goddess is dead."

With a nod, Derron stepped closer to him and Elyne joined them. Derron put one hand on his shoulder and grasped Elyne's other one. She placed her free hand on his other shoulder. They formed a circle. Henry hugged Maeve tighter to his chest as Elyne worked her magic and quickly sifted them back to the castle in the Sacred Forest.

Chapter 16

Dead Fae, Fomorians and Elves littered the ground as Henry carried Maeve inside the castle walls. He never broke stride as he headed up the stairs to her chamber. Elyne followed on his heels. Derron had stayed behind, ordering the Fae and Elven soldiers.

"I'm going to fetch Seamus," she said. "You'll stay with her?"

"I will."

Elyne sifted away. Henry gently laid Maeve on the bed. He smoothed her hair from her face. Elyne returned a moment later with the royal healer. Seamus cursed under his breath and shoved Henry aside to get to work. Henry didn't fight him. He stepped back from the bed. Elyne stood rigid next to him.

"She will live, won't she?" Elyne asked.

"Her injuries are not life threatening." Seamus never looked up from the queen. He'd rolled her to her stomach to tend the lashes on her back.

"Come, Henry. Let's allow Seamus to help my mother. And then tend your wounds."

"I'm fine. She charred me a little but it's not bad." He would do it all again for Maeve.

"As you wish."

He allowed Elyne to tug him out into the hallway. Blindly he followed her down the stairs back to the great hall where a giant of a man stood holding a bloody sword. Derron was with him.

"Ah, there you are. I was about to come find you," Derron said. "Princess, this is Conn. Former High King of the Otherworld. You'll want to hear what he has to say."

"Conn of the Hundred Wars?" She stared at him, blinking with her confusion.

He bowed in greeting. "You resemble your mother."

"But I thought you were, uh, dead."

He smiled. "I am but a spirit now. Your mother's feud with the goddess gave our restless spirits renewed purpose. We can at last rest."

"You helped my mother?"

"These were the men we didn't know when we arrived," Derron explained.

"Thank you, Conn."

"I am sorry we could not do more to keep her safe. Is she alive?"

"She is, thanks to Henry," Elyne said. "He saved her."

Conn's gaze flickered to Henry. "You did well, human, as I knew you would." Then he glanced back at Elyne. "My men and I will take our leave."

"Where will you go?" Elyne asked.

"Our spirits go to rest now."

With one last bow of his head he faded into nothingness.

"That was weird," Henry said. "He was a spirit when we first arrived. But he looked to be flesh and blood then."

"It's the magic of the Sacred Forest and the castle," Elyne said. "Nero sent my mother here. He must have known the spirits would protect her."

"The Sacred Forest won't be haunted anymore?" Henry asked.

"I don't think so." Elyne glanced around the dusty and crumbling walls of the castle. "I'd like to have this place restored as a monument. Do you think we could do that, Lord Derron?"

"Aye, we can, my princess." He smiled. "How's your mother?"

"She's in Seamus' capable hands," Elyne said. "I have faith he will heal her and she'll be fine."

"Good. I spoke with Prince Andahar," Derron said. "He has taken his father and Lord Eldrin back to the Queen's Palace. Eldrin was struck by Morrigan's magic while trying to protect Maeve. The king suffered a near-fatal injury at the hands of the Fomorian army."

"Oh, gods. I hope they're all right." Elyne scrubbed a hand down her face. "That's what he was trying to tell me before we left for the underworld. I was too distracted to listen. What of the Fomorians?"

"Most of them were killed. With no goddess and no Cormac,

they've fled the forest and have returned to their hiding place. Wherever that is," Derron said.

"The Sorrow Lands. Hopefully that's the last we'll see of them and where they'll stay."

"When can we get back to the Queen's Palace?" Henry was anxious to let Maggie know he was all right.

"As soon as my mother is able," Elyne said. "Don't worry, Henry. Maggie knows you're safe."

He blew out a breath of relief. "Thank you."

"Henry, I owe you an apology," Derron said. "I underestimated you as a human. Maeve is alive because of you."

Henry didn't hide the surprise at the unexpected compliment from Derron. Even so, he couldn't stop the guilt that flashed through him. He could have killed the goddess with the sword the moment he had her at the end of it.

"I should have listened to you and not trusted Morrigan."

"She had you under her power. She coerced you into believing her," Derron said.

"Thankfully it all turned out well."

"I'm glad it's all behind us," Elyne said. "And now that it is, I'm famished. Let's eat and rest, shall we?"

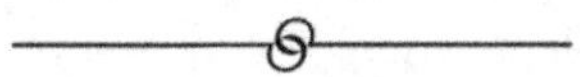

Henry waited as long as he could before knocking and entering the queen's chamber. It had seemed an eternity since the last time he'd seen her. Then she was unconscious with deep lashes on her back. Now she rested comfortably in the bed propped up on several pillows. She sat up a little straighter when Henry entered.

"I hope I'm not disturbing you."

"I thought I was going to die of boredom. Come in." She waved him inside.

Henry closed the door and walked to the bed where he sat on the edge. "How are you feeling?"

"Like I'm not going to die." She grinned.

He laughed. He'd said those words to her not long ago. "That is an improvement."

She reached for his hand and grasped it. "Henry, what you did was courageous."

"It was nothing. I couldn't let you die."

"No human has been to the underworld. No human could survive an attack from the Goddess of War." Her gaze fixed on their intertwined fingers. "I am sorry I locked you in the dungeon. You must understand it was for your own safety."

"I understand. But I could have protected you from her."

"Mayhap," she said.

He kissed her fingers, happy to have her in one piece. "I would give my life to save yours."

"Henry…" She tugged her hand away. "We must talk."

He waited while the silence stretched between them as she decided her words. The unwelcome tension grew taut as a bowstring between them.

"This…thing between us. It can never be."

"Why not?"

At last she met his gaze. Her blue eyes were full of pain and anguish and regret. "Because you are—"

"Human. Yeah, I get it. You and everyone else keep reminding me." He folded his arms. "What difference does it make?"

"It makes a lot of difference." Despite her trying to keep her tone even and unheated, frustration laced her words. "To the kingdom, to my people, to me."

"Does it? Does it matter to you? You didn't seem to complain when you were under me."

Now fire flashed in her eyes. "How dare you? Do not speak to me of that. Ever."

"Why not? Because you felt something, too? Are you so afraid of being loved that you can't allow yourself to love back? Is that it?"

"No and it's no concern of yours."

"It *is* a concern of mine. I have these feelings for you, Maeve. It's not like a switch I can flip and turn off. It's there and it's real." When she said nothing, he pressed on. "Do you deny you feel something for me?"

"How I feel doesn't matter. We cannot continue with this relationship as it is. You are human. I am queen."

Anger flared through him as he surged to his feet. "You are a coward. You're hiding behind your title because you're too scared to admit you might love me. You might have some feelings for me that matter. You might want to spend eternity with me. Am I right?"

"Get out." She pointed to the door. "I don't have to explain anything to you. And you need to return to your rightful place."

"No, you don't have to explain anything to me. But you do have to understand that when I walk out that door you will never see me again. You will never have to deal with me again. I'm going to have Elyne send me back to my 'rightful place'."

"You do that."

She wouldn't look at him. She fixed her gaze on the opposite wall. Despite the stoic look on her face, it was clear she was moments away from breaking into racking sobs. He would have missed the imperceptible quiver of her bottom had he not been looking. Her blue eyes watered with unshed tears.

She pushed him away for her kingdom and duty and honor. If that's what she truly wanted then that's what he would give her. He walked out of her chamber, her life, her world. The door slammed with a finality, closing this chapter of his life for good.

And flaring his anger to a boiling point. How could she turn away from him so easily? How could she deny her feelings for him? How could she pretend there was nothing between them? He knew damn well there was. And she threw it all away with both hands. Damn her.

His first order of business was to find Elyne and demand she send him back. He located her with Derron in the great hall, discussing plans to turn the castle into a Fae monument.

"Elyne, a word, please."

The princess took one look at him and gave a curt nod. Henry strode away from listening ears.

"Henry, what's wrong?"

"Send me back." His tone was nothing short of demanding.

"Back?" she repeated.

"Back home. My home."

"Now? Don't you want to see Maggie before you go?"

"There is no time for that. I'm done here." He crossed his arms over his chest.

Elyne looked him over, her expression cool. "Why the sense of urgency?"

"Does it matter?" He practically snarled the words.

"Does it have to do with my mother?" Now she flipped a long lock of blonde hair over her shoulder and folded her arms over her chest. "Because I know that tone. That irritation. Only my mother can produce that in someone."

"I'm ready to go home, Elyne. Can it be that simple?"

She glanced over her shoulder to where Derron shifted from one foot to the other, his hand on the hilt of his sword. "No, I don't think it can be."

Before he could answer she clamped a hand around his upper arm and dragged him away. Her blue eyes were sharp and assessing, as though she could see right through his smoke screen.

"Tell me the truth, Henry. Is there something between you and my mother?"

"There is nothing, as she so succinctly put it. And there never can be. Nor will be."

Elyne drew up tall, her back straight as she raised fine arched eyebrows. "I understand."

"Do you?" He met her gaze. Understanding was there and he realized she knew his secret.

"It's perfectly clear," she said.

"Are you going to send me back to the human realm or not?"

A long pause stretched between them as she considered. Why he didn't know. It should be easy. She should be able to do whatever Fae magic was necessary to put him back into the human realm. Why did she delay?

"No," she said at last.

"What do you mean no?"

"I mean no. I know my mother. She's stubborn as an ox. I'm not sending you back yet because I think she'll change her mind."

"About what? You don't even know anything. I haven't told you anything."

"You don't have to tell me." She gave him a secret smile. As though she knew of some covert operation to which Henry was privy. She leaned forward and whispered, "I see it in your eyes."

"See what?"

"That same look Maggie gave Finn when she fell in love with him."

Henry clamped his jaw so tight his back teeth ached. Was he that obvious? Did he wear his heart on his sleeve?

"Give her some time. She'll come around."

He didn't want to acknowledge the hope that bloomed in his breast. Didn't want to feel the excitement building around his heart. Didn't want to feel anything but the anger and pain of Maeve rebuffing him. But it was there. That hope, that faith, that desire. Could Elyne be right? Would Maeve realize her mistake and come running to him? It was almost too much to wish for.

"Are you sure about that?"

"I know my mother, Henry. Come back with us to the Queen's Palace and give her time."

It was against his better judgment. Instead of insisting Elyne send him home, he heard himself saying, "All right. I'll give her until we return to the Queen's Palace. If she still refuses then will you send me home?"

"Aye. I will. You have my word, Henry."

It was all the hope he needed.

Maeve cut short the time they lingered in the ruined castle. She was ready to move by the next morning, despite the healing lashings on her back and the throbbing still in her head from the gash. Morrigan had clubbed her with something—she still wasn't sure what—to knock her out and carry her off to the underworld.

She had been foolish to think she could take on the Goddess of War alone. She'd allowed her overconfidence to cloud her decisions. That and a desperation to be rid of the woman.

Well now she was rid of her, wasn't she?

The sooner she returned to her normal life, the sooner she could forget any of this happened. The sooner she could bury her feelings for Henry. The sooner she could erect those stones around her heart once more.

She'd hobbled her way down to the great hall where she would find her daughter and Lord Derron. She expected to see Prince

Andahar and King Urdithane as well but the Elves were nowhere in sight. Neither was Henry, much to her chagrin. The princess and her husband were finishing up a meal and both rose at the sight of her.

"Mother, good morrow. I hadn't expected to see you up yet."

"I wish to return to the Queen's Palace," Maeve said. "Today."

"Today?" Derron repeated.

"So soon? Are you certain you're healed enough, Mother?"

"I'm fine. And it's not as though we're traveling on foot. You can sift us there, can't you?"

"I can."

"Then what are you waiting for? Let's get on with it." She snapped her fingers as though that would make it so and hurry her daughter along.

"Aye, Mother." She exchanged a questioning look with Derron. "You mean now?"

"I mean now," Maeve said, her voice edged in ice. "What is so difficult to understand about that?"

"I thought…we would stay here until you were healed."

"Has Seamus put you up to this?" She glanced around but saw no sign of the healer. "I thought I made myself perfectly clear. I wish to return to the palace. Now."

"Seamus returned yesterday with the injured soldiers," Derron explained. "I'm sure he would want you to continue to rest until you are—"

"Enough of this. If you won't sift me then I'll find Nero and have him fly me."

"I'll take you now, Mother. I can always come back for the others."

"What others?"

"The…others. The Elven soldiers," Elyne offered.

"Fine. Good. Then let's go." She held out her hand to Elyne.

With one quick glance at her husband, Elyne took her hand. A moment later they flashed from the castle in the Sacred Forest to her own bedchamber in the Queen's Palace. Home at last. Maeve dropped her hand and turned away from Elyne.

"Now go. I wish to be alone."

"As you wish, Mother."

Elyne sifted away. As soon as she was gone Maeve collapsed on her oversized bed. Finally, she could allow her self-inflicted broken heart to heal.

Chapter 17

Days passed as she kept hidden in her chamber. When at last she decided to venture forth, she consoled herself with a walk through the palace. She noticed the work to repair the damage had been underway for some time. Those who saw her paused to bow as she passed. But she had no interest in the repairs or anything going on inside the palace walls.

She made her way to the gardens. Over the garden walls, she could clearly see the arched back of the scaly black dragon. He must have sensed her approach for he lifted his head and puffed out a plume of white smoke from his nostrils as if in greeting. She grinned at him. Nero. The great black dragon.

"Nero."

My queen. I am glad to see you unscathed. Are you well?

"I am. Thank you. The last I saw of you was in the Sacred Forest battling the red dragon."

Anya was not able to defeat me.

"I'm glad to see that," Maeve said.

She rounded the garden walls and exited through the gate to face Nero. He lowered his head to her as she approached so that they would see eye to eye. She placed her hand on his cold nose, the smooth scales against her palm.

"Thank you, Nero."

I regret I could not help you the way I wished. But the goddess—

"No regrets, Nero. You did what you promised you would. You protected me with your life. And for that I am grateful. I release you from your debt."

His eyes closed as he exhaled a heated breath. Steam billowed around her.

I thank you, my queen.

"It is I who thank you, my friend. Where will you go?"

There are others of my kind. I wish to seek them.

"Good luck. I'll miss you."

And I, you.

She removed her hand and turned to go but his voice in her head stopped her.

What of the human?

"The human?"

Henry. What will become of him now? Have you decided?

Had she decided? What did that mean? She turned back to him and met his red-eyed gaze. "I don't understand."

Will you send him back to the human realm alone? Or will you go with him?

"He's already returned to his home."

Nay. He remains in the Otherworld.

Excitement prickled her skin. Heat flooded her body. She quivered with surprise. The only person who would keep him here was Elyne. He was *here.* She wanted to smile, to giggle, to shout for joy. She kept her queenly façade firmly in place, her face stony.

"Surely you jest."

No jest. Your love for him runs deep. You can no longer deny it. It has set you free.

She stared at him, her heart doing a funny dance in her chest. Her stomach clenched. How could this…dragon know so much? When she herself didn't even know that?

Your thoughts betray you.

Maeve should have known she could hide nothing from the great beast. "It is not possible."

Why? Because he is human? Humans are not perfect or infallible. But this human…this Henry…offers something no Fae has ever offered you.

"And what is that?"

Unconditional love and friendship.

His words hit so close to home the pain of them lanced through her lower abdomen. She nearly doubled over. She pressed her hand against her roiling stomach. Nero knew so much about her and Henry it was eerie.

Would it be so terrible and so unimaginable for you to take the love he has offered you?

"How do I do that? I'm immortal. I'm queen. I'm Fae."

He is mortal. He is a commoner. He is human. But he loves you. And he would spend eternity with you. Your immortality can be given up. Your kingdom can be given to your daughter.

"Are you suggesting I give it all up? For him?"

He would give up everything for you. If you asked.

The heat of regret flashed through her. The damage with Henry had already been done. "But I've pushed him away."

It can be repaired. With the right gesture. Would you rather live the rest of eternity alone and without love? Or would you give all that up to be with the one man, the one human, who will love you to the end of his days?

"I'll consider it," she said. The thought of leaving everything behind scared her. But leaving Henry behind for good terrified her to her soul. "Farewell, Nero. And thank you."

Whatever your decision, may the gods bless you. Farewell.

Maeve walked back through the garden gate past the rosebushes blooming in the early evening. Past all the colorful flowers. She could not get Nero's words out of her head. All she could think about was Henry, leaving this place, and spending the rest of her days with him and him alone.

Could it be done? It had never been done.

As she entered the courtyard, Elyne and the High Druid rushed toward her. His cheeks were red from exertion, his robes flapped against his legs with his hurried pace. She could even see the beaded sweat on his forehead. She paused and waited for him to come to a jarring halt in front of her.

"Your majesty, I have great news." Akram panted and gulped in breaths. "I have finally discovered a way to restore your powers!"

Maeve didn't know whether to be happy about that or not. Her first thought was to shout no. To refuse. To tell the High Druid to go away and never return. She would not be needing her powers back. She was in love with a human.

But then her common sense prevailed. She straightened and shoved away those thoughts. She would not allow her feelings for Henry to cloud her judgment. She could never do that. She was queen.

But the thoughts still niggled at her. Mayhap Nero was right. Was she truly throwing away her happiness with both hands? Would she, could she, give up everything to be with him?

"Did you?" she asked, her voice cool and controlled. She had to return to her previous demeanor and not allow them to see how shaken she truly was by this news.

"Aye, your majesty. You, Elyne and I can go to the Tree of Life to have your magic restored. I understand there is a way to do it there."

Maeve's heart sank even more. She could agree and then she would have her magic back. All would be right with the kingdom. She glanced at Elyne, who smiled and looked a little relieved.

"See, Mother? I thought you'd want to know right away. I knew there would be a way to get your magic back. Your grace, when can we leave?"

"As soon as you're ready, your majesty." He bowed to Elyne and then to Maeve. "I am at your disposal as your most humble servant."

"The Tree of Life will assist in returning my magic?"

"Oh, aye, your majesty. It is the only way," the High Druid said.

The Tree of Life could return her magic. But could it also make her a mortal? "And if I wish to give up my immortality? Can it do that as well?"

Surprise flickered over his face. Elyne's brows knit together.

"Mother? Why would you want to do that?"

"Answer the question please," she said.

"Aye…I suppose it could do that as well," he replied. "Though there is an easier way. I don't understand why you would want to give up your immortality."

Elyne's brows went from knit together to raised. The answer was plainly written on her daughter's face. And Maeve knew that she knew why she asked.

"It's not for you to understand," Maeve said. "What is this easier way?"

"A mortality spell," Akram said, as if that were common knowledge.

"Performed by you?" Maeve asked. "Or anyone?" She refused to glance at Elyne, lest she give herself away.

But then Elyne already knew.

"By anyone. Princess Elyne could even do it."

"Do you know this spell, daughter?"

"Aye. It's a basic spell. One that any Fae magic user can perform."

His gray brows closed together to form one long one. "Why do you want to know?"

"Just a question. We shall go at first light then to the Tree of Life. I'm weary as I'm sure you all are. Make ready, your grace. My daughter and I will meet you in the courtyard."

"As you wish, your majesty." He bowed and left the two.

Maeve gave Elyne her full attention. "Have the wayward humans been returned?" It was a test to see if she would tell her the truth. If she would admit Henry remained.

"Most of them. I've invited a few to remain."

"A few?" Maeve raised a brow. "Do I know who remains?"

"Maggie, Finn and Sir Drake are honored guests. I rather like having them here."

"Hm," was her only response. Elyne hadn't included Henry in that list and she wondered where he was now. Was she hiding him? For what purpose? "And the portals?"

"They've been at last sealed with the help of the High Druid," Elyne said.

"Excellent. I think it appropriate we have a feast to celebrate our success at defeating the Goddess of War. Once we return from the Tree of Life, we can resume negotiations with King Urdithane and the rest of the Elves."

Elyne flushed. "About the Treaty of Separation, Mother…"

When she trailed off and didn't continue, Maeve said, "Aye?"

"When we learned the Goddess of War intended to kill you in the Sacred Forest, it was King Urdithane and Prince Andahar who insisted on coming with us to assist in her defeat. I thought it fitting I…well…I tear up the Treaty."

Maeve stared at her in shocked silence. "You tore up the Treaty of Separation?"

"Aye, Mother. I did. I proclaimed it null and void. The Elves and the Fae will live in peace and harmony once again." She lifted her chin a little higher to press her point.

Maeve suppressed the smile that wanted to crease her lips. Her daughter was going to make a fine queen. "I see."

"Do you not agree?" Elyne asked. She still kept her hands clasped in front of her. Mayhap to keep them still and not fidget.

How could she be angry? How could she reinstate the Treaty now? Especially since the very reason it was enacted was no longer valid. Her husband was dead, aye. And the woman who caused all the trouble was now dead in the underworld.

"It seems you made the right decision, my daughter. It also seems our feast is more than a celebration of our success at defeating Morrigan. It is also a celebration of reuniting the Fae and the Elves once again."

"I shall make the arrangements myself, Mother." Elyne couldn't hide the broad smile that creased her face. "King Urdithane and Prince Andahar will be pleased with this news. The first feast will commence this evening."

"How are the king and Lord Eldrin?"

"They're much better. Mending nicely. But with their brush with death, Andahar and Eldrin no longer felt as though they were the right ones to hold the Club of Dagda and the Spear of Lugh. Therefore, I have appointed new Fae Guardians for each of the Treasures."

"Very well. Now that the threats seemed to be over, the Elves will want to return to their own kingdom, I'm sure. Where will I find the king and his sons?"

"King Urdithane and Prince Andahar are in the great hall with the others if you care to join us to make the official celebration announcement."

"I would."

They entered the great hall and Elyne called for silence. Maeve scanned the crowd looking for their human friends. She saw no sign of Maggie, Finn, Sir Drake or…Henry. A pain stabbed her heart. She was wrong to shove him away.

"We have a wonderful announcement," Elyne said. "Mother?"

"My daughter tells me the Treaty has been abolished. In celebration of defeating the Goddess of War and unifying the Fae and the Elves once more we must have a celebration. This festival shall be week long and shall be known as the Reunification Festival from this day forward."

"Huzzah! Huzzah! Huzzah!"

The cheers rang through the ranks. Maeve was well pleased at the response, as was King Urdithane. He approached her with an obvious limp of his right leg, dodging those who were already celebrating.

"If you'll excuse me, Mother, I'd like to see to the planning."

Clearly Elyne didn't want to stick around to see what the two royal rulers had to say to each other. If Maeve had her way, she wouldn't either. But she owed it to the king to hear what he had to say.

"Your majesty." Urdithane bowed long and low. When he rose, he took her hand and kissed it. "I am most pleased about the Treaty."

"As am I. I do hope the Elves and the Fae will continue to make amends. Your help at both the Stone of Destiny and in the Sacred Forest will not be forgotten. I understand you and Lord Eldrin were wounded."

"Aye, but with the expertise of your royal healer Seamus I am much better now, as is my son." He glanced toward Elyne, who was trying to weave her way through the already celebratory crowd. "'Tis a shame your daughter is already spoken for or I would suggest a betrothal to my son Andahar. He's rather taken with the princess."

"I'm afraid Lord Derron would have something to say about that." She smiled. Derron would fight a man to the death for his fair princess. "Mayhap your son could find a suitable lady within the Fae nobles. I'm sure one of the councilmen has a daughter."

He stroked his chin, looking thoughtful. "Mayhap. Shall I send for the royal Elven builders? I'm sure they would be more than happy to help you rebuild your palace. It will help accelerate the process and get your palace walls back in place."

"I should like that. You have my thanks, your majesty."

"And mine." He gave her a surreptitious once-over before his gaze landed on her face. His very serious gaze. "I don't suppose you would be interested in an arrangement that would be mutually beneficial for both our kingdoms?"

She stared at him for a long moment, unsure what he implied. Then dawning came over her so suddenly her stomach cramped. Was he suggesting the two of them marry? To strengthen their royal bonds? Maeve pressed a hand against her stomach. She couldn't. Wouldn't. While King Urdithane was a mildly attractive man she could not possibly consider such an agreement.

That, and she knew, deep down, her heart would always and forever belong to another. This Elven king would never understand that and she wouldn't even attempt to explain it to him. She gave him a small smile.

"I thank you, King Urdithane, for the lovely offer but I'm afraid I would not make a suitable companion. Too many long years have passed since the death of my husband. I'm afraid I'm well set in my ways."

"I understand." He took her hand once again in his. "You realize, of course, I had to try. Should you ever change your mind my offer is a standing one."

He kissed her hand before walking away.

Elyne finally broke away from the crowded hall and hurried through the corridors to Maggie's chamber where she knew she would find Henry. She knocked and the door opened a moment later. Maggie greeted Elyne with a broad smile and rushed to her. She hugged her hard.

"I'm so glad everything turned out all right," she said. "Thank you for bringing my father back safely."

"I'm glad, too. But I've come to speak with Henry on a most urgent matter. Sir Henry, a word if you will?"

"I'm no longer a *sir*, princess." Henry slumped in a chair in the corner of the room, a tankard of ale in his hand. "Besides, we've nothing to talk about and I'd rather drown myself in this delicious ale."

"Please, Henry. I *must* speak with you." She beckoned him into the hall but he refused.

"Go away." He took a swig of his ale.

"Dad, you're being rude. Now go talk to Elyne."

"Giving me orders, magpie? Forget it. Not talking to her. I've nothing to say. I've used up all the words I have with the queen."

Maggie narrowed her eyes and propped her fists on her hips.

"You have not. And wallowing in self-pity is not going to make things better. Now you get up from that chair this instant and go talk to her."

Henry leveled a gaze at his daughter but Maggie wasn't intimidated one bit.

"Ye best get on with it, laddie," Finn said. "'Tis no' good to be riling the wee lassie."

"Fine," Henry grumbled.

He plunked his tankard on the ground and dragged himself to his feet. He followed Elyne into the hallway and closed the door behind him. Then he took up residence against the opposite stone wall. He crossed his arms over his chest.

"If this is about Maeve—"

"It is and you'll listen. She loves you."

He scoffed. "Says who?" He paused, then his curiosity got the better of him. "How can you tell?"

"The High Druid offered to take her to the Tree of Life to restore her magic. She agreed to go on the morrow at first light."

When Elyne didn't elaborate, Henry shrugged.

She rolled her eyes. "She also asked if the Tree of Life could remove her immortality."

Henry didn't want to acknowledge the pinprick of hope piercing his heart. "And this means what to me?"

"Don't you see? She's in love with you! If she wasn't, we'd be headed to the Tree of Life at this very moment. Not on the morrow. *Now.* Instead she's had me plan a celebration feast. A week-long celebration, mind you."

"I'm supposed to accept that as proof she's in love with me?" He knit his brows. "That seems rather weak."

"Oh, you're an impossible man." Elyne rolled her eyes. "If she wasn't in love with you, getting her magic back would be the first thing on her mind. She asked to have her immortality taken away."

He stared at her, dumbfounded. He didn't want to let her know excitement pumped through his veins. In an effort to remain passive, he shrugged a shoulder. "So what?"

"She's thinking of becoming a *mortal.* And earlier she scanned the crowd, looking for you. She looked disappointed when she didn't find you. I know you love her, too."

"It doesn't matter now, does it? She defeated Morrigan and now all is right with her kingdom. She can go back to being queen."

"Aye but she wants you."

"You can't know that."

"I can and I do. Go to her, Henry. Tell her how you feel."

"I have told her and she pushed me away. She doesn't want me."

"She *does* want you and she doesn't realize it. But she will and soon. She's stubborn. It's been many years since she's loved anyone. I want to see her happy."

Stubborn was a gross understatement.

"Her happiness does not lay with me. And I've made up my mind to return to my own world. I've asked you this more than once. Now send me back, Elyne. Please. I've already said my goodbyes to Maggie and Finn and given them my blessing on their marriage."

"So just like that? You would return to your world? Are you going to tell my mother goodbye too?"

"No. She doesn't want to see me."

"She does," Elyne insisted. "And it would kill her if you didn't tell her goodbye."

"Maybe she should have thought of that before she locked me in the dungeon." He stood straight and clenched his fists. "I'm done with the Otherworld. Sift me back. Or whatever it is you do."

She stiffened and looked down her nose at him in that stubborn way that reminded him of her mother. "I can't."

"Why not?"

Elyne pressed her lips together in a thin line. "Because you came through a standing stone. You have to return that way."

He sighed, resigned. "Fine. Tell me where. I want to start the journey."

"Go west into the setting sun. The standing stone will be approximately one day's walk."

"I have to walk? You can't even give me a horse?"

"That's how you arrived—on foot. You must return the same way."

"You have strange rules here," he grumbled.

"When you reach it step through the portal. It will send you back to Scotland where you left. Once you're through all the portals will be closed, sealing the Otherworld from the human realm."

Henry wasn't thrilled about the idea of walking. But if walking was what he had to do to get back home, then that's what he'd do.

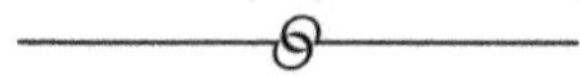

The feasting and merrymaking went long into the night but Maeve had retired early to rest. She'd bade her goodnight and entered her chamber. Her cold, empty chamber. She half hoped Henry would be there to greet her but she hadn't seen him since they returned to the Queen's Palace.

If she had any courage at all she'd question Maggie about where he was. Or Elyne. The two kept no secrets from each other.

But alas, Maeve couldn't allow those weak feelings to control her. She was strong. She was queen. She must remain that way. And in the morning, she would wake and go to the Tree of Life with Elyne and the High Druid and get her magic back.

When morning came, though, she was reluctant to leave. She'd dressed in a gown of royal blue belted at the waist with a gold braid. Her hair flowed freely around her face. She'd dressed herself, unwilling to allow even her handmaidens to assist her. She wanted to be alone. It was the best thing to soothe her aching heart.

A knock sounded on the door.

"Come."

Elyne entered, looking rather queenly. She'd chosen to put her hair up, coiling it intricately around her head in a double braid. Her gown was of the palest pink with bell sleeves, a scooped neckline and a short train. She also wore a white fur-lined cloak.

"Good morrow, Mother. I trust you slept well."

"Aye."

In truth, she tossed and turned most of the night. She hoped it didn't show in her face. Her daughter, as keen as she was, would be able to tell right away. She knew the moment had come for them to meet the High Druid and travel to the Tree of Life. But she didn't want to leave. She didn't want to go. She couldn't care less about her bloody magic.

All she cared about was…Henry. Gods, how could she be so stupid and let him go? She knew for a fact she was madly, passionately in love with the man. A *human* no less. How could this have happened? He'd snuck up on her. She hadn't been prepared for the feelings she would have for him.

She both loved and hated it.

Weak feelings be damned. She was not going to allow them to ruin her last chance at happiness.

Where was he? Had he truly returned to the human realm? Or was he still skulking around the palace?

"Mother? Are you all right?"

"I'm fine." She rose from the edge of her bed.

"You look pale. Mayhap we should postpone the trip to the Tree of Life so you can get more rest," Elyne suggested.

"No," she said sharply. "We will go today." She wanted to get this over with. She reached for her cloak and slipped it over her shoulders.

"If you want to wait a day or two, it's no problem to send a message to the High Druid."

Suddenly Maeve knew something was amiss. She peered at her daughter, who seemed to be scheming. "What do you know?"

At least Elyne had the good sense to look abashed. "I'm not sure what you mean, Mother."

"You know something. What is it?"

Elyne flushed, her skin turning a pale pink. "I…I know nothing of consequence."

"Poppycock." She wasn't going to take her word for it. She would also make a decision that would forever change the future of the realm. "I'm not going."

Now Elyne's eyes flew wide. "What? A moment ago, you said—"

"I know what I said. I've changed my mind." She flung her cloak on the bed. "I'm not going to the Tree of Life. I'm not getting my magic back, Elyne." She softened as she stepped toward her daughter and grasped her hands. "You have proven to me you can rule the Otherworld without me."

"No, Mother, I—"

"For that I am so proud of you, my daughter. So proud. You will make a wonderful queen."

"What are you saying?"

"I'm saying I'm stepping down as Queen of the Otherworld. I hereby grant you the title to rule over the realm as you see fit. You and your husband, Lord Derron. Though I suppose he will be King Derron now, won't he?"

"Mother, I-I don't understand." She shook her head slowly.

"You will be queen now. I am relinquishing the throne to you. You will need to travel to the Stone of Destiny to make if official. And then mayhap this celebration can be extended into a coronation."

Elyne stared at her, her cheeks flushed. "Are you certain?"

"More certain than I've ever been."

"But what are you planning to do if you're not queen?"

She knew she had to tell her daughter what her plans were but she was afraid. Afraid that if she spoke the words out loud it would somehow curse her plans and they would not come true.

"I plan to find Henry and return with him."

"Henry?"

"Aye. Does that displease you?"

"No, Mother. You would give up your crown for him?"

"I love him." There. She'd said it. And with the words her stomach fluttered. She resisted the urge to press a hand against her abdomen.

If Elyne was surprised or otherwise, she hid her emotions well. "He's a human. You realize that?"

"Aye. Exactly why I am also giving up my immortality for him."

She stared wide-eyed at her with her mouth hanging open. Maeve huffed.

"Would you, Elyne? If Derron were human, would you give up all you had to be with him?"

"Aye," she said without hesitation. "There is no greater thing in this world—in any world—than loving the man of your dreams and him loving you back."

"Then you understand."

"Aye, I do.

Maeve wasn't sure but she thought Elyne blinked away tears.

"I would rather spend the rest of my days with Henry than eternity as queen. Alone. I've been alone long enough. Now perform that mortality spell and let's get on with this."

"I must ask again. Are you certain?"

"As certain as I have ever been about anything."

With a nod, Elyne grasped her by the hands, squeezing them tight before chanting the spell in the language of the Fae. Maeve sensed her immortality leaving her. The Fae light inside her that once burned bright and gave her everlasting life now diminished. Making her into a mortal—though not quite human. Now she would age and eventually die. Like Henry. And once her immortal life was gone all her feelings for Henry intensified threefold. She nearly doubled over but managed to stay upright. Once they were finished, Elyne grabbed her and hugged her hard.

"Go, Mother. Before it's too late. He's gone to the stone circle to return home."

"That's why he stayed. Because you knew. You knew I loved him."

"Aye. I had to give you both one last chance. He begged me to sift him home but I…told a little lie. I told him I couldn't and he would have to exit the Otherworld the same way he came in. I sent him to the stone circle. He left yesterday." Tears shimmered in her eyes. Tears of happiness.

But Maeve's stomach clenched with worry. What if he'd already made it there and disappeared through the portal?

"You still have time," Elyne said as though reading her thoughts. "He couldn't have made it there yet on foot."

"He's on foot?"

"Aye. If you take, say, a dragon…well, then you would make it there before him. And anyway, the portals have all been closed." Elyne flashed a grin.

Maeve realized then her daughter knew her better than she even knew herself. Elyne had made sure Henry had no way to get back to the human realm. Her daughter knew she would come to her senses later rather than sooner and she made sure to give her one last chance with Henry.

She knew the dragon she would call. The fastest beast in the air. Nero could get her to Henry with great speed.

Maeve hugged Elyne so hard she thought she might break her

bones. But Elyne hugged her back, squeezing her. "Thank you." And she kissed her on the cheek. "'Tis farewell."

"For now, Mother. I expect I'll be checking on you."

"Cheeky girl." She tweaked her nose. "If you must. I should like to know how the realm fares without me."

"Go now. Before it's too late. Go and be happy. I will open the portal for you."

One last hug and Maeve dashed from the room. She bolted through the palace walls. All those she passed looked at her, surprise on their faces. They had never seen their queen do anything out of character such as run through the palace. She had to get to the courtyard. She had to call Nero to her.

At the palace gates the guards blocked her way. "The roads are not safe, your majesty."

"Stand aside," she ordered. "And let me out of the gates."

The two soldiers exchanged a glance. She would not let them stand between her and her beloved Henry. Without waiting for them to act or reply, she gave them a violent shove and ran out the gates, her hair flying behind her.

A quick glance over her shoulder told her they were too stunned to move or call for help. Good. She wound her way to the edge of the tree line where she looked up into the predawn sky. Pale-pink light pushed away night's shadows to welcome another day.

"Nero!"

After several heartbeats, she heard the flutter of the beast's wings and a moment later he alighted in front of her. He bowed his head in greeting.

My queen.

"Take me to Henry. He heads to the stone circle. I must reach him before he steps through the portal."

It is my greatest honor to take you, by your command.

She climbed on his back and they were airborne, heading toward the stone circle. She knew she could count on Nero to get her there. As they flew, she saw Henry paused outside it. His hand on the rock as though contemplating stepping through. She patted Nero and pointed.

He dove toward the ground. Henry turned to watch her land

and slide off Nero's back. She stood rooted in place as the great dragon flew away and she and Henry stared at each other. Her heart rammed hard in her chest as though it might burst through.

He no longer wore the glamour that masked his human appearance. This Henry was as dashing, if not more, than the Fae version. He still had the tall, slender build with the hint of muscle curving his chest and upper arms. That was unmistakable beneath the material of his cotton shirt. He still had the auburn hair with red strands glinting in the morning light. He still had the depthless green eyes that held so much mirth and life it made her want to dive in.

And yet something was different about him. He wore his human clothes—jeans, shirt and spectacles. She'd never seen him with glasses before.

He looked entirely too handsome.

It made her heart sing with delight.

Finally, she took a step toward him. He stiffened, his face a mask of unreadable emotion.

"Henry." Because it was all she could think to say. And it was completely inadequate.

"Maeve." He gave her a curt nod. "What are you doing here? Come to see me off? To make sure I return to my 'rightful place' in the world. Back to the human realm which you so loathe."

The words stung. Words he flung carelessly back at her. She deserved it. "Henry, I…"

"Fear not, my queen. I shall step through and be gone from your realm once and for all." He started to take a step into the stone circle.

"No, wait!" He halted. "Please."

He looked at her, waiting for her to say something. She knew it was now or never. "My words to you were…harsh. I hope you can accept my apology." She clasped her hands to keep from fidgeting.

He looked her over, as though considering whether or not to forgive her. He gave a swift nod. "Accepted."

Relief flooded her.

"Goodbye, Maeve." Again, he started to step into the circle.

"Wait, Henry. Please. I'm not finished."

"What more is there to say?" he demanded. "Haven't we said it all?"

"No. No, we haven't. I haven't. There is…more. So much more." Oh, she was such a coward. Why couldn't she say the words rattling around in her head? She took a tentative step toward him. "I've come to tell you something."

He stood a little straighter as she took another step toward him. He was close now. So close. She could smell his musky scent that was ever present. She wanted to touch him but she was too afraid he would rebuff her. What if he decided she wasn't worth it? That she'd damaged their relationship forever? What if she had given up everything for nothing?

No, she didn't. Couldn't have. Henry was the one. She could not walk through the rest of her days without him.

"Henry, I've been such a fool. An idiotic fool."

"That's a good start."

"Those things I said were meant to hurt you. To make you go away from me because I didn't think I could…" Her eyes closed and she wavered on her feet. Her heart pounded so hard it rattled her entire body.

"You could what?"

"That I could love you." Her gaze met his as she said it.

And there in the depths of his green eyes she saw hope flicker to life. "You what?"

"I love you." A giggle bubbled up her throat. She liked saying it. No, she *loved* saying it. She pressed her cold fingers to her lips and said it again. "I love you so much, Henry."

"You love me," he repeated, as though he wasn't sure he heard her correctly.

She nodded. "Madly. Passionately. Always. Forever. I cannot stay here alone. I was wrong to treat you so badly. I was afraid we would never be able to be together. Because you are human. Mortal. And I am Fae. Immortal."

He didn't reply. Didn't say a word. Merely stared at her. Did his expression soften? Or was that a figment of her imagination? She rushed on.

"My daughter told me you would be here. I knew I had to come. I…had to see you again. To tell you my true feelings."

Again, he stiffened. "Is that all then?"

She didn't want to acknowledge her heart sinking to her toes. He didn't understand. Not yet. She would have to make him understand.

"No, Henry. Not by far. I have relinquished the throne to Elyne. She will be crowned in the coming days."

"You…did…what?"

"I have stepped down as queen. I am no longer ruler of the Otherworld."

"But why?"

"Because I love you, Henry, and I want to be with you. Because I no longer wish to hide behind my title and my kingdom. Can you not see?"

"You love me. A human?"

"Aye, a human. A human I never thought to have feelings for. A human who is maddening in every way." She reached for him to rest her palms on his chest. "A human who has captured my heart and made me feel alive again. Please tell me it's not too late."

His gaze softened. He looked at her with such tenderness she thought she might faint. Her knees threatened to buckle. Her body threatened to crumple. And all the while her heart did a silly thumping dance in her chest.

Henry lifted his hand and stroked the back of it across her cheek. She turned her head and planted a soft kiss on his palm. With that small gesture she heard the ragged exhalation of his breath shudder out of him. She was hopeful it was a sign he had forgiven her. That he wanted her. That he would love her forever as she would him. That it wasn't too late. Oh gods, why didn't he say something? Anything?

He broke his silence. "Why are you here, Maeve?"

"I want to come with you. I have given up my crown and my immortality to be with you."

"You gave all that up? For me?" He sounded incredulous. As though he couldn't believe what he heard. What she said.

"I did. All for you."

"I…don't know what to say."

"Say you love me."

"I do love you. I will always love you."

His breath shuddered out of him as his hand slipped from her cheek to sweep through the strands of her hair. "Are you sure?" But he was smiling as he asked it.

She couldn't stop the smile pulling at the corners of her mouth. "I am sure, Henry. I love you. Of that I will always be sure."

"I'm honored. And touched."

"I can't live without you."

"Nor I you."

A cry of relief broke form her lips as he pulled her into his arms. A warm glow flowed through her and for the first time in her very long life she was blissfully happy and fully alive. When his lips met hers, it sent new spirals of delight through her right down to the tips of her toes. It was a kiss of such reckless abandon it stole her breath. He loved her and she loved him.

When he pulled away, he said, "You may not be the queen of the Otherworld but you will always be the queen of my heart."

"And you, Henry, will always be my knight. The knight who saved me from my loneliness."

"I guess there's one thing left to do then."

"Aye, there is."

Henry took her by the hand and turned toward the stone circle. So sure was she about her decision, she didn't look back as they stepped through the stone circle together.

Realm of Honor Cast of Characters

The Humans

Sir Finian "Finn" McCullough: Scottish knight
Maggie Chase McCullough: Finn's wife
Sir Drake Attenborough: English knight and jousting hero
Henry Chase: Maggie's father

The Fae

Princess Elyne: crown princess of the Fae Otherworld
Lord Derron: Knight of the Realm, Protector of the Otherworld
Queen Maeve: ruler of the Otherworld and the Seelie Court
Lord Roderick: member of the High Council
Lord Aldun: member of the High Council
Lord Vaughan: member of the High Council
Seamus: healer for the Fae
King Adhamh: the queen's husband who was murdered
Morrigan: Goddess of War
Lord/Dark King Kieran: dark elf bent on human and Otherworld domination
Lord Gawaine: Queen Maeve's high councilor
Dark King Fergus mac Delbaith: dark king of the Unseelie court
Lord Pwyll: Guardian of the Stone of Destiny
Lord Malcolm: Guardian of the Sword of Light and Derron's father
Lord Llewelyn: Guardian of the Club of Dagda
Lord Udrich: Guardian of the Spear of Lugh

The Elves

King Urdithane emar'Rudul: ruler of the Wood Elves
Andahar emar'Rudul: crown prince of the Woodlands Elven throne
Leopold: Wood Elves royal advisor
Eldrin emar'Rudul: brother to Andahar, Elven ranger
Allanna emar'Rudul: sister to Andahar and Elven Princess

Lord Navin emar'Rudul: brother to Andahar, Woodlands Gatekeeper
Lord-Regent Marath: Wood Elves liege lord
Lord Randir: Fire Elf and Laerwen's betrothed
Laerwen emer'Aranhil Bloodfire: Fire Elf and Princess of the Hin'dar Rhule
Hiram: Laerwen's royal advisor
Lady Talaiel: ruler of the Skye Elves
Turin: healer for the Skye Elves
Brom: healer for the Wood Elves
Lord Malack: one of the noble Wood Elves
Queen Lucinda and King Aleron: ruler of the Fire Elves

The Fomorians

Cormac: Fomorian mage forced to help Kieran
Lorcann: Fomorian mage

The Dragons

Ambrielle: the emerald dragon
Aura: the azure dragon
Luna: the silver dragon
Nero: the black dragon
Moon dragons: silver dragons of the Skye Elves

The Realms

Fae Otherworld: home of the Fae, includes Seelie and Unseelie Courts
Woodlands: a humid forest region and home of the Wood Elves
Hin'dar Rhule: dry, arid volcanic region and home of the Fire Elves
Skye Realm in the clouds: home of the Skye Elves and the moon dragons
Human Realm: home for Maggie and Finn
Underworld: where Morrigan was banished

The Races

The Fae: also known as Faeries, a race of magical beings who can alter time and travel from their realm to the human realm.

Fire Elves: Elves who live in the volcanic realm known as the

Hin'dar Rhule. Their bodies can withstand the hottest heat of the fires, but the lava is still deadly to them. They seek help from the Wood Elves when the Fomorians destroy their home.

Fomorians: an ancient race of vile creatures who wreak havoc. They were banished to a watery prison but one powerful Fomorian mage managed to break out and free his people so they could rampage once more.

Skye Elves: a reclusive Elven race living among the clouds with their moon dragons. The legend of the Skye Elves says one is as strong as ten men and they are undefeatable in battle.

Wood Elves: Elves who live in the trees of the Woodlands and who had a long-standing Treaty of Separation with the Fae, dividing the two races. The Treaty has since been abolished, uniting the two and allowing them to work together to defeat the evil in the realm.

Did you love *A Knight to Remember*?

Pick up the fourth book in the Realm of Honor series, *A Knight Like No Other*, on sale now at your favorite retailer.

By the king's order, Princess Allanna is betrothed to Lord-Regent Marath, an Elven noble with an evil agenda who's manipulated his way into royal favor. Marrying him will be a fate worse than death, especially when Allanna yearns for the sexy and irresistible English knight, Sir Drake—the knight who holds her heart and a knight she is forbidden to love. She flees her family to be with him, giving up everything she knows.

Enraged at her defiance, Marath summons a mage to kidnap and kill Allanna. Drake, determined to protect the woman he loves, will stop at nothing to see her safe. Their desire for one another burns hot and nothing can keep the two lovers apart. Nothing but Marath's evil plan to do away with the Fae and separate Drake and Allanna forever.

Read more at <u>www.michellemiles.net</u>

ALSO BY MICHELLE MILES

Dream Walker
Call of the Dark

Age of Wizards
In the Tower of the Wizard King
On the Hunt for the Wizard King

A Ransom & Fortune Adventure
Highland Fling, Vol 1
Dead of Winter, Vol 2
The Citadel, Vol 3
Lord of the Underworld, Vol 4

Dragon Protectors
Desiring the Dragon Lord
Seducing the Dragon Knight
Tempting Her Dragon Bodyguard

Realm of Honor
One Knight Only
Only for a Knight
A Knight to Remember
A Knight Like No Other
Shadows of the Knight

Guardians of Atlantis
Tempting Eden
Seducing Eve
Ravishing Helene
Guardians of Atlantis Box Set

Coffee House Chronicles
Talk Dirty to Me
Nice Girls Do
Have Yourself a Merry Little Latte
Take Me I'm Yours
Sex, Lust & Martinis

Forever Yours
A Little Taste of Heaven

Shorts and Anthologies
A Dance Among the Faeries, Short Story
Eorwulf, Short Story
The Soul of Sharah, Short Story
Sinfully Sweet, Short Story
Flights of Fantasy: A Collection of Short Stories

Watch for more at www.michellemiles.net

Sign up and get your free book!

I love interacting with readers and the best way to do that is through email. Sign up for my VIP Reader's List and get a free book, notifications of upcoming releases, join the review team and much, much more. It's a great way for me to connect with you!

You can get the free book by signing up at:

https://www.subscribepage.com/ VIP

Your privacy is important to me. I will never sell or share your email address.

Did you enjoy this book? You can make a difference!

Reviews are an indie author's most powerful marketing tool. Honest reviews help us get noticed by other readers and increase vis- ibility in the marketplace. It's the best way for indie authors like me to be discovered by fabulous readers like you.

If you enjoyed this book, I would be ever so grateful if you could spend a few minutes leaving a review at your favorite e-retailer. It can be as short as you like. And if you're interested in joining my re- view team, email me a note to let me know! I personally answer every email I receive.

Thank you very much!

About the Author

Michelle Miles believes in fairy tales, true love and magic. She is the award-winning author of the epic fantasy, IN THE TOWER OF THE WIZARD KING, as well as the fantasy romance series, REALM OF HONOR, featuring knights and their ladies fair, and the paranormal dragon-shifter romance series, DRAGON PROTECTORS.

In her spare time, she enjoys listening to music, reading, cross-stitching and watching movies. Even though she's a native Texan, she loves castles, dragons, fairies and elves and is an avid Game of Thrones fan. She can be found online at Facebook, Twitter, Instagram, Pinterest, and Goodreads.